Matt merely stood gazing at her, his hand drifting up her arm, caressing her shoulder, making her heart pound with excitement.

Why didn't Matt kiss her? The air between them was so charged it was practically crackling.

"Stefanie, when we were trapped . . . when we thought we might drown . . . I kept thinking about what I'd be missing—what we'd be missing—if we didn't get out. Until then, I hadn't realized what I was feeling for you. I . . . It isn't something I'm used to feeling."

"Funny," she managed, "for some reason I was thinking about what we'd be missing, too."

"I'm glad," Matt whispered. His hand cradling the back of her neck, he drew her toward him. Then his mouth closed hotly over hers. . . .

ABOUT THE AUTHOR

Toronto author Dawn Stewardson travels as much as she can. So naturally she went to Scotland to do research before writing *Deep Secrets*. "I didn't see the Loch Ness monster," says Dawn, "but I did encounter the Hooray Henries and the Cheerless Charlies." And who are they? "Well, you'll have to read the book to find out," says Dawn, "or go to Scotland, of course."

Books by Dawn Stewardson

HARLEQUIN SUPERROMANCE
329—VANISHING ACT

HARLEQUIN INTRIGUE
80—PERIL IN PARADISE
90—NO RHYME OR REASON

Dawn Stewardson

DEEP SECRETS

Harlequin Books

TORONTO • NEW YORK • LONDON
AMSTERDAM • PARIS • SYDNEY • HAMBURG
STOCKHOLM • ATHENS • TOKYO • MILAN

This one's for Grace!
With special thanks to Ian McKenzie,
who provided the magic of Culloden House.
And to John, always.

Published May 1989

First printing March 1989

ISBN 0-373-70355-4

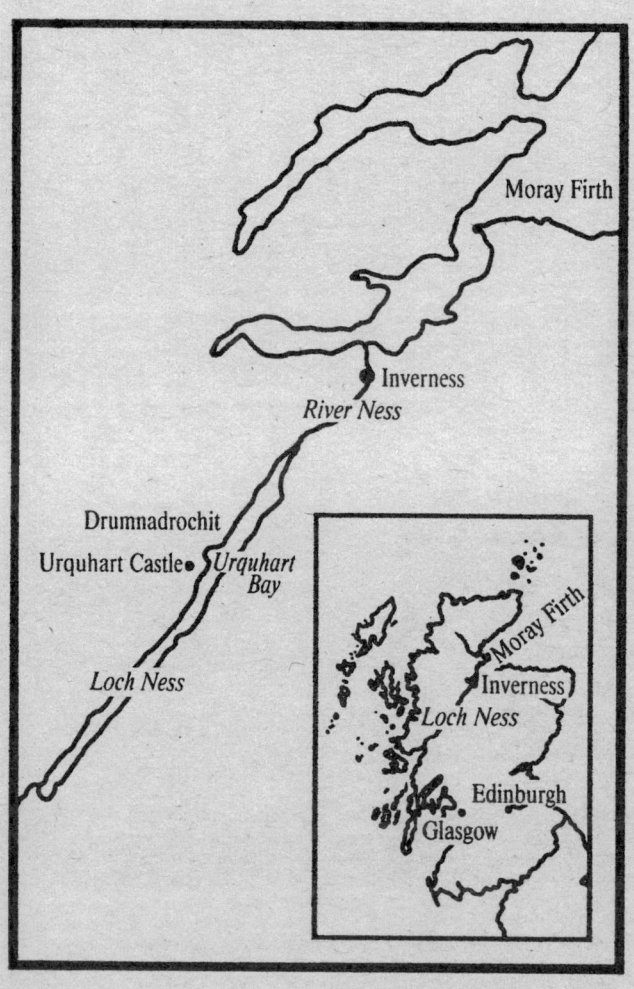

Moray Firth

Inverness
River Ness

Drumnadrochit
Urquhart Castle● *Urquhart Bay*

Loch Ness

Moray Firth

Inverness

Loch Ness

Edinburgh

Glasgow

CHAPTER ONE

"LOOK, MISS TAYLOR, I apologize for being evasive. But our competitors would kill for details about this project. I can't discuss specifics from halfway across the country. Once you're here tomorrow, I'll answer all your questions."

Stefanie twisted the phone cord absently, gazing out from her apartment over the sun-drenched city below. In the distance, tiny waves shimmered on Lake Michigan. She turned away from the view, forcing herself to concentrate on David Finch's proposition.

"Mr. Finch . . . I haven't agreed to be there at all, let alone tomorrow. Frankly, I'm not keen on spending July anywhere but in Chicago. I'm in desperate need of a recharge. I've barely been home a week out of the past two months."

"Hold off on that recharge until August and I promise you'll never regret it. I'm talking about a photographer's dream opportunity here. A few weeks from now, everyone who's involved in this project is going to be famous."

"Then why," Stefanie asked curiously, "did Nancy Goitano back out at the last minute?"

"That's something else I can't go into on the phone. Look, I hate to press, but Nancy's left us in a bit of a bind. The rest of the team arrived in Scotland three days ago. They need a photographer over there like yesterday. You've been highly recommended, but if we can't set up an interview for tomorrow . . ."

There are—Stefanie silently concluded his sentence—*a hundred other good wildlife photographers who'd jump at the amount of money Sound Research is offering.*

She thought rapidly, conscious of David Finch's impatience at the other end of the line. She definitely needed the money. She'd made almost nothing on her Brazilian assignment, had probably come out behind the game if she was honest about it. The Naturalist Federation of Brazil hadn't exactly been awash in cruzeiros.

Yes, hooking into whatever Sound Research was doing certainly made economic sense. If she didn't want to be forced into choosing between eating and coming up with next month's rent, she'd better at least agree to talk with Finch in person.

"This is strictly a nature shoot, isn't it, Mr. Finch? Underwater and animal life are all I do."

"Miss Taylor, from what I've been told about you, this is right up your alley."

"All right, then. I'll fly out and see you tomorrow."

"Wonderful! You've made the right decision. Just one last thing. You aren't claustrophobic, are you?"

"No. Not in the least." Stefanie paused, expecting David Finch to elaborate.

Instead she heard a barely audible sigh of relief and realized the man had been holding his breath while he'd waited for her answer.

"Good," he went on, as if there'd been nothing unusual about his question. "I'll look forward to seeing you tomorrow afternoon, then. There's a nine-fifteen

American flight out of O'Hare. I'll have a ticket waiting for you at the check-in counter there, and a car reserved at this end—at the Hertz desk in Logan International. You're sure you'll be all right getting up here on your own? The traffic around Boston can be pretty fierce.''

"I'll be fine. Chicago traffic isn't any picnic, either. And I've just spent a month driving some of the worst roads in Brazil. A hundred-mile trip up the New England coast is likely to seem tame in comparison.''

"Yes. Yes, of course. Well…tomorrow, then. You'll reach the turnoff for Chandler's Cove a few miles after you cross into Maine.''

"All right. Till tomorrow.''

"And, Miss Taylor, please bring your passport along.''

"Yes…I'll do that.'' Stefanie hung up, wishing she'd had a little more time to consider these plans. Finch's cloak-and-dagger routine had been annoying. He'd made the project sound more like a CIA assignment than a nature session. And bring her passport along? To an interview? He must want proof of her citizenship. That was bordering on the insulting. Well, she'd definitely draw the line if he wanted to fingerprint her!

She headed into the bedroom, reviewing their conversation in her head. It had left her with far more questions than answers. All she'd learned was that Sound Research had developed some new type of equipment they wanted to demonstrate, and her photographs would verify its effectiveness.

Maybe it was a revolutionary, fast-action shutter. That was a logical guess—a shutter that could capture wildlife moving at top speed.

But why do the demonstration in Scotland? Her mind flipped through an imaginary nature book about the country, coming across nothing extraordinary. "Famous," Finch had said. Even shots of some of the rarer birds of prey or waterfowl wouldn't be unusual enough to make any photographer famous.

He'd undoubtedly been exaggerating. And her agreeing to go racing off to New England for the interview had probably been foolish. No...that wasn't true at all.

In fact, it was one of the more sensible things she'd done lately. She simply couldn't afford to pass up the job...or others it might lead to.

Finch had mentioned his company often collaborated on government projects. And the government did a fair number of nature shoots. Maybe not exciting ones, but she wasn't getting any younger. With the big three-zero staring her in the face, she had to start being more practical. If David Finch offered her that assignment tomorrow, she'd grab it.

As STEFANIE CROSSED the New Hampshire-Maine state line, she eased up on the accelerator, letting the Pontiac's speed drift down to the posted limit. She hadn't driven since Brazil, and this car was an Indy contender compared to the one she'd rented there. A few miles farther along, she spotted a sign for the Chandler's Cove exit.

Once she was off the turnpike, the Atlantic stretched in front of her. Since Boston she'd been catching glimpses of the ocean, appearing, then vanishing, then reappearing, on the right-hand side of the car. Now she was close enough to see the white surf crashing onto shore.

The air, rushing in through the open driver's window, had taken on a pungent, saltwater scent. Above, gulls screeched messages to their friends.

Minutes along the secondary highway, she reached a private road. No building was visible—only a sedate sign betrayed the presence of Sound Research Inc. She pulled up to the barrier, pushed her sunglasses onto the top of her head and smiled at the guard. "Hi, I'm Stefanie Taylor. Mr. Finch is expecting me."

The young man checked his book, then pressed a button, allowing the barrier to swing up. "Yes, Miss Taylor. Just follow along to your right."

Ahead, the road curved, affording her first view of the enormous, glass-and-marble Sound Research building. Its glitzy architecture struck her as totally incongruous with the pastoral Maine setting.

Stefanie felt a strong twinge of dismay, knowing she didn't want to work for any company as insensitive to its surroundings as this one clearly was. The offices of Sound Research Inc. smacked of downtown Houston, not traditional New England.

She pulled into a parking space marked for visitors and cut her engine, wondering if the gold-colored glass of the building's windows had been tinted with real gold dust. Every detail of this complex screamed "money."

The outrageous sum Finch was offering for the photo assignment suddenly didn't seem so unbelievable. If Sound Research Inc. wasn't a Fortune 500 company, it must be right up there at number 501 or 502.

Stefanie stared unhappily at the polished-brass front door, tempted to restart the Pontiac and head directly back to the Boston airport. And then what? Sit in her apartment, waiting for an assignment that suited her fancy to turn up? Cringing every time she used a credit card, afraid she'd be over her limit? And knowing that, when an offer she liked did come her way, it would pay about as much as the Brazilian fiasco had?

No. There comes a time, she told herself firmly, to bite the bullet. Besides, what did it matter whether she liked the looks of this building or didn't really want to go to Scotland? Hadn't she decided only yesterday to be more practical? Yet here she was, wavering already.

"I resolve," she whispered firmly into the rearview mirror as she checked her makeup, "to be more practical from this moment on."

Stefanie freed her portfolio from the confines of the back seat, locked the car and headed along the walkway.

Air-conditioned coolness, Muzak and a perfectly groomed receptionist greeted her inside. An ornately mirrored elevator whisked her to the tenth floor. She felt it slowing, took a deep breath, then pasted a smile firmly on her face as the doors opened.

A second, equally perfect receptionist returned Stefanie's smile from behind a desk. "Miss Taylor?"

Stefanie nodded, hearing the elevator doors close behind her, sealing her fate.

The receptionist pressed an intercom button, murmured a few words, then led the way down a corridor to an office. Its open door bore a sign reading David Finch, Vice President.

"Stefanie Taylor! A pleasure to meet you." David Finch rose from his desk, keenly aware of the surge of relief he felt at seeing her. She'd do! She'd more than do. She was damned attractive. Thank the Lord he didn't have to start looking all over again. Nancy Goitano's disappearance had caused them enough delay.

He extended his hand, his eyes sweeping Stefanie in a quick, practiced assessment. A little thin, certainly not a classic beauty, but she'd be fine. Her eyebrows were a touch heavy, her mouth was too wide, but the skin was good—pale and smooth. And her eyes were nice. Very nice. Large, warm, hazel eyes—the color of sherry aged in oak. And her riotous dark hair was wonderfully elemental. She looked almost like a wild thing herself.

Yes, she'd be an asset with the press and in the public relations pictures. And PR was the name of this particular game.

"So, I see you made the drive up from Boston all right, Miss Taylor. Please sit down. Tell me how your trip was."

"Quite pleasant...no problems at all." Stefanie glanced casually about Finch's office. It was both impeccable and formal, like the man himself. He was clearly "Mr. Finch," not "David." The gray wallpaper was the precise shade of his gray, pinstripe suit, and only a tone or two darker than the silvery gray of his hair. She imagined an entire closet filled with suits that matched various rooms.

"Well, now that you're here, let's not waste any more time. I'll fill you in on the details of the project, then you can ask me all the questions you like."

"Before you divulge your secrets," Stefanie said with a smile, "wouldn't you like to look at my portfolio?" She picked up her case from beside the chair and began unzipping it. "My work might not be exactly what you want."

Finch brushed the idea off with a wave of his hand. "I've already checked your credentials and your reputation, Miss Taylor. You're what we want."

Stefanie smiled uneasily. This entire situation was making her uncomfortable. She wasn't certain precisely what was bothering her—Finch's secretiveness on the phone yesterday, the exorbitant pay, or the apparent urgency. There was something very strange about this project, something vaguely unreal. From the intent way he was watching her, she knew she was about to learn what it was.

"Let's get down to specifics, Miss Taylor. First off, the equipment we're testing is something we've developed here at Sound Research, something we're extremely proud of. We have an engineer on staff—name of Jeffery Osborne—who's absolutely brilliant. He's developed an incredibly enhanced variation of sonar. Know much about the technology?"

SONAR. Stefanie tried to recall what the acronym stood for. The phrase came to her—Sound Navigation And Ranging. Basically sonar was an underwater echo-sounding system that could locate solid masses. So the photography part of the project must involve shooting aquatic creatures, not land animals.

"I know a little about sonar," she said in answer to Finch's question. "But not much. I've scuba dived to get most of my underwater shots. But I've done a few projects with teams that were using sonar-equipped submersibles."

Finch nodded, a knowing smile creeping across his face. "Yes. You got your shot of the coelacanth on one of those assignments, didn't you?"

"My compliments, Mr. Finch. You've obviously done your homework on me."

"That shot is one of the reasons we knew you'd be interested in this project, Miss Taylor. You're already famous for getting a picture of a fish thought to be extinct for seventy million years."

"I'm afraid," Stefanie admitted with a wry smile, "it didn't make me the least bit famous. If I'd gotten the first picture of a coelacanth, maybe. Unfortunately someone beat me to it by a good many years. All I ended up with were minor mentions in a few photography magazines."

"Well, as I told you yesterday, the Sound Research shoot is going to make your name a household word. This time you're going to be first. And what you're going to photograph will excite the entire world."

Stefanie realized she was leaning forward, eagerly curious, willing Finch to continue.

"Miss Taylor... Sound Research is about to demonstrate the capabilities of its new sonar by tracking down the Loch Ness Monster."

Stefanie sank back into her chair, disappointment overwhelming her. Talk about fame being fleeting! She'd barely gotten a whiff of the idea of being famous, let alone a taste of fame itself. She'd come all the way from Chicago, only to learn David Finch was a member of the lunatic fringe. Terrific! She'd known there was something weird about this deal. Weird? Try downright crazy! She tried to think of something to say. Nothing came to mind that wasn't incredibly rude.

Finch grinned at her. "I gather I've left you speechless."

"That isn't," she managed civilly, "exactly how I'd phrase it. Mr. Finch, minor as my professional reputation may be, I take it seriously. If you'd told me what you were up to over the phone yesterday, you could have saved the expense of my trip.''

"Look, Miss Taylor. I apologize for being blunt, but I suspect you've jumped to conclusions."

"And I suspect," Stefanie replied evenly, "it was an eminently reasonable jump. I can understand why Nancy Goitano backed out. I'm sure she had no more interest in a search for a nonexistent monster than I have."

"The fact is..." Finch paused for a moment, looking uncomfortable. "The fact is, Nancy was thrilled with the idea of this search. She's done underwater work for us before—on projects we've conducted for the U.S. Navy. She knows how Sound Research operates, knows we'd never be involved in anything frivolous. She was eager to be part of the team."

"What happened, then?"

"I have no idea," Finch admitted slowly. "Nancy seems to have disappeared into thin air. She organized all the photographic equipment for the shoot, was apparently set to go, then didn't turn up here for the final meeting before the team left for Scotland. She'd booked a flight from New York to Boston, but wasn't on it.

"We're worried about her, of course, but we can hardly cancel the sonar demonstration because of it. There's too much at stake, too many people committed to it."

Stefanie eyed him closely, deciding he was telling the truth about the other woman not simply backing out. A disquieting chill seized her. Finch was talking again. She tried to push the issue of Nancy Goitano's disappearance aside, tried to concentrate on what he was saying.

"I assume you've heard of Rossmuir University?" he asked.

"Of course. It's as well regarded as the large Ivy League schools, isn't it?"

"Even more so in some disciplines. In fact, Rossmuir's Marine Biology Department is considered the finest in America. And our project is a collaboration between Sound Research and Rossmuir.

"Our sonar will do the tracking. Jeffery Osborne is looking after that, of course. And he has overall responsibility for the search. But Matthew Garrett, head of marine biology at Rossmuir, is in charge of the nature aspect. He and his assistant will be doing a lot of environmental testing in the lake. And our photographer will report to him. The shots of the Loch Ness Monster will constitute much of his scientific validation."

"Scientific validation?" Stefanie repeated uncertainly.

"Yes. You see, despite what you think, we aren't talking about a fictitious creature at all. We're talking about an existent, but unconfirmed, species."

Stefanie stared at the man, feeling like crying and laughing at the same time. He couldn't be serious. His face told her he was. She glanced around the elegant office. Rossmuir University and a major high-tech company. This wasn't adding up. At least, she couldn't believe what it was adding up to.

She looked at Finch again, her mind racing. Either he was an awfully good actor or he actually believed this nonsense he was spouting. He couldn't!

"Well," she tried, "I'm sure there could be *something* in the lake, but the Loch Ness Monster's a joke! A myth, right? Folklore?"

Finch shook his head. "You probably have no idea how many countries, how many individuals, have mounted searches in that lake over the years, how much money has been spent trying to find the Loch Ness Monster. I'm not talking about any *joke*."

Stefanie swallowed hard, wishing she could take back her words, realizing she had just implied the vice president of Sound Research was a moron. Clearly he wasn't. But that meant...

No! There was no way this inconceivable project could be for real. That wasn't possible! But what if it was and she'd just blown her chance to be part of it?

She had to back up and listen for a minute. Frantically she searched for something to say that would appease Finch, that would at least wipe the look of annoyance from his face. "What I mean...I guess what I was trying to say...is there's never been any scientific evidence. There hasn't...has there?"

Finch smiled wryly. "Relax, Miss Taylor. I must admit, my initial reaction to this whole idea was much like yours. But, to answer your question, yes. In recent years there's been considerable interest from the scientific community. The species has even been given a name, *Nessiteras rhombopteryx*. And there've been articles about Nessie searches published in serious scientific journals—the *New Scientist* and *Technology Review* to name only two."

"Nessie," Stefanie repeated quietly. "Nessie...named after Loch Ness."

"You may be making that connection backward. *'Niseag'* is the Gaelic word for water horse. According to locals, the lake was named, centuries ago, for the monster that lived in it."

Stefanie looked at Finch skeptically. "Do they seriously believe that story? Or is it just a come-on for tourists?"

Finch shrugged. "I'm not certain. They are awfully enthusiastic about their monster legend. But, of course, Nessie isn't really a monster at all.

"Matthew Garrett figures the creatures are descended from some sort of prehistoric sea lion. He holds to a theory that there's a breeding population in Loch Ness—probably been there since the ice age. Recorded sightings date back to the sixth century."

"But...cameras have been around for over a hundred years. And there's never been a definitive photograph taken? If these creatures are living in the lake, then surely by now..."

"Someone has to be first, Miss Taylor. It's just like your coelacanth. Until someone got that first picture, no one knew the fish still existed. We're offering you the chance to be first this time."

Stefanie pushed her hair back, trying to think. Finch was sitting here, straight-faced, telling her Nessies existed. That was absurd! But Rossmuir University? Sound Research Inc.? She certainly didn't know more about the subject than their experts. In fact, everyone involved in this project probably knew a zillion times more than she did. What if there really were Nessies in that lake? What if she actually captured one of the creatures on film?

"Are you familiar with the 'Surgeon's' photograph?" Finch asked, interrupting her thoughts. "It's the most famous of the Nessie shots." He reached for a folder on his desk and passed her a photograph from it.

Stefanie stared at it. "Yes. I've seen this reproduced in books. It certainly looks like there's some sort of huge animal in the water but..."

"A vacationer—a reputable gynecologist—took that picture way back in 1934. Tests were done on the negative to prove it hadn't been tampered with. There've been other photographs since this one that have been just as tantalizingly suggestive. But no one has ever gotten close enough, none of the pictures have been quite clear enough, to provide absolute proof. You could get the shot that is."

"I...Mr. Finch, if people have been trying to get that shot for decades, what makes you think this search is going to succeed where so many others have failed?"

"Because of our sonar. Jeffery Osborne has come up with a sonar that's so accurate, has such a wide sweep, that we can't fail to hone in on one of the creatures. Loch Ness is an enormous area even to think about pinpointing an object in. Other search parties have used sonar, but never sonar with our capabilities. That's what we're demonstrating, Miss Taylor. Our sonar can do things no previous type has ever been able to do."

Stefanie watched Finch as he spoke. He seemed so sincere, sounded so convincing.

"Just think of it!" He slapped the top of his desk emphatically. "Submarines can still hide in the fjords of Sweden, can avoid the Swedish navy's sophisticated sonar. And we're going to show the world a sonar that enables us to track a thirty-foot-long animal at such close range that Miss Stefanie Taylor will be able to shoot a definitive picture of it—the very first one."

"I'd be first," Stefanie whispered, vaguely aware she was trembling with excitement.

"You'd be first. And every government in the world, every private concern in the field of underwater investigation, would be looking at your photographs and wanting to buy Sound Research's product. Your reputation would soar from minor to monumental. You'd be able to write your own ticket from there on in."

The office was silent. Stefanie could hear herself breathing, could feel her heart pounding.

"Well?" Finch asked quietly.

She smiled nervously at him, still uncertain whether Sound Research was involved in a scientific project or a wild-goose chase. But, whatever it was, she was hooked.

How could she be? What had happened to "practical"? Less than an hour ago she'd resolved to be practical. Rushing off to join in a search for Nessie might be the most impractical thing she'd ever done. Except the money was still practical, wasn't it? *Be honest,* a little voice whispered inside her head. *It isn't the money. You simply can't take a chance on missing out on the opportunity of a lifetime.*

Stefanie cleared her throat. "Well, Mr. Finch... you've got yourself a photographer."

David Finch extended his hand. "Welcome to the team, Miss Taylor. Now all we have to do is sign your contract and get you to Scotland." He buzzed the intercom on his desk. "Miss Levitt, please get that contract ready for signatures, then book Miss Taylor a flight to Glasgow—the first one you can get her on out of Logan International."

"Wait a minute, Mr. Finch! I'm used to traveling fast and light, but there are limits. I didn't even bring a change of clothes with me today, let alone any equipment."

"I thought I'd mentioned equipment. Nancy arranged for everything. It went over on the same flight as the search team. As far as clothes go, do some shopping in Boston before you get on the plane—or wait till you get to Scotland. We're not on a tight budget. I'll give you a company card you can use."

Stefanie shook her head firmly. "Regardless of what Nancy's already shipped over, I have to go back to Chicago for some of my own gear. The big equipment, things like floodlights and strobes, don't matter much. But I have to take a couple of cameras I know inside out—the same with lenses and range finders."

"Miss Taylor, we have top-of-the-line equipment waiting there for you."

"I'm sure you do. But it isn't *my* equipment. I have a few things that are almost impossible to buy. They won't be waiting there for me. And it would take me weeks of trial and error to feel comfortable with a new camera. Mr. Finch, if we do find Nessie, I want the best pictures possible. I'm sure you do, as well. Underwater photography's awfully tricky. I assume all the shots will be from some type of submersible?"

"Yes, of course. The lake's too cold and deep for anything else. We're using a very small research submarine. Loch Ness has a lot of underwater caverns and Osborne wanted a sub that could get into most of them. Things may be a little crowded, but what we sacrifice in space we make up for in maneuverability."

Stefanie nodded, finally making sense of Finch's question about claustrophobia. "Well," she went on, "having to shoot through a sub's windows just adds to the complexity. But, even without the additional glare, there are all kinds of problems with refraction, reflection, dispersion, light absorption, attenuation—"

Finch threw up his hands. "I concede your point. You need your own camera. How soon can you get things together?"

"As far as my clothes and equipment are concerned, it's simply a matter of going home and packing. The only other thing I need is film."

"Film we have tons of."

"I don't mean to sound like a perfectionist..." Stefanie paused, laughing at herself. "I guess that's what I am when it comes to my shots. I need to have film I know will perform exactly as I expect it to.

"Nancy may have chosen what I want. But if she didn't specify the type I always use, or order the variety of speeds I'll want on hand, I'll be at a major disadvantage. I've got a supplier in Chicago who'll have everything in stock. The only thing is," she added, glancing at her watch, "he'll be closed by the time I get back."

"Phone ahead. Have him courier whatever film you want to your apartment. Then we can book you onto a flight out of O'Hare tonight. That'll get you into Glasgow in the morning."

Finch sounded as if the world would collapse if there was any further delay.

"For some reason," Stefanie teased gently, "I'm feeling more than a little rushed. Am I allowed to call my parents—let them know where I'm going? Or isn't there time for that?"

"I don't know. Are they long-winded?" Finch paused, grinning at her for a moment. "You look after your packing and your parents and I'll arrange a flight and make sure there's someone to pick you up at the airport in Glasgow. You'll need a ride up to Drumnadrochit—the little town on Loch Ness where the team is staying. Just be sure to get some sleep on the plane. You'll undoubtedly need that, as well.''

"Mr. Finch, I'm getting the distinct impression you're a slave driver.''

"Me, a slave driver? Miss Taylor, at the risk of misquoting Al Jolson, 'you ain't seen nothin' yet!' Wait until you meet your bosses on the search. By the time you've spent a couple of days with Jeffery Osborne and Matthew Garrett, you'll be thinking of me as positively laid-back.''

STEFANIE CLOSED her apartment door and slid her portfolio into the hall closet. It was one thing she wouldn't be needing in Scotland.

Scotland. The reality—or was it the unreality?—of this assignment hadn't quite sunk in yet. Her glance swept slowly around the living room. This was reality—a room filled with reminders of special people and places.

She studiously ignored an enormous dust bunny lurking in one corner and focused on her three-legged Moroccan stool. She'd bought that stool the same day she'd braved her first camel ride.

Her gaze shifted to a life-size parrot created out of delicate coral wood. It had shared her seat on a flight home from Venezuela years ago.

On one end table sat the hand-carved, teak photograph frame she'd found in an Indian bazaar. She stared wistfully at Peter's face, looking out at her from inside the frame.

She picked up the photograph. It brought back so many memories. But Peter was more than a memory. He was her friend—he and his *adorable* bride, Cindy.

Stefanie realized she was gritting her teeth and consciously unclenched her jaw muscles. What was the saying? "Gentlemen prefer blondes." It was certainly true. Absently, she brushed back her long tangle of dark, curly hair. Peter always referred to it as "frizzy." Her fingers caught in a snarl. Well, maybe it did tend to frizz a little. But who wanted long, pale, silky-straight hair like Cindy's?

Peter did. That's who. Peter, who'd relegated himself to the role of friend, not lover. Stefanie stared at the strong, smiling face. She'd taken that photograph. When? Six years ago? Seven? She and Peter had been together a long time.

It seemed as if he'd always been there for her, been her comfortable refuge in Chicago, always accepting her as she was, always telling her she was beautiful, not seeming to realize she was actually far too tall and skinny.

He'd never pushed her, had just lived his own life when she was gone. But he'd always been there waiting when she arrived back in the city, back in his life.

Until a few months ago. Oh, he'd still been in Chicago, had still told her to come over the moment she'd called. But he'd had adorable Cindy waiting with him, hanging on to his arm for dear life, devouring him with catlike eyes the entire, torturous hour Stefanie had spent with them. Cindy—the slinky blond leech!

Cindy, with her perfect hair and perfect figure and those perfect, pearly fangs. *Teeth*, Stefanie's brain corrected automatically. Cindy was Miss Blond Perfection. And what was Stefanie? Miss Brunette Imperfection, with kinky dark hair, a string-bean body and front teeth with a space between them.

Stefanie sighed wearily. She had only herself to blame about Peter. If she'd wanted him as a permanent fixture in her life she could have had him—could have spent more time at home, could have married him. She'd loved him. Maybe she still did. But not enough. Not enough to give up the life-style that meant more to her than any man. She opened the drawer of the end table, stuck Peter facedown inside, then went into her bedroom to pack.

CHAPTER TWO

STEFANIE RESCUED her cartons of film and battered suitcase from the carousel at Prestwick Airport and piled them onto the luggage cart she'd nabbed. She tossed her raincoat on top of the pile, shifted her gadget bag from one shoulder to the other and wearily started through the crush of bodies to join a customs line. No, not line—the sign on the wall read Queue Here For Customs.

Whichever it was—line or queue—it was moving slowly. Stefanie shuffled forward a few feet, adjusting her bag once more, wondering how two cameras, four extra lenses and a couple of range finders could possibly weigh so much. To make matters worse, her imagination insisted they were growing heavier by the second. They weighed at least two hundred pounds by the time she reached a customs officer.

He glanced routinely at her passport, gave her belongings a cursory check, then asked the purpose of her visit. His eyes lit up at her reply. "Aye, so all this film is for Nessie, then. Well, you'll find our beastie's far too canny for mere humans. But I wish you luck."

"Thank you." Stefanie smiled at his obvious amusement. "I'm sure I'll need all the luck I can get."

She reorganized her luggage cart and maneuvered it over to a wall, glancing about for the someone who should be there to meet her. A stocky man with short-cropped brown hair was hurrying across the arrivals level in her direction. He made eye contact with her and nodded a curt greeting.

"Stefanie Taylor?"

She glanced away from the approaching man, her eyes searching for whoever had spoken her name. The deep, male voice belonged to a lanky, pleasant-looking fellow in his mid-thirties.

"Yes, I'm Stefanie Taylor." She looked quickly back to the stocky man. He'd paused some fifteen feet away and stood watching her. Puzzled, she turned once more to the man who'd spoken.

He smiled a broad, easy smile that transformed his face from pleasant looking to attractive. "I'm Matt Garrett. David Finch asked me to meet you."

"But..." Stefanie stared over at the other man again or rather, at where he'd been moments before. A little girl clutching a tattered teddy bear now stood on the spot.

"Is something wrong?"

"No. Nothing's wrong," she answered absently, still picturing the stocky, brown-haired man. David Finch had sent Matt Garrett to meet her. Then who was the other man? No one, she decided quickly. Merely a man who'd mistaken her for someone else.

She forced her attention to Matt. "Finch told me he'd arrange for someone to collect me. It's just...I guess I wasn't expecting it to be the boss."

"The first rule you'll have to remember," Matt warned with a quiet chuckle, "is never to let Jeffery Osborne catch you referring to me as the 'boss.'"

"But...Finch said I'd be reporting to you...that you're in charge of the biological end of the project."

"I am. But Osborne's in charge of the overall search, and as far as he's concerned, the nature angle exists solely to demonstrate the wonders of his sonar."

Matt paused, grinning at her. "Don't look so concerned. That's only his view. And he won't run roughshod over us. Without my scientific credentials and your photographs to back him up, his sonar might as well be dead in the water. Just keep in mind he has the final say about things. This is very much a Sound Research show. It's their money, their equipment, and they get to make the rules."

Stefanie nodded her understanding. "Finch did give me that impression. The contract he had me sign practically bound me into slavery for the next few weeks." She silently congratulated herself when Matt laughed, surprised she could even think straight after an overnight flight, let alone manage to say something amusing.

"Well, I wouldn't go quite so far as accusing Finch of being a slave driver, Stefanie, but I know what you mean. Sound Research is being incredibly thorough. They're taking this search very seriously."

"And are you, Matt?" Damn! She hadn't meant to blurt the question out so bluntly. She should at least have waited until they'd gotten out of the airport. But she was desperately curious to know what a biologist thought of this monster hunt.

He stared into space for a moment, his ambivalence apparent.

Stefanie watched him, revising her impression from attractive to *very* attractive. The zoom lens in her mind zeroed in on his face, focusing on his expressive eyes. They were the rich color of dark chocolate. His longish hair, equally dark, was starting to gray at the temples.

The lower part of his face was darkened by a five-o'clock shadow. At—what time was it? She'd never been very sharp when it came to traveling through time zones, but it couldn't be noon here yet. She smiled to herself, deciding his five-o'clock shadow was extremely virile looking.

"I'm here in Scotland," Matt finally replied. "That should say a fair bit about my belief in this project."

"Finch mentioned you have a theory about the Nessies," Stefanie pressed, deciding that since she'd jumped in she might as well make the most of the opportunity. "That they're a type of prehistoric sea lion?"

"Well . . . that's one possibility. It's logical from an evolutionary perspective. And the description of them fits. According to eye witnesses, the animal has a small, almost delicate head, a proportionately long neck and a sleek, slender body with seallike flippers. Nessie sounds like either a giant otter or an elongated seal— elongated to about thirty feet.

"Of course," Matt added, "the sea-lion theory and reality might be entirely different. The creatures could turn out to be nothing more than giant sea serpents. But if they are something unique, I sure want to be in on discovering what."

"That sounds a lot like my rationale for being here. If someone's going to photograph the Loch Ness Monster, I want it to be me."

"Maybe it will be, Stefanie."

"Maybe. Maybe as in 'highly likely,' or maybe as in 'there's a ghost of a chance'?"

"I'm a scientist, not a bookmaker," Matt admonished her with a grin. "I don't give odds. But I'll certainly tell you what I know, give you an idea what you might be facing as far as the photography goes. In fact, I figured we'd use the trip back to Drumnadrochit to talk about the Nessies."

"Drum..." Stefanie laughed at herself. "How can I be heading for a place when I can't even pronounce its name? I'd be far happier if Loch Ness was near Aberdeen or some other city that didn't sound as if it belonged in a fairy tale."

"Well, the name just takes a couple of tries to get your tongue around. You have to break it down. The *drum* you've got. And the *na* is easy. Try thinking of the *droch* part like *dock* with an *R* stuck in." Matt paused, his gaze sweeping her. "But I guess bombarding you with both biology and phonetics lessons right off the bat isn't the greatest idea. You look absolutely beat."

Stefanie self-consciously brushed her hair back, trying to smooth it's tangles with her hand. Terrific! She'd obviously made a wonderful first impression. She glanced down at her wrinkled outfit, wishing she'd had more time to organize. Her pale blue cotton jumpsuit had been hanging in the closet, clean, and she'd thrown it on. Now, ten hours later, it looked as if she'd pulled it from a rag bin.

Matt was eyeing her gadget bag. "Let's get going. I'll take that for you. It looks awfully heavy."

"It is. But I'd rather stick you with this luggage cart. I've learned the knack of balancing my bag. If you take it now, I'm liable to tilt."

Matt reached for the cart's handle, rewarding her with another easy smile.

Stefanie cranked her rating of his looks up one more notch, noting the whiteness of his even teeth and the crinkly laugh lines that had appeared beside his eyes. Her glance flickered involuntarily to his left hand, to his naked third finger.

She fell in behind him, silently reminding herself the lack of a ring meant absolutely nothing. Any man who looked like a young James Garner was either gay or taken . . . and she'd bet her bottom dollar Matt Garrett wasn't gay.

He stopped near the exit. "They don't let these carts out of the terminal and there's not much point lugging your things all the way to my car. You wait here while I get it. I'll be back in ten minutes or so."

Matt had barely disappeared, when a loudspeaker burbled out a message. Something in the garbled words caught Stefanie's attention. She listened for them to be repeated.

The speaker crackled again. "Would Mr. Matthew Garrett please pick up one of the white telephones on the arrivals level."

Stefanie glanced about for a white phone, spying one on a counter several yards away.

Keeping an eye on the cart, she pushed her way through the crowd and picked up the receiver. "I'm answering the page for Matthew Garrett."

There was a momentary silence, then a vaguely familiar voice responded. "Miss Taylor?"

"Yes?"

"David Finch here."

His voice sounded strained, not as heartily confident as she recalled it.

"Matt's here at the airport, Mr. Finch, but he's gone to get his car—said he'd be about ten minutes. Could I take a message, or do you want to hold?"

There was a long pause before Finch answered. "I'll talk to you about it. Now I don't mean to alarm you, Miss Taylor. There's no problem. It's just that I tried to reach Osborne and Garrett in Drumnadrochit this morning and missed them both. I wanted to catch someone in case... Look, the reason I'm calling is I thought I'd better let the team know about something.

"It has nothing to do with the search, but I didn't want you all to hear it from some other source and start worrying about anything."

Get to the point! Stefanie ordered silently.

"I know how people can work themselves into a state over nothing." Finch coughed out a nervous little laugh. "It's about Nancy Goitano."

Oh, Lord! Stefanie closed her eyes, certain of what was coming. Nancy had turned up and wanted her job back. She was probably on her way to Scotland this very minute. And that would leave one Stefanie Taylor completely out in the cold.

"Miss Taylor... Nancy's dead."

"Dead?" Stefanie realized the word had been soundless and tried again. "Dead?" This time it squeaked out.

"I'm afraid so. As I said, it had absolutely nothing to do with our project. I just thought the news might be upsetting to you people. I know Osborne often picks up the *New York Times* when he's out of the country. When I called Drumnadrochit and learned he'd gone into Inverness this morning... I really didn't want the team to learn about this from a front page."

Stefanie's mind whirled. "Mr. Finch... why would it be front-page news?"

"Well, the fact is, Nancy was murdered. The police haven't released any details, but apparently it was a rather gruesome business, even for New York. Now I don't want you to think there might be something..."

Finch continued his rambling. Stefanie heard only the drone of his voice, not the words. There were too many questions racing around in her head, demanding answers, for her to listen to what he was saying.

Why was Finch so extremely upset? This wasn't the forceful, assured man she'd met in Maine. Today he was having trouble putting sentences together. Why? Because he'd known Nancy far better than he'd implied? Or because there really *was* some relation between her murder and the project?

Stefanie realized Finch had stopped talking. She mumbled something that was undoubtedly incoherent, hung up and walked shakily back to the luggage cart. She'd barely reached it, when Matt appeared in the doorway.

She watched him stride toward her, and wished she knew him better, wished she didn't feel so alone.

He stared at her face as he approached. "Problems?"

Stefanie nodded, quickly filling him in on her conversation.

He shook his head. "That's an awfully tough way to go. I just met Nancy briefly. Did you know her?"

"No. Only by reputation. She was a top notch photographer. Matt... there isn't anything strange about this search, is there? Nothing that might have to do with Nancy's murder?"

"What do you mean? Did Finch say something to give you that idea?"

"Completely the opposite. He kept telling me there wasn't any connection. But he seemed so upset, so anxious to reassure me, that he made me nervous."

"I can't imagine there's anything to be nervous about, Stefanie. Nancy disappeared before the project even got under way. And murder isn't exactly a rarity in New York City. It's a terrible thing to have happened, but the possibility that it's somehow related to this search strikes me as pretty remote."

He placed a hand tentatively on Stefanie's arm. "Look, you're tired. That always makes things seem worse than they are. I know this has been a rotten welcome to Scotland, but work on putting it out of your mind, okay? A woman you didn't know and whom I'd barely met was murdered thousands of miles away. There's not a thing we can do about it. So we'll both try not to think about it. Deal?"

Stefanie nodded. A stranger's murder was definitely something she didn't want to dwell on. Matt was right. What could it possibly have to do with the search?

"Good. Now let's get out of here. You'll feel better once we're on our way. If you grab your coat and suitcase, I'll take those boxes."

He stared, with apparent amusement, as she moved her things off the two cartons of film. "I hadn't noticed what these were. We brought over enough film to shoot every cubic inch of water in Loch Ness. Didn't Finch tell you that?"

"Well . . . yes. I was just worried it wouldn't be the kind and speeds I wanted."

Matt glanced at the brand name. "Ektachrome. Yeah, that's what we've got. There's a truckload of it stashed in the research sub—takes up half our storage space. There must be a hundred rolls of every speed available."

"Oh." Stefanie shrugged her embarrassment, recalling the fuss she'd made with Finch.

OUTSIDE THE TERMINAL the day was sunny and warm, without a trace of Scotland's legendary drizzle. Matt had left his little red hatchback parked in a No Stopping zone near the door. He opened the hatch, shoved the cartons and suitcase into the car and reached for Stefanie's gadget bag.

"No, that's okay, Matt. I always keep this with me. Old photographer's habit," she explained at his questioning look. "The moment you let your camera out of reach, you miss a fantastic shot."

"That a law of nature I've never heard of?"

"Well, it's definitely a law of something. It never fails."

Stefanie reached to open the car door, then stopped, realizing the hatchback was right-hand drive. "I'll have to get my mind in gear," she told Matt, heading around and slipping into the passenger's side. "I hope you aren't expecting any work from me today. Until I've had some sleep, I'd probably start shooting with the lens cap still on my camera."

Matt grinned, bending his long legs under the steering wheel. "Well, I won't ask you to take any pictures, but do you think you could make it through a lunch stop? I'm starving and we have a couple of hours' drive ahead of us. If you give me time to eat, I'll let you sleep in the car during the trip."

"And will you save me from drowning if I nod off into my soup during lunch?"

"Word of honor! I once earned a Boy Scout badge for lifesaving, so I can certainly handle the treacherous tides in a bowl of soup."

Matt started the car and wheeled it away from the terminal. "The woman who owns the guest house we're staying in recommended a place to eat, a restaurant called the Auld Highland House. Sound all right?"

"Sounds too authentic to be true!" Stefanie gazed out the side window as Matt drove, refusing to think about Nancy Goitano, concentrating on the grimy stone buildings of Glasgow. The sheer age of Old World cities always impressed her. These sooty slums they were passing through must have been here for hundreds of years.

"It looks even more depressing without the sunshine." Matt's voice drew her attention back to him. "You hit a good day. When Osborne, Mary and I arrived, it was raining to beat the band. Mary spent a year studying in Scotland, and according to her, rain's standard fare."

"Mary's your wife?" The words popped out before Stefanie could stop them. She mentally kicked herself for being so transparent.

"No." Matt gazed across the car for a moment, as if trying to decode her question. "No. I've been divorced for over five years."

Stefanie ordered herself to look nonchalant, but the way Matt was biting back a knowing grin made her squirm.

Mercifully he stared out through the windshield again. "I'd assumed Finch filled you in about Mary. She's a post-grad student at Rossmuir—doing a doctorate in oceanography. I'm her thesis adviser. She's along as my assistant.''

"A trip back to Scotland sounds like a major treat for a student.''

"It is. She likes the country—was eager to come. Whereas,'' he added with a wry glance, ''most of my faculty associates wouldn't have touched this project with the proverbial ten-foot pole. In their view, a search for the Loch Ness Monster is a little too far-out.''

"And that doesn't bother you, Matt?''

"Not particularly. I've learned not to take my professional image too seriously.''

"Does that mean you have an inheritance tucked away as insurance?'' Stefanie teased.

Matt grinned at her. "No...but it means I have tenure at Rossmuir. And I'm head of the department. My position's pretty secure. Besides, Sound Research does top scientific work. Their name alone makes this search quasi-respectable.''

"I guess that's true. And what about the rest of the team? Finch only told me about you and Jeffery Osborne. Who else is there?''

"No one. We're the team—Osborne, Mary, you and me.''

"That's it? You mean you rate an assistant and Jeffery Osborne, mighty sonar inventor, doesn't?''

"It isn't exactly a question of rating. I'm running too many tests to handle them alone. Besides, Osborne's a bit of a workaholic. He seems to relish the idea of doing everything himself.''

Matt drove quietly for a few moments, then looked back over at her. "By the way, when I told you I didn't have a wife, you were supposed to reciprocate with details of your personal life.''

Stefanie laughed at his candor. ''Is that so? Those are the rules you play by in Maine, are they? In Illinois we fancy ourselves a little more subtle. But just to satisfy your curiosity, I don't have a wife, either.''

''Very funny!''

''Nor a husband…nor a live-in.'' Stefanie turned her head away, hoping her pleasure at Matt's interest wasn't painfully obvious. Since Peter had removed himself from her life, she'd developed a nagging suspicion that she was over-the-hill in the appeal department. Matt apparently didn't think so. She glanced across the car again, expecting him to pursue their train of conversation.

Instead he pointed to a narrow river on the left, visible through occasional breaks in the rows of derelict waterfront buildings. ''That's the Clyde over there.''

''Oh.'' Stefanie scrambled for a more intelligent response. This man certainly jumped tracks quickly. ''The water looks filthy. Glasgow isn't exactly picture pretty, is it?''

''It's nicer downtown—famous for its parks.'' Matt checked a handwritten note lying on the dashboard. ''The Auld Highland House is on Queen. Watch for a main street called Gorbals. We turn there and take a bridge across the river. Then we should reach Queen after a few blocks.''

The restaurant materialized as expected. From the outside, it was a skinny three-story granite building—one of a series stretching along Queen. The solid row of shops was broken, here and there, by entrances to narrow alleyways.

Inside, the Auld Highland was full of warm woods and crisp white linens, and dominated by an enormous stone fireplace.

Stefanie spotted a sign pointing to the ladies' room as she was about to sit down, and hesitated, smoothing one hand across the wrinkles in her jumpsuit, remembering how awful she must look.

She put her gadget bag on a chair. "Excuse me. I'll just be a minute. Why don't you go ahead and order. I had breakfast shortly before we landed. All I could handle now is tea."

"You're going off and trusting me with that?" Matt nodded at the gadget bag. "I'm honored."

Stefanie made a face at him. "I expect you to guard it with your life."

Once in front of a mirror she groaned, seeing that wrinkled cotton was the least of her worries. This clearly wasn't the time to play "mirror, mirror on the wall." She was in even worse shape than she'd expected. Trying to sleep on the plane had left her hair looking as if she'd been tossed through a wind tunnel. And the makeup she'd applied after breakfast had completely vanished, leaving her face pale and shiny. Tired circles surrounded her eyes.

She dragged a brush through her hair, spent longer than she'd intended redoing her makeup, then stared critically into the mirror.

Is that the best you can manage? her image silently asked.

She turned away, realizing she was far more concerned about her appearance than usual. She opened the door of the ladies' room and gazed down the hall and across the breadth of the restaurant at Matt, aware she was looking at the reason for her concern.

Stefanie took only a few steps along the hallway before an urgent, husky whisper reached her.

"Still waters run deep."

She whirled toward the sound, catching her breath audibly as she recognized its source. Pressed into an alcove, out of view of the dining area, was the stocky, brown-haired man who'd been at the airport. His pale eyes bore icily into hers, fixing her to the spot.

Stefanie stared at him, feeling her throat constricting. He stared back. She realized he was expecting her to speak. "Wha...what?" she managed.

"Still waters run deep!" he hissed insistently.

"Uh...right. I guess...they do...sometimes."

She sensed, rather than saw, him start to move and forced her legs into action. She raced toward Matt, spinning back around as she reached their table, fully expecting the man to be on her heels.

No one! Nothing! Nothing except puzzled faces peering at her from other tables. Nothing except Matt's hand on her arm, his concerned voice slicing through her fear.

"Stefanie? What's wrong? What happened?"

"There was a man, Matt! A man hiding outside the ladies' room. He—"

Matt bolted from the table, across the restaurant and checked along the corridor. He paused outside the ladies' room, tapped on its door, then disappeared inside. Moments later he was striding back.

"There's not a soul there now, Stefanie."

Shakily she sank onto a chair.

A gray-haired waitress neared the table and stopped, glancing uncertainly from the tray in her hands to Matt and Stefanie. "Are you all right, ma'am?"

"Yes . . . it was just a man by the ladies' room . . . he startled me."

"I'll look, ma'am."

The waitress placed a huge sandwich before Matt, tea in front of Stefanie, then hurried off, her now empty tray clutched like a shield.

Stefanie reached for the teacup, realized her hands were trembling and changed her mind. She waited anxiously until the waitress returned.

"I didn't see anyone, ma'am. But the door into the close wasn't locked. He likely left through it."

"The 'close'?"

"Oh, the lane, ma'am . . . between the buildings. I'm sorry you were frightened. Can I get you anything else?"

"No. I'm fine, thank you."

The waitress nodded and moved off.

"I guess there are crazies the world over," Matt said once she was out of earshot. "You sure you're okay?"

"Yes, I am. But the man wasn't a crazy, Matt. At least, not just a random crazy. I saw him earlier—at the airport. He was heading over to me when you introduced yourself. Then he vanished. But he followed us here. He must have."

"You're certain it was the same man?"

Stefanie nodded.

"Stefanie . . . you're awfully tired. Maybe—"

"Matt, I'm a photographer! I look at people's faces. And I'm not mistaking that man. He was walking directly toward me in the airport, was staring straight at me. I assumed he'd been sent to meet me." She took a sip of tea, relieved to find her hands were steady.

"Matt...he spoke to me in the hallway just now...as if he were giving me a message. He said, 'Still waters run deep.'"

"Which means?"

"How do I know? It was *his* message. It didn't mean a thing to me."

"Still waters run deep," Matt repeated slowly. "I've heard the saying, of course, but it doesn't mean anything special to me, either. What did he look like?"

"Thirtyish, short brown hair, light blue eyes, bushy eyebrows, about five-foot-ten, heavy build, had on jeans, sneakers and a plaid shirt."

Matt grinned across the table at her. "What do you do? Take pictures with your eyes?"

"I told you, I look."

"Well, that description doesn't sound like anyone I've seen before. Maybe," he went on, his expression teasing, "when he saw you at the airport you bewitched him and he felt compelled to see you again."

"Oh, sure! The last thing I am at the moment is a bewitching sight. Witching is more like it! I look as if I should be riding a broom."

"I think...I think you look very pretty."

"Oh." Stefanie gulped down a mouthful of tea so quickly that she almost choked. Matt was watching her, his dark eyes confirming his words. "Oh...well, thank you. You're much kinder than the mirror in the ladies' room."

"What does a hunk of glass know about anything?" He smiled reassuringly. "Give me a minute to finish off this sandwich and we'll leave. I haven't forgotten my promise to let you sleep in the car. A little rest will probably do wonders."

"I intend to take you up on that promise, Matt. I travel so much I've learned to sleep just about anywhere." Stefanie drank the remainder of her tea, telling herself to calm down. Her brain didn't obey.

The man with the message refused to leave her thoughts. Try as she might, she couldn't make any sense of his words. The other patrons were still shooting curious glances in her direction. They obviously figured she'd escaped from a loony bin.

"I feel," she finally whispered, "like an idiot on display."

Matt laughed quietly. "Come on, then, idiot. We'll hit the road and get the hell out of Glasgow, away from Mr. Still Waters—whatever he meant. He probably didn't even know what he was talking about himself. Maybe he gets his jollies following women from the airport and scaring the hell out of them. But he's certainly not going to trail us all the way to Loch Ness."

CHAPTER THREE

BY THE TIME Matt cleared the outskirts of Glasgow, Stefanie was fast asleep beside him. He found himself glancing over at her now and then, each time wondering what was attracting him to her. She wasn't his type at all. He didn't go for tall, thin women.

Although *thin* didn't seem precisely the word to describe her. She definitely wasn't so slight that she didn't have a nice figure . . . quite the opposite. Maybe *fragile looking* was the right term. And she certainly had nice brown eyes. Hazel, actually—large, warm, hazel eyes. He'd noticed them right off. But, all in all, Stefanie Taylor wasn't his type.

Strange, then, that he'd felt a twinge of interest the first moment he'd seen her. She'd looked so vulnerable—as if she'd barely been able to cope with her luggage. He knew that wasn't the case, but he'd caught one glimpse of her and felt protective as hell.

He frowned, aware that was a dangerous feeling, especially if Stefanie Taylor turned out to be a little off kilter. Lord! He certainly hoped that wasn't the case. Desperate as they'd been for a replacement photographer, Finch surely hadn't sent him one with loose boards in her attic. That was all he'd need!

Since the first day in Drumnadrochit, he'd been spending all his spare time either dealing with Osborne's tantrums or trying to fend off the stray males who'd been sniffing around Mary. If his photographer turned out to be paranoid, he might as well throw in the towel.

He glanced at Stefanie again, wondering just how active her imagination was, hoping *overactive* wasn't the operative word. Not that he doubted there'd been a man in the restaurant—some lunatic who went around muttering nonsense to attractive women—but he couldn't believe the fellow had followed them from the airport. Stefanie must have been mistaken about that.

She'd had a long trip. She'd been tired and Finch's phone call had upset her. Hearing about a murder was enough to make anyone anxious—make anyone think someone was following them. A mistaken identity was understandable.

Matt checked the rearview mirror once more. The blue sedan he'd noticed as they left Glasgow was still behind them. Or was it a different blue car? For pete's sake! What difference did it make? He was on the major route between Glasgow and Inverness. Was it surprising he wasn't the only driver on the road? He drove on, drumming the steering wheel absently, hoping paranoia hadn't become a communicable disease.

"WAKE UP, Stefanie."

"Mmm..." She didn't want to wake up. She wanted to stay just as she was, curled into a half-asleep ball, her head nestled against Peter's shoulder. "Peter, I'm so tired...can't I have just ten more—" Reality struck like lightning. The solid, warm shoulder and comfortingly male scent didn't belong to Peter.

Stefanie jerked herself alert and stared, embarrassed, at Matt, feeling her face growing warm under his amused gaze.

"Sorry, Matt. I don't generally fall asleep on strange men's shoulders. Hope I didn't put yours out of wack."

"No permanent damage. Feel better for the sleep?"

"Yes. Much better, thanks. All I need is about ten more hours."

"Well, you can start getting them any time you like. We're here. That's the Galloway Guest House."

Stefanie stared through the windshield at the old, two-story stone house. A lush lawn sprawled in front of a colorful garden. A tiny ripple of relief washed over her. The Galloway Guest House looked like a place she'd enjoy staying at.

Her arrival in Glasgow had been a horror show. But that was past history. She wasn't going to even think about it again. If what she could see at the moment was typical, the tiny village of Drumnadrochit comprised a wonderful little world of its own.

"Now look behind us," Matt was saying. "The lake on the far side of the road is Loch Ness. Welcome to Nessiedom, Stefanie."

She turned, her eyes sweeping the breathtaking view, her hand automatically reaching into the back seat for her camera. She stopped herself. There'd be weeks to get shots of Loch Ness.

The far side of the glittering lake, a mile or more across, was clearly visible—a rocky mountain of land rising straight up from glass-smooth water. But in length the lake stretched out of sight in both directions.

"It's beautiful, Matt . . . and enormous. Finch told me it was large, but I hadn't expected this."

"It's almost twenty-five miles long—and incredibly deep. Probably over a thousand feet in some places."

Stefanie stared out over the water, the possibility of finding a thirty-foot-long creature in its depths seeming even more remote.

"You really think we can track down a Nessie in a lake that size, Matt?"

"It's possible. What we can turn up will depend on whether Osborne's sonar is as good as he claims. That remains to be seen. So far we've only taken the *Sea Horse* out for a few short trials—just to collect some offshore water samples and shale for testing and to play around with our equipment."

"*Sea Horse*. That's the name of your research sub?"

"*Our* research sub," Matt corrected her with a smile. "You're part of the team. In fact, we figured there was no sense in launching even a preliminary search until you'd arrived. If we'd located a Nessie without our photographer along, Osborne would have been suicidal."

"I get the impression Jeffery Osborne's more than a little temperamental."

"Well, I can't imagine anyone describing him as 'placid.' But he's reputed to be a genius when it comes to sonar. That's what matters." Matt opened his car door. "Come on. Let's go on in. If Mary or Osborne are around, I'll introduce you. Then you really should try for a little more sleep. The couple of hours you just had aren't enough."

Stefanie grabbed her gadget bag and followed Matt up the driveway. As they neared the house, its front door flew open and a round, cheery-looking woman of about sixty appeared. She smiled broadly, brushing back of strand of gray hair that had escaped her bun.

"So this is the lass you've all been waiting for, Matthew. Welcome to the Galloway Guest House, dear. I'm Florrie McFarlane."

Florrie grabbed Stefanie's hand, shook it heartily, then bustled her inside. "You look tired, dear. Would you like tea?"

"Well... I'm not sure what Matt has planned."

"We thought that if Mary and Osborne were here, Stefanie could meet them."

"Aye. Mary's in her room. But your Mr. Osborne hasn't come back from Inverness yet. I'll just show this lass the kitchen before we go up." Florrie propelled Stefanie down the hall, giving her a whirlwind tour.

"Breakfast is served in the dining room between seven and nine. But make yourself tea anytime you like—day or night. And there are usually scones in the bread box. I do love to bake, so whenever you want a snack, go right ahead."

"Thank you. You're certainly making me feel at home."

Florrie beamed at her. "That," she went on, gesturing to a door just outside the kitchen, "leads to the private part of the house—where Mr. McFarlane and I live. If you've a problem, you need only knock. I'll take you upstairs now, dear. Your room's ready and waiting."

"Don't bother, Florrie," Matt told her. "I'll show Stefanie which room is hers."

"You're a good lad, Matthew. I spend half my life running up and down those stairs. The room's not locked. I'll try to find a key later if you feel you need one, Stefanie."

Stefanie followed Matt along the main-floor hall-way to the stairs. "She seems nice."

"She's a gem. But I think I've been gaining a pound a day eating her baking."

"And her husband? Does he help run the place?"

Matt grinned back down at her as he reached the top of the staircase. "Running a guest house is hardly a fitting job for the lord provost of Drumnadrochit, Stefanie."

"I'm sure that's true . . . I'd probably be even surer if I knew what a lord provost was."

"The village mayor." Matt stopped at the first room along the hall and opened its door. "This is it."

Stefanie paused in the doorway, glancing around the airy, comfortable room, then toted her gadget bag over to the bed and dumped it on top of the chenille bed-spread. "Very nice. So tell me about Lord Provost McFarlane. What's his wife doing renting out rooms?"

"She says it's a way of keeping busy since her family grew up. I don't imagine the income hurts, either. Apparently things have changed in rural Scotland. Historically lord provosts were wealthy land owners. Nowadays I gather they're more likely to tend bar in the local tavern or clerk in a grocery store."

"And what about ours. Bartender? Grocery clerk?"

"Neither. Ours . . . are you ready for this?"

Stefanie grinned at Matt's teasing tone. "Hopefully I can handle whatever it is."

"Our Angus McFarlane is the proprietor of Ye Olde Loch Ness Monster Souvenir and Gift Shoppe, one of the major tourist traps in the village. Here we are, at-tempting to demystify the Nessies, and he capitalizes on the monster myth."

"And we're staying in his house...while we conduct a serious search?"

"Well, the Sound Research people weren't aware of his nefarious occupation when they booked us in here. Osborne was in a bit of a snit when he learned about it—insisted we should move out immediately. But that's just an example of his underdeveloped sense of humor. I think the situation's wonderfully ironic.

"I suspect Angus does, too, although the locals have mixed feelings about these searches. The activity on Loch Ness helps publicize the monster and helps bring in the tourists. But if the true facts about Nessie are discovered, the tourist trade is likely to drop off. It's the mystery that fascinates people.

"At any rate, regardless of who owns the guest house, we didn't want to be driving twenty miles back and forth to Inverness every day. And it turned out there wasn't any other accommodation available in Drumnadrochit. This little place is packed in the summers. At the moment there are three other teams searching Loch Ness."

"Good grief! We'll be banging into one another left, right and center."

"Not likely. You saw the size of the lake. And during off hours, everyone avoids members of other teams like the plague. I guess they figure they might let secrets slip out. Nobody wants another country's expedition to find Nessie—national pride or something."

Stefanie laughed. "Nessie searching sounds like an Olympic event. Which countries are we competing against?"

"Right now there's a crew here from Japan, one from West Germany and one from Russia. Fortunately we've staked out the Highland Shires as the

American after-hours stronghold. It's the local pub—
and home of the Hooray Henries.''

"Matt, this isn't fair! You've been here for days already. You know all the local lore and I'm right out of
it. Who on earth are the Hooray Henries?''

"They're the cheerful counterparts of the Cheerless
Charlies, of course.''

"Matt!''

"Don't be so impatient, Stefanie. You'll meet them
the first time you hit the Highland Shires. Unless,'' he
added, his smile fading, "you meet a Hooray Henry
sooner than that.''

"Who—''

"Let's go introduce you to Mary.'' Matt turned
abruptly back into the hall.

"My cameras are in here,'' Stefanie called after him.
"Don't I need to lock up?''

"Not really. There are only four guest rooms. The
team's it as far as guests go. We haven't been bothering with locks. In fact, I think Florrie was insulted we
even asked about keys.''

Stefanie glanced uncertainly at her gadget bag, not
wanting to make an issue of this. "You sure?''

"Sure. It's perfectly safe. And we're just going along
the hall.''

Reluctantly Stefanie closed the bedroom door and
followed Matt.

"That's my room.'' He pointed to the door next to
hers. "And across the hall there's Osborne's room,
then the bathroom at the end.''

Stefanie heard voices coming from the last room on
their side of the hall. The conversation ceased as Matt
reached the open doorway.

"Hi, Mary...Rob." Matt took Stefanie's arm and drew her into the room. "Stefanie Taylor, meet Mary Johanson and Rob McFarlane."

Stefanie barely heard the man's name, didn't even glance at him. She simply stared at Peter's adorable Cindy...sitting there at an enormous desk decked out like a research lab. Cindy was smiling one of her perfect, pearly smiles.

Stefanie's tongue automatically searched out the space between her own front teeth. She closed her eyes for an instant, realizing she must be so jet-lagged she was hallucinating. This woman couldn't be Cindy. Matt had said *Mary*. She opened her eyes, braving another look.

Of course it wasn't Cindy! But Mary Johanson was the spitting image of Peter's bride—another Miss Blond Perfection, all of twenty-three or four, with long, silky hair and an oh-so-pretty face. Was the entire world being taken over by Olivia Newton-John clones? Stefanie's piece of it certainly seemed to be!

Mary was murmuring a greeting in a precious, little-girl voice that practically made Stefanie gag. She forced herself to smile and nod, feeling like Howdy-Doody must have felt on his off days. She looked away from Mary to the man with her. "I'm sorry. I didn't catch your name."

"'Tis Rob McFarlane, Stefanie."

The invisible puppet string jerked her head up and down again as *McFarlane* clicked into place in her mind. Rob appeared to be about thirty. That probably meant he was Florrie's son. Stefanie smiled just looking at him. He was a huge bear of a man, with reddish hair and a bushy red beard that seemed totally at odds with his dark business suit. But it probably made him look wonderful in traditional Scottish regalia.

"Pleased to meet you, Rob. Pleased to meet you both." Stefanie looked at Mary once more, ordering herself to stop being irrational. It wasn't the girl's fault she was a gorgeous blonde.

"Bankers seem able to keep nice hours in Inverness, Rob."

The edge in Matt's voice pulled Stefanie's attention back to the two men. Matt's expression was distinctly unfriendly.

"It's being an investment banker that gives me the freedom, Matt. We manage to get out and about a fair bit. I was checking on some property today. Didn't see much point in going back to the office just in time to close up.

"Mary was explaining her peat tests to me," he offered, waving a large hand at the test tubes on Mary's desk. "But I imagine you three want a little time to talk. I'll be going now. Told my father I'd drive some things over to the shop for him, anyway. See you later, Mary."

Stefanie glanced at Matt in time to catch the annoyed, territorial glare he shot Mary. So that was the lay of the land. Well, it certainly didn't surprise her. Mary Johanson was the type of woman men always went for. Matt's student coming along as his assistant suddenly made perfect sense. Their relationship obviously went a good deal farther than student-teacher.

Stefanie swallowed the little flutter of disappointment that welled up in her throat. "Tell me about the peat tests, Mary. I'm days behind the rest of you."

"Don't worry. You haven't missed anything exciting. Mainly, we've been establishing levels of nutrient growth in the lake. We want to prove the environment's rich enough to support creatures as large as the Nessies are said to be.

"But what I'm checking at the moment is primarily for your use, Stefanie. The bottom of Loch Ness is a virtual bog and the water has an incredibly high concentration of peat." Mary held one of the test tubes up to the window. Dark particles hung suspended in the water.

"I've been trying to establish the range of visibility you're going to have for your photography. It won't be very good. Even with the floodlights and strobes we've set up in the *Sea Horse*, you'll only have about twenty feet—maybe thirty if we're lucky. But that's the outer distance your camera will be able to pick anything up at."

"Only thirty feet? With the lights and a telephoto lens?"

"I'm afraid these peat particles will defeat any lens you try. After a certain distance, the water's like a black velvet curtain."

Stefanie turned to Matt, her hopes sinking. "Even if we locate a Nessie, do we have a chance of getting within twenty or thirty feet?"

"Well, the *Sea Horse* is powerful. If we make contact...if Osborne's sonar is good enough...we should be able to close in."

If. The tiny word kept looming larger in Stefanie's mind. This entire search was nothing more than a series of ifs. The more details she learned, the less likely, it struck her, that those ifs would all come together. But, hopefully, the prospect would seem brighter after she'd had more sleep.

"Matt . . . would you mind if we got the rest of my things from the car now? You were right. I could do with a nap."

"Sure. We'll leave the analyst to her work."

"See you later, Stefanie." Mary smiled sweetly. "Did Matt tell you about the Highland Shires Pub? Maybe you'd like to come with us tonight. The locals hang out there. It's a lot of fun."

"Maybe . . . thanks." Stefanie turned and followed Matt out. Going to the pub with Matt and Mary. That certainly sounded like a barrel of laughs. Being a third wheel always added something to an evening.

She clomped down the stairs after Matt. Outside, across the road, sunlight danced cheerfully on the lake. They'd almost reached the car when Matt stopped—so suddenly she practically bumped into him.

Stefanie peered past him. The little car's hatch stood open; its storage area was empty.

Matt looked back at her, his expression anxious. "Maybe Florrie took your things in. Wait here a sec. I'll check with her."

Stefanie waited, gazing out across Loch Ness, wishing Matt hadn't seemed so concerned. The front door slammed. She heard his footsteps on the driveway and turned. His face told her what she didn't want to know. She'd just been hit with the knockout ending to this ghastly day. So much for Drumnadrochit being a wonderful little world.

She felt the last ounce of energy draining from her body. Maybe she should pinch herself. If she could manage that, maybe she'd wake up to find this entire trip was simply a nightmare, that she was actually still home in Chicago. Maybe . . . but somehow it didn't seem likely.

Matt strode rapidly to the car, slammed the hatch closed and turned back to her, his angry expression confirming this was reality. "Was there anything valuable in your case, Stefanie?"

"No, just my clothes." Just her clothes. Wonderful! Unconsciously she smoothed one hand down the front of her jumpsuit. Its wrinkles had multiplied by at least ten times during the trip from Glasgow. If it looked like a rag now, what was it going to look like after she'd worn it every day for the entire month of July? If she had the energy, she'd cry.

"We should report this, Stefanie. There isn't a local police force so we'll have to go into Inverness."

"Oh, Matt! Not now. I couldn't face it. And what good would it do? I can't imagine the police treating this as a major crime."

"Well...the film doesn't matter. We have enough. But your clothes?"

Stefanie shrugged miserably. "I don't know, Matt. Nobody would be interested in them. With any luck, once the thief sees there are only clothes in my case, he'll discard it someplace nearby. Maybe if Florrie asked the neighbors to check around for it...?"

"Damned hatchbacks," Matt muttered. "Those cartons of film were so tempting, sitting right out in the open. If they'd been in a trunk, this wouldn't have happened. Well, let's get back inside. I'll talk to Florrie—see what she thinks we should do. If we don't get your clothes back, we can always go shopping."

Stefanie dragged along after Matt, back into the house.

"Why don't you hit the sack?" he suggested. "I'll let you know later what Florrie says."

Stefanie nodded and headed up the stairs, suddenly wanting reassurance that her cameras were safe. Anxiously she opened the bedroom door. Her gadget bag was exactly where she'd left it.

She moved it into the wardrobe and sank onto her bed, considering a quick shower. But the mattress was decadently soft—far too inviting to ignore. Besides, she had no robe. She'd have to trot back to her room draped in a towel. A shower could wait.

She undressed quickly, then crawled between the sheets. They were cool and welcoming against her skin, smelled faintly of lemony soap and fresh air. She glanced momentarily at the door, realizing she'd forgotten to ask about a key. Did it matter?

No. She couldn't face getting dressed again. She'd be fine. Matt had assured her the house was safe. Besides, after everything that had happened today, the Fates couldn't possibly have anything further in store for her.

MATT CLEARED HIS THROAT, certain Mary was aware of him standing in her doorway, certain she knew precisely why he was there.

"Just a minute, Matt. Just let me make a note of these last densities." She jotted down a few figures, then looked over at him. "I should have the final nutrient growth analysis finished in an hour or so. Will you be in your room? I can bring it along to you."

"Good idea. I'm going to hang around at least until Osborne gets back." He paused, feeling ridiculous as hell. Mary was more like a colleague than a student, and he didn't like pulling rank on her. But something had better be said before Osborne learned about this latest incident.

"What's up?" Mary finally prompted.

"Look...I thought Rob had an apartment in Inverness."

"You know he does." Mary stared pointedly back down at her figures.

"Well, no one would ever suspect that from the past few days. Every time I turn around I practically fall over him."

"Then why don't you stop turning around?"

Matt glanced away from Mary's teasing grin, resisting the impulse to smile back, reminding himself Osborne's suspicions might be founded. There was no denying someone had been nosing around the *Sea Horse*, had been interested in their search equipment. Now Stefanie's film had vanished from the car. And every time something suspicious happened, Rob McFarlane seemed to be on the scene.

Matt looked back at Mary, concentrating on being stern. "Don't make this hard on me, okay? You know what I'm getting at. And I feel like a damn fool. I don't have any experience meddling in other people's social lives and I don't like doing it."

"Fine. I don't like you doing it, either, so stop. This may be a guest house, but it's also Rob's parent's home. If he wants to visit them, it really isn't any of our business, is it?"

"Come off it, Mary! You know damn well he's not hanging around Drumnadrochit to visit his parents. He's hanging around you. The least you can do is be a little more discreet. Osborne has a fit every time he sees Rob."

"Osborne's fits," Mary snapped, "are insulting. Rob's spending time here because he likes me. No other reason. He couldn't care less about our search. He doesn't care about any of them—except for thinking they're good for some fun. And he certainly isn't trying to use me to find out anything.

"Matt, Osborne's so obsessed with proving how fantastic his sonar is, I think he's becoming unhinged. I'm just glad you're my boss, not him."

"Well, keep in mind he's *my* boss. And you aren't making that any easier for me."

Mary shot him a guilty look, making him wonder if that fact had even occurred to her.

"Look, Matt, I'm sorry. Really. I didn't mean to cause you trouble. If 'discreet' will help, you've got it. Just don't ask me to send Rob packing. Please? That wouldn't be fair. I'm pulling my weight here. We've already run more tests than we'd initially intended to. But sitting alone in my room every night wasn't one of the job requirements—and spending time with Rob doesn't make me Mata Hari. Tell Osborne we never discuss the search. It's the truth."

"Mary...somebody just stole Stefanie's luggage from my car."

"Oh, no! What an awful thing to happen. She must be feeling sick about it, Matt. Do you want me to go talk to her? I can lend her some clothes, take her into Inverness to shop if she'd like."

"Thanks. But the point is, my car was parked halfway up the driveway. Who would have even noticed there was anything in it...unless he was in the yard?"

"For heaven's sake, Matt! You aren't really implying that Rob would steal a woman's clothes, are you? What does he strike you as, a transvestite?" Mary's grin suddenly reappeared. "Aside from anything else, Stefanie's skinny. Rob would never fit into her things."

Matt shook his head, determined Mary wasn't going to end this discussion by making him laugh. "Stefanie had a couple of cartons of film in the car. They're gone, too."

"We have a million rolls of film on the *Sea Horse*."

"I know that. But the thief didn't. The point is...it's like the strobes that went astray."

"They turned up."

"Yes, but Rob—"

"Matt, Rob's a terrific guy. Really he is. So trust me, okay? He has nothing to do with whatever Osborne suspects is going on...if there even is anything going on."

Matt exhaled slowly. There was obviously no point in continuing this conversation. The stars in Mary's eyes were affecting her vision. "Yeah...well...I guess you're right. From what I've seen, Rob does seem like a nice guy. I didn't mean to take my jumping to conclusions out on you. It's just been a beast of a day."

"You mean there's more?"

Matt briefly explained about Nancy Goitano and the man in the Auld Highland House.

"Wow! That does qualify as a bad day. I wondered why you were so bent out of shape. Now I understand. Poor Nancy! And poor Stefanie. It all must have seemed like a welcome to the Twilight Zone! Then having someone steal her things on top of everything else? We'll have to be supernice to her, Matt. She probably wishes she were anywhere but here."

Matt nodded. The idea of being supernice to Stefanie didn't strike him as the least bit onerous. He turned to leave, then paused, noticing the newspaper lying on Mary's bed. It was opened to an article headed "Nessie Mania."

"Rob brought that to show me," Mary told him. "It mentions the Hooray Henries. He thought it was hilarious they'd been written up in a paper as staid as the *Financial Times*. He says the paper's given him more press about being leader of the Henries than they ever have about any investment deal he's been involved with."

Matt picked up the newspaper and skimmed until he reached a bit that mentioned the Highland Shires was the headquarters of the fun-loving Henries. "The members are affable, gregarious and off the wall," the article continued, "so intoxicated with their belief in the monster that they suppress all thought that she might not exist."

In typical *Financial Times* fashion, the article went on to talk about the monetary value of the Nessie mystery to the Scottish tourist industry. Annual revenue in the form of lodging, souvenirs, tours and monster burgers was estimated at...Matt's brain translated the pounds figure into dollars...was estimated at $160 million.

"Interesting." He tossed the paper back onto the bed, wondering just how concerned the locals really might be about the possibility of their monster being demystified.

CHAPTER FOUR

MATT SAT AT HIS DESK, trying to concentrate on the nutrient analysis Mary had dropped off. But the number 160 million, preceded by an enormous dollar sign, kept flashing inside his head, distracting him.

How much would that amount decline if Nessie turned out to be a far more mundane creature than myth portrayed her? Tourists wouldn't continue flocking to Loch Ness, hoping for a glimpse of the "prehistoric monster," if Nessie proved to be nothing more than an overgrown eel.

He ran his fingers through his hair, thinking about Rob, coming back once more to the fact that Rob's father depended on the tourist trade... And Osborne was so darn sure that someone, for some reason, was up to no good, was out to disrupt their search.

Could it really be because of tourist dollars? And could it possibly be Rob? He didn't fit the role of villain. He really did seem to be a carefree, fun-loving fellow—not at all the dastardly character Osborne kept trying to paint him.

But Osborne was certain someone wanted to keep them from using his sonar...or wanted to learn exactly how it worked. That was the man's other fear. Someone might be out to steal his invention. In one way that possibility seemed even more remote, but in another it was more realistic.

Details about the sonar, with its military applications, were classified. Could there actually be some plot afoot to pirate Osborne's technology? Matt paused, his head spinning.

Whatever the truth, Osborne's suspicions were going to drive them all crazy. In Osborne's eyes, anything that happened instantly became conclusive evidence of some devious plot. So someone had poked around the *Sea Horse*. Should that really be a surprise? It was by far the most advanced research sub on the lake at the moment—probably the most sophisticated that had ever searched there. Why wouldn't people be curious?

Maybe that's all things came down to. Simple curiosity. Maybe there was no plot at all—no villain. Maybe all Osborne's clues were merely products of his overactive imagination. The longer Matt spent with the man, the more reasonable that possibility seemed.

But there was Stefanie's luggage…and the film she'd brought along. If Rob hadn't been trying to cause them grief by taking it, then what? Had someone simply been passing by and nabbed it? Or…

His mind's eye pictured the blue sedan he'd noticed on the trip up from Glasgow. He shook his head wearily. It had been an awfully peculiar day. All those strange events, all happening within such a short time frame—learning of Nancy's murder, Mr. Still Waters appearing, Stefanie's things being stolen. It seemed impossible that any, let alone all, of them could be connected. And yet…

The sound of Jeffery Osborne coming up the stairs interrupted Matt's thoughts—or rather, the sound of Osborne's whistling. For an overweight man Osborne moved very quietly, but his whistle was like a bell on a cat.

No, Matt corrected himself, rising from his desk and heading over to the open door. A belled cat was a poor analogy. Its bell only tinkled occasionally. Osborne whistled under his breath almost constantly.

The tuneless sound he produced was intensely annoying. An hour of it had everyone within hearing range twitching. If he was going to keep it up in the close quarters of the *Sea Horse*, the rest of them would have to wear earplugs.

The man's short, stout frame rounded the corner at the top of the stairs and he grunted a greeting along the hall. He looked even more worried than usual. A frown was drawing his scraggly eyebrows so closely together that they formed an unbroken line over his dark eyes. His lips, now that the whistling had ceased, were clenched. It was probably just the dim light in the hall, but Osborne looked more like a down-on-his-luck bum who was pushing fifty than a thirty-eight-year-old genius about to stand the world of sonar on its ear with his invention.

"Photographer get here okay?" he demanded.

"Fine."

Osborne jerked his head in the direction of his own room. "Want to talk to you a minute."

Matt followed the other man across the hall. The largest of the four bedrooms, it had become the team's official meeting place away from the *Sea Horse*. Osborne closed the door securely behind them, put his briefcase on the bed, snapped it open and pulled out a newspaper. He thrust it toward Matt. "Look at this!"

A glance told Matt it was a *New York Times*. "I know. Finch called earlier."

Osborne eyed him anxiously, tossing the newspaper aside. "What did he say?"

"Nothing much. Actually, I didn't talk to him. Stefanie did. But I gather he figured we'd be upset when we learned Nancy was dead, wanted to let us know about the murder himself. He mentioned you often pick up a *Times*. I guess he hoped he'd catch us before you found out about it this way."

"Yes, yes. But what did he think?"

"I gather he was upset. Most people would be."

"That isn't what I mean! What did he think about the murder, maybe . . . you know . . . about Nancy having signed on with us . . . and then this."

Matt shook his head slowly, telling himself once again that idea was crazy. But Stefanie had been concerned about Finch's denials of any connection. Now the possibility of some relationship between their search and Nancy's murder had occurred to Osborne. Of course it had, Matt chided himself. Osborne worried at the drop of a hat.

But no connection had occurred to Mary, or she'd have mentioned it. And he simply couldn't see any logical relationship. So why was a nagging worry gnawing at him, telling him there were too many unusual things happening all at once for them to be entirely coincidental?

Well, nagging worry or not, he wasn't about to admit his concerns to Osborne. Reinforcing the man's suspicions would only make things more difficult for them all.

"Finch said the murder was just one of those things, Osborne. What does the *Times* say?"

"No details. Nancy's body was tossed into the Hudson River. There aren't any clues or possible motives that they're talking about."

"Another murder in the Big Apple," Matt said, carefully keeping his tone casual. "How many are committed in a year—hundreds? Or are they up to thousands by now? So you and I and Mary happen to have been at a meeting with one of the victims. I imagine that's as close as Nancy's murder gets to us."

"Yeah . . . yeah, you're probably right."

Matt breathed a silent sigh of relief and quickly changed the subject. "What were you doing in Inverness?"

Osborne's anxious expression switched to one of excitement. "I had an idea for a new piece of search equipment—stayed up half last night finishing the design. I went into town to see about getting the components for it."

"What is it?"

Osborne shrugged. "Just something I thought we could attach to the remote manipulator arm."

Matt eyed the engineer closely, curious about what he was up to. Their manipulator arm was practically as efficient as the space shuttle's Canadarm. What more could they possibly want?

Osborne stared back at him with a studiously innocent look, offering no further details.

"You figure we need another attachment for picking up underwater samples?" Matt tried. "We already have two grapplers and an expandable clamp we can hook onto the arm. What else are we likely to need?"

"Oh . . . it's just something."

Osborne grinned a patently phony grin, which Matt assumed was supposed to look conspiratorial.

"You know how inventors are, Garrett. We never like to talk about something we've dreamed up until we're sure it isn't just pie in the sky. I'll tell you all the details once I've got the prototype ready—just as soon as I'm sure it'll do what I want it to do."

"Which is?"

"Oh, this and that. Problem right now is that the exact components I need aren't available in Inverness. And there's a part that's going to take precise skill to assemble. Apparently there's no one around here with the technical expertise. But I talked to a few people, and a couple of them came up with the same name—a fellow in Edinburgh who's supposed to be top-notch.

"I called him an hour or so ago. Luckily he figures he can get the required components there and he's agreed to give us priority. He'll start breadboarding my design first thing in the morning."

"For a suitable price," Matt commented wryly.

Osborne grinned. "That's a major difference between private industry and your university community, Garrett. Sound Research plays hardball. And we expect to pay top dollar.

"There's only one other thing," Osborne went on. "Someone has to get my plans to Edinburgh tonight, then bring the assembled prototype back once it's ready. I thought . . . maybe Mary could drive down?"

"Mary? Isn't that asking a bit much? Besides, she's busy here."

"Well, she's the most expendable. You told me she was running ahead of schedule on the environmental tests. And I think you, I and the photographer—"

"Stefanie. Her name's Stefanie."

"Yes. Well, you and I and Stefanie should do at least a few trial runs as soon as possible—get her familiar with the sub's interior. Mary's not expecting to go down in the *Sea Horse* very often, anyway. Four people would be packed like sardines. So Mary's the obvious one to send to Edinburgh.''

"I don't know, Osborne. I'm not keen about the idea of her going off on her own. This new invention of yours—is it really likely to do a whole lot extra for us?''

"It could make the entire search, Garrett. Believe me. It could make the entire search.''

"Even so . . . why not send a courier?''

"No good. I'm not trusting my plans to some local yokel who could do heaven knows what with them. Look, Garrett, Mary's been talking about how she didn't manage to see much of Scotland while she was studying here . . . how she'd like to see a bit more than Inverness this month. Now's a perfect opportunity. I've booked a room at the Royal Scot. She'll have a luxurious place to stay, her time will be her own and she can spend it seeing Edinburgh. Walking the Royal Mile will put her in seventh heaven. Anyway, she shouldn't be away more than one night—two at the most.''

Matt considered the idea. Mary did want to see more of the country than the Highlands. And she had the testing well in hand. "All right, I'll go talk to her, Osborne. If she's agreeable to the trip, fine—but only if she's agreeable.''

Matt paused at the door. "I almost forgot. Stefanie's sleeping now, but tomorrow someone will have to take her into Inverness. Her luggage disappeared.''

"Damned airlines,'' Osborne snapped.

"Well . . . actually, it wasn't that. Her things were stolen from the back of my car.''

Osborne's face turned white. "Where?''

"From out front . . . just after we got here.''

"You see! You see what I've been telling you?''

Matt shrugged noncommittally and opened the door to leave. He had no answer that would pacify Osborne. And there was definitely nothing to be gained by elaborating. If the man learned Stefanie had lost film, as well, and that Rob had been around the house at the time, he'd probably want to call in Scotland Yard.

"It's a damn good idea to get Mary out of Drumnadrochit for a couple of days, Garrett! One less problem to worry about! I only wish—"

Matt stepped into the hall and closed the door behind him.

STEFANIE LAY PERFECTLY STILL, the yellowy orange haze of light behind her closed eyelids telling her it was early morning. She struggled groggily to consciousness, playing the game she always played when traveling, trying to remember where she was before she opened her eyes for a clue. Finally she cheated, smoothing her hand across the bedspread. The soft, nubby chenille triggered recall.

She opened her eyes and checked her watch. Five-thirty. She'd slept for practically twelve hours. She stretched, feeling ready for anything. Then her glance caught her blue jumpsuit, tossed carelessly over the armchair beside the window. Well, maybe she wasn't ready for quite anything—certainly not for putting that jumpsuit back on. It was a miracle it wasn't standing up on its own.

She listened to the silence for a moment. There wasn't a sound in the house. Waking this early would give her a chance at the shower before anyone else got up. She tugged the edges of the creamy bedspread out from under her mattress, promising herself she'd remake the bed perfectly. Wrapping the spread around herself, she scuttled down the hall, leaving the problem of clothes until she was fully awake and clean.

The bathroom door, she noted with relief, locked. Bottles of shampoo and conditioner sat beside a stack of bath towels on a large shelf. She silently blessed Florrie McFarlane, let the bedspread drop and clambered over the three-foot-high side of the old bathtub.

It was equipped with a modern, hand-held shower. She pulled the shower curtain across and, after only four unsuccessful tries, figured out how the spray control worked. The trickle of lukewarm water the shower produced felt heavenly.

Fifteen minutes later and a hundred times cleaner, Stefanie wrapped one large towel around her wet hair and a second one about her body. Bundling the bedspread under one arm, she unlocked the bathroom door and peeked out into the hall. All clear! Clutching the towel securely around her, she started for her room.

She'd taken two steps, when the door of Jeffery Osborne's room opened and a short, chubby man stepped into the hall. Hairy legs protruded from beneath his ratty bathrobe.

Stefanie stopped short, trying not to think about how much of her own legs were exposed. There was definitely a view of her knobby knees...and then some.

The man paused, staring suspiciously at her, pulling the plaid bathrobe more tightly across his stomach. "Stefanie Taylor?"

She nodded. The movement was enough to loosen the towel on her head. It began to slip down over her forehead. She didn't have a free hand. The towel continued its slide, the tuck that held the ends together gradually loosening.

Finally it slipped entirely off her head, coming to a precarious rest over one shoulder. Suddenly her other, completely naked shoulder, seemed totally indecent. She clutched the top of her remaining towel even more tightly, casting the man a weak smile. "Jeffery Osborne?"

"Yes. Pleased to meet you," he added stiffly, obviously not the least bit pleased.

For a horrible instant, Stefanie thought Jeffery was going to extend his hand. Then Matt's door opened and they both turned toward him. He was wearing a pair of tight jeans. That was it.

He had, Stefanie noted fleetingly, a very nicely muscled upper body, a thick mat of dark chest hair. The beard stubble that darkened his face, combined with his tousled hair, made him appear positively rakish.

He grinned at them for a moment. "I see you've met."

Jeffery nodded.

Stefanie stood perfectly still, praying nothing else would begin to slip.

Matt eyed her as if he were hopeful something might. "Mary's gone for a day or two, Stefanie, but she said you could borrow some clothes from her. We'll go into Inverness as soon as we have a chance so you can shop."

"Hurry and find what you need to wear," Jeffery ordered curtly. "I want to get down to the *Sea Horse* right after breakfast. The majority of Nessie sightings have been in the morning. That must be when the creatures are most active." Jeffery adjusted his robe once more, then hurried along to the bathroom.

Stefanie waited until he had closed the door before speaking. "What's going on, Matt? Where's Mary?"

Matt walked the few steps to Mary's door, opened it and gestured Stefanie inside.

She hesitated. "Could I . . . these towels . . ."

Matt laughed. "You do look a little like a refugee from a bathhouse. Just wait there a second."

He disappeared into Mary's room. A moment later he was back in the hall, a silky satin robe clutched in his hand.

Stefanie eyed it critically. Absolutely gorgeous. Exactly the type of housecoat she'd have expected Miss Blond Perfection to own. The satin was precisely the same color as Mary's hair.

Matt handed Stefanie the robe. "Why don't you go into Mary's room and put this on? I'll wait out here for a minute, but I do need to talk with you briefly."

Stefanie did as Matt had suggested, then peered back out at him. "Now I feel like an escapee from a British sex farce. Satin is definitely not my style!"

Matt grinned at her. "Looks good on you. Anyway, I won't keep you long.

"What's going on with Mary," he explained, coming into the bedroom and closing the door behind himself, "is that Osborne sent her down to Edinburgh to look after the details of some invention he's dreamed up. She's left most of her clothes behind, though, so you should be fine. And, Stefanie . . ."

"Yes?"

"Don't mention anything to Osborne about that film you brought from the States. I told him your suitcase had been taken, but I didn't mention the film...or tell him about your encounter with Mr. Still Waters, for that matter."

Stefanie looked at Matt curiously, waiting for him to explain.

He hesitated, then shrugged. "It's just that Osborne's got the crazy idea someone's trying to disrupt our search. I don't want to add any fuel to his fire."

Stefanie felt a flutter of concern. "Someone's trying to disrupt the search?"

Matt shook his head firmly. "Only in Osborne's mind. But he's undoubtedly added your stolen luggage to his list of clues."

"And...you're certain he has no reason to, Matt?"

"Certain? You had such a strange day yesterday I wouldn't count on anything being certain." He shot her a reassuring smile. "But let's go with incredibly unlikely—so unlikely there's absolutely no reason for you to start worrying."

"But . . . but, if there's nothing to worry about, then where did Jeffery's list of clues come from?"

"From his imagination. We had a couple of minor problems, and he blew them into major incidents. Our strobes temporarily went astray. Then he discovered a couple of scratches around the lock mechanism on the *Sea Horse* and decided someone had tried to break into it. But the scratches could have gotten there a hundred different ways. Also, he's come up with the theory that Rob McFarlane..."

Matt paused. "I hear Florrie moving around downstairs. I have to talk to her about something. I'll let you get on with finding something to wear."

Matt left, giving Stefanie no further opportunity to press the subject of Osborne's imaginings. She rubbed her wet hair absently with the towel, wondering what the theory about Rob McFarlane involved, wondering whether Matt had covered the complete list of Jeffery's "clues."

She hoped he had...hoped if there actually was something going on he'd tell her the whole truth, not try to prevent her from worrying by keeping her in the dark.

She ordered herself to set the issue aside for the moment. There'd be plenty of time to learn exactly what was happening. Right now, top priority was getting dressed.

Staring at the contents of Mary's wardrobe, Stefanie realized the younger woman had been sitting down when they'd met. From the looks of her clothes, she had to be about five-foot compared to Stefanie's five-foot-eight, and a size eleven petite to Stefanie's size seven. She finally chose an oversize, emerald cotton shirt and a pair of jeans that looked as if they would at least reach her calves. Holding the waistband to her waist, she decided that as long as she could find a belt, they'd probably stay up.

She tossed the shirt and jeans onto the bed and poked uncomfortably through the lingerie in Mary's top drawer. The idea of wearing another woman's underwear might be distasteful, but her choice was between Mary's clean things and the lingerie she'd worn forever during the trip here.

A little rummaging turned up a pair of bikini panties that seemed smaller than most of the others. Then she selected a silk camisole, knowing it would be pointless even to try on any of Mary's bras—she'd clearly fall out of them the first time she bent over.

Once dressed, she took a quick look in the mirror. The sight wasn't half as bad as she'd expected. In fact, it wouldn't be at all bad if short, baggy pants happened to be the rage in Scotland.

At any rate, her appearance didn't matter much. Not when she was going to be stuck in a submarine with one man who was clearly Mary Johanson's private property and another who, on first meeting at least, had exuded all the warmth and charm of a dead fish. Jeffery Osborne, she mused, was definitely not the sort of person one would ever call "Jeff."

Stefanie stopped in her own room for a moment, tossed the bed back together and combed the majority of the tangles out of her hair. Then she grabbed her gadget bag from the floor of her wardrobe and headed downstairs to join the others.

BY THE TIME they started off in Jeffery's car, a thick fog had descended, banishing the sunlight and cutting visibility drastically. The far side of Loch Ness had vanished into haze.

Jeffery drove silently along the two-lane highway that paralleled the shoreline below it. A mile or so from the Galloway Guest House, he turned onto a dirt road and guided the little car cautiously down the steep, winding route leading to the water.

Scrunched into the back seat, Stefanie peered between the two heads in front, anxious to get her first glimpse of the *Sea Horse*. She could see the lake's surface, but much of the shoreline was hidden by bushes.

Matt glanced back at her. "This is Urquhart Bay. And that," he added, pointing to their right, "is Urquhart Castle."

Stefanie looked over. A fog-shrouded promontory of land jutted out into the lake, its sheer cliff dropping off into Loch Ness. Across the table of land sprawled a ruin.

The huge, crumbling stone tower perched at the edge of the precipice would seem ghostly even without the fog's assistance. The castle was probably worth investigating, but right now her interest lay in seeing the little research submarine.

As they neared the lake, she spied it—a sleek, silvery shape, lying low in the water. Except for a handrail stretching on either side along the length of its smooth main deck, the *Sea Horse* looked much like a giant, sleeping porpoise. The back end even had a...a *thing* sticking up into the air. Whatever its technical name was, it reminded her of a dorsal fin.

"What's that...fin called?" She pointed between heads at it.

"Sail structure," Jeffery replied. "It houses the retracting periscope and the radar and radio antennae." He jerked the car to a halt and shoved his door open. "Let's move it, guys."

Matt got out of the passenger side and headed after Jeffery, leaving Stefanie to fend for herself.

She struggled with the front seat, trying to flip it forward. Finally Matt looked around, then strode back to help her, wearing an apologetic grin.

"Sorry, Stefanie." He released a catch, flipped the seat up and reached for her hand to help her out. "I forgot this was a two-door. I'll make an effort to remember my manners from here on in."

Stefanie shrugged, bending back in to get her gadget bag. "Don't worry about it. I'm just one of the guys."

Matt laughed quietly. "You may be just one of the team, but you're definitely not just one of the guys. Don't forget, I saw you wearing only a towel this morning."

Stefanie glanced at his face, uncertain how to take the remark. She decided he was merely joking. "Jeffery saw me straight out of the shower, as well. And I distinctly heard him say, 'Let's move it, guys.'"

"Well, you should have realized by now that he only has eyes for his sonar. But I'm definitely not Osborne."

This time there was no misconstruing Matt's implication. She stared at him coolly. All she needed was a come-on while his adorable little Mary was out of the picture. *When the cat's away the mice will play.* Or was it *The rats will play?* Whichever—she wasn't interested in playing games with rodents.

Matt's smile faded under her level gaze. "We'd better get going before Osborne leaves without us." Wheeling around, he started rapidly in the direction of the pier.

Stefanie shifted her gadget bag and followed along, disappointed in Matt. He hadn't struck her as the kind of man who played around behind his lady's back.

They walked to the *Sea Horse* without speaking. Matt stopped at the entrance hatch. "Hold my hand while you back onto the ladder. I'll just release us from the mooring, then close up and follow you down. Watch your step at the bottom. It's pretty dim down there. The observation level is completely below water."

Stefanie carefully descended the six rungs and turned. The little submarine was crammed, fore to aft, with equipment. She glanced to the back, where Jeffery was already tinkering with something, whistling an annoyingly tuneless whistle, apparently oblivious to her arrival.

She quickly detailed the *Sea Horse*'s interior with her eyes. Its observation chamber couldn't be much longer than twelve feet, and if she stretched her arms out, she could probably touch either side. It's nose, the craft's navigation area, was a large, circular window surrounded by instrument panels, monitor screens and receivers.

The observation windows she'd shoot through, at the midpoint of each side wall, were a good size—about four feet in diameter—and huge lighting units had been secured, flush to the glass, around each window. In addition, several powerful strobes were stationed at regular intervals to allow for pinpointing objects.

She stepped over and checked one of the lighting unit's mountings. Good. There shouldn't be any problem with reflection. And she'd certainly need those lights. The dark water outside was absorbing the surface light like crazy.

But the illumination from these lighting banks would be brilliant. Nancy Goitano had done a good job of selecting equipment. All they'd need now to ensure a photograph was a little cooperation from a Nessie. *All?* Stefanie shook her head ruefully. Did she expect one of the creatures to swim over to a window and say "cheese"?

"Something wrong?" Jeffery asked, his tone anxious.

Stefanie looked toward the back of the sub. Jeffery was hunkered down over a large, cylindrical object that reminded her of a fat torpedo.

"No, nothing's wrong. In fact, I was thinking you'd done a great job of setting up. You've practically got a studio in here for me."

"Glad you approve. The way you were shaking your head had me worried."

"No...nothing to worry about." Stefanie stared at the cylinder curiously.

Jeffery smiled up at her. She realized that was the first time she'd seen him smile since they'd met.

"This is it." He patted the cylinder lovingly.

"It?" Lord, she hoped she didn't sound as stupid as she felt. She continued to stare, trying to puzzle out what *it* was.

"The famous Osborne sonar." Matt's arrival rescued her.

Stefanie cast a quick, grateful glance back at him.

"The shape's a little unusual," he added, stepping off the bottom rung of the ladder.

"Yes, the sonar, naturally," Stefanie mumbled, turning back to Jeffery. "I was just trying to remember precisely..."

Jeffery stroked the front of the cylinder with his palm. "The transmitting and receiving transducers are right up here, of course. But the way I've positioned the pulsing and gating units behind them gives this baby much of its advantage—that and the special components I invented."

He gave her a second smile and rushed on. "With most sonar, the intensity of underwater sound decreases at twelve decibels per doubling of range for the echo signal. With my invention, that decrease is cut to four decibels. Would you like me to explain that using logarithmic ratios?"

"No, that's all right." Stefanie forced a weak smile of her own, certain it was making her look as moronic as she felt. "I think I understand."

Jeffery apparently accepted her lie. "To use the sonar system, Garrett and I suspend it on a cable from the side of the sub. Once we're submerged, we tow it far enough behind and beneath the *Sea Horse* that our own vibrations don't interfere with the sonar readings."

Stefanie nodded, pleased she'd at least been able to make sense of that last bit.

"Once it's out of the hull, there's more room for us to move around. We can even get into our storage area." He gestured at a locker door the sonar was blocking.

"There's a mountain of film in there for you. Here, have a quick look." Jeffery shifted one end of the sonar enough that he could open the door partway.

Stefanie peered inside, taking a quick, mental inventory of the film cartons. Every speed she'd possibly want was there. "What about developer...and darkroom supplies? Did Nancy ship that sort of thing?"

"No. She mentioned something about getting it locally. All that's in the locker is film and our diving gear."

"Diving? Will we be working outside the sub? I thought all my shots would be from inside."

"They will be," Matt assured her. "The currents are too treacherous once we get very deep to chance diving. They could easily sweep a person away. We probably won't use the gear at all."

"Then why have it?"

"It's just an example of Sound Research equipping us for every possibility."

"I'm going to leave the sonar unit where it is for this preliminary dive," Jeffery interrupted. "There's no point activating it when we just want Stefanie to get familiar with the visibility underwater. Check out whatever you need to as far as the photographic equipment goes, Stefanie.'' He turned back to Matt. ''Want to take her out?''

''Sure.'' Matt stepped over to the wheel and began flipping switches on the instrument panels.

''I didn't realize you were captain, Matt.''

''What kind of marine biologist would I make,'' he asked, smiling back at her, ''if I didn't know how to get around underwater? But I'm not captain. Osborne's the senior pilot here. When it comes to anything more than simple navigation, he's welcome to the controls. Sometimes I think I only know enough to get into trouble.''

''If that were true,'' Jeffery said, ''I wouldn't let you loose on her. You do well . . . for someone who isn't an engineer, of course.''

''Of course,'' Matt agreed, his tone solemn, his sidelong grin only for Stefanie's eyes. He turned away and stared out the front window into the water.

Stefanie could feel the motor pulsating as they began to move slowly away from the pier. This was it. Her job had begun.

She felt the sub start its descent and stared out of one of the observation windows. The water was getting blacker by the moment. Mary's estimated twenty to thirty feet of visibility began to seem like an exaggeration.

Stefanie could barely differentiate between the salmon and lake trout swimming by. She switched on a bank of lights, instantly making the fish more visible. This assignment wasn't going to be any piece of cake, though. She'd never been in such dense water.

She turned on all the remaining lights, then pulled the Pentax from her gadget bag and began trying out different lenses and filters. With each combination, she tested a strobe or two in addition to the mounted lighting units.

"What do you think?" Jeffery finally asked.

She grinned at him. "I think your sonar had better be awfully darned good."

"My sonar has twice the capabilities of any other ever developed."

Stefanie merely nodded and turned back to the window, away from Mr. Modesty. Even if he was right, this was going to be one tough shoot—or one impossible shoot if the Nessies played shy.

"This is awful," Matt muttered. "We'd be better off in a rowboat on the surface."

"Surface sightings are nothing but chance!" Jeffery snapped. "And pretty rare chance at that. On a lake this size, we could sit in a rowboat every day for the rest of our lives without spotting a surfacing. With the sonar we're doing something active, not just hoping Lady Luck's ready to smile on us."

Stefanie adjusted her f-stop a final time and looked back at Jeffery again. "That's about it for my checking. Mary's tests were accurate. If you can get us within thirty feet of a creature, I'll have a possible shot. Within twenty feet and I'll definitely have a picture."

"Make any difference to you if we're inside an underwater cavern?" Jeffery asked.

"Doesn't matter a bit. We're not getting a single ray of light from the surface, anyway. Everything's coming from the *Sea Horse*."

"Let's take her up, then, Matt. I'll map out an underwater route and we can get going for real this afternoon."

"What about Stefanie's clothes? I was thinking about taking her into Inverness later."

Jeffery scowled at Matt, then at Stefanie. "Oh, yeah. All right. She can go shopping today."

Stefanie tried a smile. "While we're in town, I can pick up developer and the darkroom supplies I'll need."

Jeffery nodded, looking somewhat appeased by the fact that at least part of her shopping would be search related.

"All right. You get what you need. I'll map out several routes and we'll start in earnest first thing tomorrow."

Stefanie had barely finished repacking her gadget bag when she saw the underwater piles of the pier through an observation window. "Nice navigating, Matt."

He laughed. "I don't deserve an ounce of credit. That's what all this sophisticated equipment's for."

He cut the engine and they drifted a little before gliding to a halt. "Come on, Stefanie. Grab your bag."

Stefanie followed Matt up the ladder and onto the pier. Fog had settled in even more thickly. The two men secured the *Sea Horse*. Then they all started for the car. Stefanie stared out over the glassy smoothness of Loch Ness as they walked. Haze was rising from it, forming a gray mist that obliterated everything in the distance.

They'd just reached the end of the pier, when a ripple suddenly broke the surface a hundred-odd feet offshore. Stefanie wrenched her gadget bag from her shoulder and tore its zipper open, her eyes never leaving the water. In the haze a smooth, slender dark shape emerged from beneath the water. It rolled lazily over once...twice. Then, just as she got her camera focused, the creature dived, leaving a vee-shaped wake of tiny bubbles as the only picture in her viewfinder.

CHAPTER FIVE

STEFANIE CLICKED THE SHUTTER frantically, as if her refusal to believe the effort was futile would make things right. The motor drive whirred her film ahead, automatically recording exposure after exposure. But they were exposures of the air bubbles. She'd already missed the shot. Tears of frustration formed in her eyes. "I didn't get it! I'm sorry! All I've got is a picture of the damn wake. It happened so fast . . . I wasn't expecting . . ."

Matt rested one hand gently on her shoulder and turned her to face him.

She couldn't meet his gaze.

"Stefanie . . . it's okay. That wasn't a Nessie."

She glanced first at Matt's face, then at Jeffery's. Neither of them looked angry. In fact, Jeffery even appeared marginally sympathetic.

"But I saw her, Matt! I just wasn't quick enough. I should have had my camera ready."

"Stefanie, it was only a log. You wanted it to be a Nessie and that was what you saw. In the fog, at that distance, it could have been. But it wasn't."

Stefanie shook her head. Matt was merely trying to make her feel better. It wouldn't work. She wasn't a child. She was a grown woman who'd just missed the photograph of her professional career.

"Garrett's right, Stefanie."

She stared at Jeffery. Matt might have shifted into a kindness mode, but Jeffery? She doubted he had one. "But it fit the description—long, sleek and dark. And I saw her dive. Logs can't dive!"

Matt wrapped one arm around her shoulders. "Come on. Let's get back to the car. I'll give you my official marine biologist explanation on the way. And don't feel badly." He squeezed her shoulder reassuringly. "You're certainly not the first one to be taken in."

Stefanie forced one foot ahead of the other, matching Matt's steps, keenly aware of his arm around her, of how comforting it felt.

"There's a lot of decomposition going on at the bottom of Loch Ness, Stefanie—causes all kinds of chemical reactions. As Mary was saying yesterday, it's a veritable peat bog down there."

Mary! She'd forgotten about Miss Blond Perfection for a moment. She paused, adjusting her gadget bag, casually slipping out from under Matt's arm.

He glanced at her curiously, then continued. "That old log has been lying on the bottom, slowly decomposing for a long time. The decomposition process causes gasses to form inside objects, and eventually the gas level in the log got so high the log became lighter than water. That's why it surfaced. Then, once it was above water, the gas was released. Since it was still waterlogged, that made it heavier again and it sank."

"But, Matt, it was swimming. It didn't just bob up and sink again like a hunk of waterlogged wood. It rolled over like a giant seal playing games."

Matt shrugged. "Looked that way. But it was simply that gas escaped from the first side exposed to the air. The topside immediately became heavier and rolled back under the water. Then the gas was released from the other side of the log and the whole thing rolled over and sank again.''

Stefanie stared at him suspiciously. "So fast?"

"Have you ever been in a car that's blown a tire?"

"Yes."

"Well, it's the same principle. Air, or any other gas under pressure, escapes instantly once it gets a chance. Loch Ness plays all kinds of tricks, Stefanie—has all sorts of ways of causing illusions. That's one reason there's so much skepticism about the Loch Ness Monster.

"The vast majority of 'sightings' have proven to be nothing more than a salmon jumping, or the wake of a boat...or a log," Matt explained. "Everyone wants to see Nessie so badly that anything moving in the water seems to look like her. But don't worry about what just happened. There's an up side to it."

Stefanie glanced ruefully at him. "Sure there is. If you call making an idiot of myself an up side."

Matt laughed quietly. "That's not it at all. Anyone could have jumped to the same assumption—thousands of people have. The up side is that you didn't miss a million-dollar picture. All you missed was a shot of some old log."

"As I was saying," Jeffery interjected, "surface sightings are rare. But we'll get her. You'll get your pictures. Garrett will get his scientific discovery. And I'll get..."

Jeffery's words trailed off as he continued toward the car, smiling smugly to himself.

Stefanie welcomed the silence on the trip home, certain that if either man spoke, they'd bring up the subject of the log again. She felt stupid enough without listening to a rehash.

After what seemed like a million miles, Jeffery pulled into the driveway of the Galloway Guest House. He stopped the car, hopped out and glanced back in at Stefanie and Matt. "I'll see you guys later. I'm going to head up to my room and start mapping out search routes."

Matt helped Stefanie out of the back. "Osborne almost makes me feel guilty. He spends every waking minute working on some aspect of this search, while I seem to have all kinds of free time. Speaking of which, how soon would you like to go into Inverness?"

"Matt . . . as long as you wouldn't mind lending me your car . . . there's no point in my dragging you along with me."

"I don't mind."

Stefanie bit her lip, uncertain how to proceed. She'd gotten the distinct impression Matt was interested in being far more than friends. She didn't want to come on like Goody-Two-Shoes, but she certainly wasn't getting involved with someone else's man.

Aside from any other consideration, "someone else" would be back in a day or two and they'd all be working together. Adding that to the fact Matt was her boss, avoiding him seemed like a far better idea than finding herself involved in a confrontation.

"Well, it's awfully nice of you to offer, Matt, but I know most men hate shopping."

"I haven't really got anything else to do this afternoon. Besides, you don't have much choice. I'm the only one who's authorized to drive my rental car."

"Oh."

"In fact, I haven't got anything special to do to-night, either. Why don't we go out somewhere nice for dinner? Sound Research can afford to spring for a dress you could wear. And I've heard about a place I'll bet you'd love. How does dinner in a hotel that has a history a mile long strike you?"

"Matt... Look, Matt, I'm sure that suggestion is completely innocent, but I don't want to cause any trouble, any misunderstanding between you and Mary. I think we'd be better off to skip the socializing... just in case she saw it in the wrong light."

Matt leaned against the car, watching Stefanie. "Let's back this up for a minute. Mary's my assistant. Period. I don't imagine she has any concerns about who I do my socializing with."

Oh, great! Stefanie's sense of disappointment in Matt came flooding back. With the cat away, the mouse was going to *lie*, as well as play. And he had the gall to stare her straight in the eye while he did it.

"Come on, Matt. Don't kid around. I saw the way you looked at Mary when you found Rob with her. That was pure, unadulterated jealousy. If looks could kill, she'd be dead."

A grin tugged at the corners of Matt's mouth. "Ah... so my black look was what clued you in. And are you always that sharp at reading people's looks?"

Stefanie breathed a silent little sigh of relief. She'd nailed him. "Yeah... yeah, I've got a pretty good batting average. I'm a photographer, remember? I observe people's faces."

"So, what do you figure you bat? Right up there at a thousand?"

"Pretty near."

The grin stopped merely tugging and spread across Matt's face. "Well, knock your stat down to nine hundred, Ms Taylor. Mary is my twenty-four-year-old student. I'm her thirty-five-year-old professor. That's the total extent of our relationship. I'm not interested in anyone who's more than a decade younger than me. My God, she's not even finished school! I'll bet she doesn't even know George Harrison was originally a Beatle!"

Stefanie stared at him skeptically. "If that look you shot her wasn't jealousy, what was it?"

"It was pure and simple annoyance. Osborne's upset about Mary seeing Rob and she's been practically flaunting him in Osborne's face."

"Jeffery cares who she sees? Why?"

Matt shrugged. "Who knows why he cares about a lot of things? In this case, though, it's because he's developed a crazy theory about Rob."

"Which is?"

"Well . . . you remember I told you he figures someone's out to disrupt our search?"

Stefanie nodded.

"He's got Rob McFarlane lined up as his prime suspect. What with Rob's father depending on the tourist industry and Rob himself being leader of a zany group of Nessie fans, Osborne's convinced Rob's only hanging around Mary to get information from her, that he's some sort of spy."

"Isn't that pretty farfetched, Matt?"

"Yes...likely. But the problem is Rob seems to have been around every time something unusual's happened—like yesterday when your luggage was taken. Even so, I'm more inclined to think the entire sabotage idea is just a figment of Osborne's imagination.

My bet is Rob's hanging around Mary simply because he's fallen for her. He stares at her with such a moon-struck look it's difficult to buy any other reason."

Stefanie nodded, realizing she'd been only half listening to Matt. Instead she'd been musing about Mary being involved with Rob...not Matt. That must be the truth. Surely Matt wouldn't have the nerve to out-and-out lie to her when Mary was due back so soon.

She smiled a little, thinking how she usually hated finding she'd been wrong about something. But in this instance she liked it. She also suddenly liked Mary a lot more.

"By the way," Matt said, interrupting her thoughts. "How old are you?"

"Ah...twenty-nine."

"You're just lucky! Six years is my outermost limit. If you were twenty-eight, I'd have to retract my dinner invitation."

Stefanie laughed. "Okay. I was wrong. You can stop teasing now. There must be something in the Scottish air that's affecting me strangely. I keep seeing things that aren't at all what they seem to be—first you and Mary, then that log."

"That must be it," Matt agreed with a grin. "It's something in the air. But have I relieved your concerns about going out with me? Absolutely nobody will care."

"All right. I'll buy that. But there are two sides to this. Don't you have any concerns about going out with me? At least this afternoon? I've got to be looking as if I'm wearing my midget sister's clothes."

"Well, Inverness isn't exactly the fashion capital of Great Britain. Likely nobody will even give you a second glance before you find something to fit you. Not," he added with an exaggerated leer, "that I object to short pants and an expanse of bare legs."

STEFANIE SPREAD HER PURCHASES out on her bed, then pulled a handful of hangers from the wardrobe. Matt had been right. Inverness was far from a fashion capital—in more than just miles. But she'd easily managed to find jeans and shoes that fit, and enough tops to get her through.

The dress he'd insisted she buy to wear out for dinner tonight had caused more difficulty. She and Matt must have been in every shop in the city. Even so, at his urging, she'd ended up with something she would never have bought in Chicago.

She gazed down at it uncertainly. The white, calf-length, gossamer dress was absolutely gorgeous, but it wasn't her. She was Plain Jane. This dress was Zsa Zsa Gabor.

She picked it up and moved to look in the mirror, holding it against herself. The delicate silk nestled against her body, clinging to every curve it found. She stared critically into the mirror, then back at the bed, at the white, pearl-encrusted hair combs the saleswoman had told her would be the perfect accent.

Maybe the woman had been right. Maybe . . . if she tried something different with her hair. She pushed the dark tangles onto the top of her head with one hand and eyed the result.

An hour later, when Matt tapped on her door, her stomach was turning flip-flops. Either she looked more elegant than she'd thought possible or she looked ready for a masquerade ball. Terrified it was the latter, she took a deep breath, grabbed her purse and opened the door.

Instead of Matt, Florrie McFarlane stood gazing up at her. "Oh, you look wonderful, dear. It's amazing what a little rest will do. And that dress!"

Stefanie brushed the fabric self-consciously. "Thank you."

"Very nice. Very nice, indeed." Florrie paused, glancing furtively along the empty hallway, then back at Stefanie.

"There's a man downstairs," she whispered. "Asked to see you, dear. A man with a foreign accent, he is!"

Florrie led the way. From halfway down the staircase, Stefanie could see a man standing just inside the front door. He was probably thirty-one or thirty-two, tall and blond and Nordic looking, with blue eyes and a prominent, square jaw. If she was allowed only one word to describe him, it would have to be *hunk*.

They reached the bottom of the stairs and Florrie scurried off to the kitchen. Stefanie looked at the man curiously. "Hello. I'm Stefanie Taylor."

"Miss Taylor." He gazed steadily at her until she began to feel uncomfortable.

"And you are Mr....?"

"Chernovsky. Vladimir Chernovsky. Am pleased to meet with you."

Stefanie nodded uncertainly. "What can I do for you, Mr. Chernovsky?"

"Vladimir." He grinned engagingly.

"Vladimir, then. What can I do for you, Vladimir?"

"Is what I do for you." Vladimir opened the front door, stepped outside and returned a moment later with her suitcase.

Stefanie stared at it in surprise.

"Is full." Vladimir proceeded to lay her case on the floor and open it, exposing a mishmash of her clothes.

"Oh, Mr. Chernovsky... Vladimir. This is wonderful! I didn't really expect to get it back. Where was it?"

"Is messy. When I find, clothes are on ground. I put back in... not neat."

"Don't worry about that! I'm so glad you found it at all. And thank you very much for returning it."

Vladimir shot her another grin and snapped her case closed. "Was not hard. I find near this house. Your name is on tag. I ask few people. One of them tells me here."

"Well, I really appreciate your taking the trouble to return it."

"Is good I did. I meet beautiful woman."

"Why... thank you. That's very kind."

"There you are!" Matt's voice came from the staircase. "I wondered, when you weren't in your room..."

Matt paused on the bottom step, looking curiously at Vladimir.

"Matthew Garrett, Vladimir Chernovsky." Stefanie pointed at her suitcase. "Look what Vladimir found, Matt."

Matt nodded slowly. "Good for him. Stefanie must be awfully happy to have this back, Vladimir. Where was it?"

"Not far. Under bush." Vladimir stepped back to the door. "I am seeing you again, Stefanie?"

"Ah... perhaps, Vladimir. Will you be in Drumnadrochit long?"

"*Da*. Long. I think for weeks."

"Then perhaps we'll see each other. The village isn't very large."

Vladimir smiled and opened the door. "Good night, Stefanie. And Matthew," he added, his eyes never leaving Stefanie. "I see you."

The door had barely closed behind Vladimir, when a deep voice boomed from behind them. "What's that Russkie after, lass?"

Stefanie turned and stared at the strange man, a big, burly fellow in his early sixties. He sported a mane of graying hair that had obviously once been red.

"Stefanie," Matt said, "you haven't met our host yet. This is Angus McFarlane."

"Pleased to meet you, lass. What's that Russkie after?"

"Vladimir?"

"Aye, Vladimir or Boris or Ivan—whichever one he was. They've all been into the Olde Loch Ness several times—the entire Russian search team's been there, in fact. The Japanese team only came by to take pictures of the rustic exterior. And I haven't seen a sign of the Germans. But the Russkies all want souvenirs. The way they buy, they must be rolling in rubles."

"Vladimir found my suitcase. He was just returning it."

Angus stared at the case for a moment. "Aye, so he found it, did he? Probably right where he hid it. They're a canny lot, those Russkies."

Stefanie glanced to Matt for help.

He grinned at Angus. "We should probably have at least a shred of evidence before we jump to conclusions, shouldn't we?"

Angus snorted. "'Tis only a wee jump. The Russkies can't buy many consumer goods at home. They take what they can when they're away. Blue jeans. Had blue jeans in that case, dinna ye, lass?"

"Yes. But," Stefanie protested, "all my things seem to be here—including my jeans."

"Aye, that's it, then. They're a canny lot, those Russkies." Angus turned abruptly and headed along to the private area of his house.

Stefanie stared at Matt, wondering if Angus's parting logic had made any sense to him.

He shrugged. "Angus is a bit of a character. They probably elected him lord provost because he adds color to the village." He gave Stefanie an exaggerated once-over as he spoke, then whistled softly.

"You look absolutely fantastic! No wonder Vladimir's eyes were popping out of his head when I came downstairs."

"Well, thank you. Too bad I'll have to return everything, seeing my own clothes have shown up. In fact, I guess I should go upstairs right now and take this dress off."

Matt grabbed her hand as she turned. "Don't you dare! That dress looks perfect. You can't possibly return it. Besides, there's no way we can spend another day in Inverness, not just to go trotting around returning things. Osborne would have a fit. He'll be far happier to sign for the cost of those clothes. Anyway, you don't have time to change now. Not unless you want to miss the piper."

"What piper?"

"The one who pipes at six-thirty, of course."

"Matt! Don't be annoying!"

Matt laughed. "There's a piper who marches around the grounds of Culloden House at six-thirty, playing his bagpipes to welcome the dinner guests. But we won't be dinner guests if we stand here playing Twenty

Questions instead of hitting the road." He tightened his grip on her hand and headed for the door.

"Matt! We can't leave my suitcase sitting in the middle of the foyer."

"Right." Matt moved it over five feet so it was out of the way, against a wall. "Satisfied? Can we go now?"

"Why not? The last thing I want to miss in Scotland is a piper."

STEFANIE SPOTTED A SIGN for Culloden House and glanced at her watch. "Hurry, Matt. It's almost six-thirty." She half suspected he'd been teasing her about the piper, but just in case...

Matt turned off the highway onto a narrow road lined with enormous trees. A few hundred yards along, he slowed the car. A large gateway lay before them. Two huge stone pillars, supporting an open iron gate, guarded the entrance and framed Culloden House in the distance.

The hotel was a large, three-story, brick-and-stone structure with adjoining two-story wings on either side. Ivy meandered gracefully over much of the exterior. A white, wrought-iron railing ran decoratively across the front, sweeping up either side of the central staircase leading to the main entrance.

"This looks more like a private estate than a hotel, Matt."

"It was originally. And I understand it's still privately owned—the owners operate the hotel. Are you a history buff?"

Stefanie shook her head.

"Neither am I. But apparently in the seventeen hundreds, Culloden House was one of Bonnie Prince

Charlie's headquarters during his attempt to defeat the British. In fact, it was his loss at the Battle of Culloden that ended his hopes of gaining the English throne.''

Stefanie stared out at the enormous expanse of lush grass enclosed within the hotel's circular drive. ''It's difficult to imagine a battle here. It looks so peaceful.''

Several cars were parked along one side of the drive. Matt pulled to a stop at the end of the line and cut the engine. The faint, mournful strains of a bagpipe wafted through the car's open windows.

''Where is he, Matt? Inside?''

Matt pointed to the far edge of the hotel. Just coming into view from the side yard was a piper dressed in traditional regalia. He walked slowly, his green-and-white plaid kilt swirling gently at his knees. The bagpipe's volume gradually increased as he crossed onto the lawn and came closer to them.

''He's wonderful, Matt. It's all wonderful! I should have brought my camera.''

''This is a night off, Stefanie. If you aren't careful, that damned gadget bag of yours is going to attach itself permanently to your shoulder. Come on. Let's go inside. I'm sure we'll still be able to hear the music loud and clear.''

As they neared the staircase, Stefanie realized there were two dogs on the top landing, one on either side of the entrance. They sat like a pair of matched statues, regal sentinels at the door.

''Scotch collies, Matt!''

''What did you expect?'' he teased. ''German shepherds? French poodles?''

"Don't be so smart! They're beautiful, aren't they? I love dogs. If I didn't travel so much, if I had a house, I'd definitely want a dog."

"I have one."

"Do you? What kind is he?"

"She. Her name's Buffy. And she's no particular breed—just a big, lovable, dumb dog."

"Those are the best kind. I wouldn't want one that was smarter than me." Stefanie paused to pat the collies. One acknowledged her with a disdainful glance. The other seemed completely oblivious to her.

"If that were Buffy," Matt said, "she'd have you down on the stairs and be licking you to death by now."

"In that case, I think I prefer Buffy."

Matt smiled, then opened the door and ushered Stefanie into the opulence of Culloden House.

The interior was overwhelming—a wonderful assemblage of burnished woods, high ceilings, elegant moldings, arches, pillars, crystal chandeliers and luxurious patterned carpeting. On one marquetry table sat a delicate china bowl filled with potpourri, imparting a faint scent of heather.

A distinquished-looking man, wearing a dark dinner jacket and a kilt of the same tartan as the piper, greeted them. "Welcome to Culloden House. I'm Ian McKenzie, the owner. Please come and join our other dinner guests in the drawing room."

He led the way to an immense, formal room overlooking a garden. Entering it was like walking into a time warp, into a space that had stood still through the ages.

In the drawing room Ian McKenzie served a smoky-tasting scotch.

"This is wonderful," Stefanie murmured. "I've never drunk anything quite like it."

Their host smiled. "It's private stock. You won't get it outside Scotland. We're selfish enough to keep our best scotch for ourselves."

One of the other guests began speaking to Ian McKenzie. Stefanie turned to Matt. "How on earth did you find out about this place?"

"Rob McFarlane."

"Then I don't ever want to hear you voice another suspicious thought about him. This is amazing. I feel as if I've been dropped into the past."

"According to what Rob told me, you have been. Much of Culloden House is as it's been for centuries. Look at those portraits. Apparently they're all paintings of the Forbes family. Duncan Forbes was Scotland's top judge in Bonnie Prince Charlie's time. He owned Culloden House."

Stefanie wandered in the direction of the portraits. Matt rested his hand gently on her arm as they stood gazing at the row of faces.

"They seem very alive," Stefanie murmured. The faces gazed back at her, making her wish they could speak.

"I wonder what they'd say," Matt mused quietly.

"Strange, Matt. That's exactly what I was wondering."

They slowly walked the length of the drawing room, examining each of the portraits in turn. These men and women, in their old-fashioned clothes, belonged here, among the museum pieces that decorated their ancestral home.

"You know, Stefanie, with your hair all piled up the way it is, you look very much like some of the women in these paintings. None of the other guests do."

Stefanie glanced about at the half-dozen other couples in the room. She'd barely been aware of them. They were merely bit players, peripheral to what she and Matt were sharing, to this special, almost unreal experience that was unfolding.

As dusk fell, Ian McKenzie escorted the guests, couple by couple, into the dining room. Candles flickered on each table, providing the room's only light, throwing dancing shadows onto the emerald walls.

Dinner passed in a marvelous dream. Everything was perfect—the food, the wine and Matt—especially Matt. Throughout the meal, he repeatedly touched her hand as they talked. She liked his touch . . . very much. She liked him . . . very much.

And he liked her. There was no mistaking that. From the moment he'd come down the stairs of the Galloway Guest House hours earlier, he'd been treating her as if she were the loveliest creature in the world— hanging on her every word, telling her with his eyes that she was an exquisite beauty.

Now he was smiling across the table at her, sending little tingles through her.

But she knew both of them were being influenced by the magic of Culloden House—by the candlelight, the wine, the sense of history, the countless romantic dinners these walls had witnessed. The place was both enchanted and enchanting. There was absolutely no doubt it had enchanted her.

And Matt Garrett, gazing at her with his warm, brown eyes, was every bit as captivating as the hotel. He seemed the most desirable man in the world.

Keep in mind, a little voice inside her head reminded her, *this world isn't real.*

"What do you think about leaving?" Matt asked quietly. "It's after midnight."

"It can't be!"

Matt laughed and reached across the table, covering her hand with his. Her heart leaped at his touch. His hand, warm on hers, felt utterly perfect. She stared down at it, knowing she'd be content to be frozen in time at this instant.

"Don't sound so worried, Stefanie. My car won't have turned into a pumpkin...and you still look absolutely gorgeous..."

The silence lasted so long that she thought he'd decided not to go on. Then, when he finally spoke again, his words enveloped her in a rosy glow.

"Stefanie, this evening has been the most enjoyable one I've had in years. And it's because I've been with you."

She glanced at him, scarcely able to believe he was feeling the same way she was. Maybe the magic wasn't the house's after all. Maybe they were creating their own.

"I've had a wonderful time, too, Matt...because I've been with you. With you and in this place. I think the Scottish air is doing me in again. There's a spell at work. Either that," she added with a wistful smile, "or our host mixes a potion into his drinks."

"I doubt that's it, Stefanie. The effect of a potion wears off with time. I don't think that's going to happen...not with me, at least."

Matt gently squeezed her hand. She looked down again, uncertain how much she wanted to say, how much she could trust herself to say. It had been so long since she'd felt what she was feeling right now. Or had she ever felt quite this way? Even with Peter?

She didn't think so. Some divine, overwhelming insanity seemed to be possessing her mind, threatening to cause her to say and do all kinds of things no rational, sane person would even contemplate.

"If you'd like," Matt continued quietly, "we can stay here drinking coffee till dawn...not let the evening end just yet. I imagine Ian McKenzie would even offer us a champagne breakfast. But Osborne's still going to expect us to be on the ball first thing in the morning."

Stefanie sighed at the intrusion of reality. "I hate 'first thing in the morning.' And I hate the thought of leaving here. But I guess it'll already be awfully late by the time we get back."

"There'll be other evenings, Stefanie." Matt squeezed her hand again before he rose. "We'll have a whole lot of other evenings."

MATT PAUSED outside the door of Stefanie's bedroom, still holding her hand tightly in his. During the entire drive home, cuddled against him in the dark confines of the car, her body had ached to be even closer to him, cried out to be held in his arms. Now she could barely breathe, knowing he was about to kiss her.

He smiled at her in the dim light of the hall and gently brushed a stray strand of hair from her cheek. The slight caress of his fingertips was electrifying. Then he leaned forward, and the world exploded around her.

His kiss engulfed her, promising pleasure beyond her wildest imaginings. The feelings pounding inside her were a hundred times more powerful than any she'd ever felt with Peter. Instead of warm familiarity, Matt's kiss engendered sizzling excitement, excruciatingly exquisite desire.

His lips burned hers; his tongue sent shivers of anticipation racing through her body. His clean, male scent delighted her. His hands, smoothing their way down her back, drawing her body tightly to his own arousal, made her certain she could never again exist without his touch. Her body throbbed against his, so strongly that she knew he could feel her longing.

Her lips, her tongue, her body, responded to Matt's advances with a primordial urge she couldn't control, had no wish to control. Her fingers wound tiny circles up the back of his neck, catching stray locks of his hair, pulling him ever more tightly to her, telling him how much she wanted him, needed him.

The strength of her desire was frightening, but instinct told her she had no need to fear Matt Garrett. He would never hurt her.

Finally Matt released her from his kiss, his arms still encircling her, his hands caressing her back, his lips gently nuzzling her neck.

She was certain, if he released her, she wouldn't have the strength to stand.

"Wow..." he whispered against her ear. "*Wow*...that's such a totally inadequate word for what I'm feeling, Stefanie. I'm sorry. I can't seem to make my mind work. Will *wow* do for the moment?"

Stefanie nodded into the hollow of his neck. At least he was speaking in complete sentences. She was certain she couldn't manage a single word.

Matt opened her door, one arm still around her, and kissed her again, this time with infinite gentleness. "Good night, Stefanie. Sleep tight. I'll see you in the morning."

He brushed her forehead with his lips, then walked the few steps to his own room. He opened the door, turned and blew her a kiss. "Till morning," he whispered.

Stefanie waited until Matt's door had closed behind him, then floated into her room. She closed her door quietly and leaned back against it, trying to control the smile she knew was a mile wide.

"Sleep tight," he'd said. Sleep tight? She doubted she'd be able to sleep a wink. This had been the most marvelous night of her entire life. And Matt was the most wonderful man she'd ever met. It wasn't the magic of Culloden House that had captured her heart. It was the magic of Matt Garrett.

She threw off her clothes, hung up the dress Matt had chosen for her and crawled into bed. She lay listening to her heart beating, recalling every word they'd spoken, every glance they'd exchanged.

A cautious tapping, barely audible, came from the hall. She waited, concentrating, until she heard it again—a light knocking, so faint she might be imagining it. Curious, she rolled out of bed, crept to the door and inched it open a crack. Her heart stopped beating.

Mary Johanson stood outside Matt's door, wearing her silky satin robe, the same robe Matt had given Stefanie to wear.

Matt's door opened quietly. Mary whispered something. Then Matt stepped into the doorway, his naked chest shadowy in the hall's dim light. He wrapped his arm around Mary's shoulders, drew her inside and closed the door quietly behind her.

CHAPTER SIX

STEFANIE STOOD STARING through the crack long after Matt's door had closed, her heart on the floor, memories of their evening ashes in her mouth. Her throat hurt. She closed her eyes for a moment, forbidding any tears to fall but unable to prevent waves of hurt, humiliation and anger from washing over her.

So much for her instincts! If their telling her Matt Garrett would never hurt her was an example of their accuracy, she'd better trade them in on a crystal ball.

And so much for Matt being wonderful! Anything even resembling wonderful had been illusion, had been the magic of Culloden House disguising his true, despicable character.

What had he said? He'd had the most enjoyable evening in years because he'd been with her? Ha! Double ha! She'd simply been a pinch hitter while Mary was in Edinburgh.

But Mary was back—ever so clearly back! And Matt Garrett's enjoyable evening was obviously just getting started. What nerve! Did he actually think he could have two women on the line when the three of them were living in adjoining rooms?

And then there was that hogwash he'd fed her about Mary and Rob McFarlane being an item. Talk about playing her for a fool! Apparently Matt figured she was so gullible she'd believe anything he told her. A fresh

wave of humiliation swept her. Damn! She'd been
every bit as gullible as he'd given her credit for. She'd
bought that story hook, line and sinker.

Well, never again! Matt Garrett could take his lies
and go jump in Loch Ness as far as she was concerned.

Gradually her hurt gave way to a desire to kill. The
only question was, which one of them should she do
in? The answer didn't take long to arrive at. Not Mary.
It wasn't Miss Blond Perfection's fault Matt was a total jerk. Or that Stefanie Taylor was an utter fool.
There was no sense hating Mary. The girl had enough
problems—she had Matt. And she was welcome to
him!

All right, then. That left Stefanie free to devote all
her hating to one person. She quietly clicked her door
shut and got back into bed, trying to ignore the residual pain in her heart. She wasn't going to have it inter-
fering with her will to hate.

What was the saying about revenge being sweet? If
she got the slightest opportunity, she certainly intended to find out whether that was true.

She lay with her eyes tightly closed, her pillow
scrunched over her ears, telling her mind to go blank.
But no matter how hard she tried to banish the recollections of Matt's kisses, of Matt's touch, they per-
sisted in taunting her. Despite her resolve, an ache
continued to worm away at her heart. Finally tears
trickled down her cheeks. Long after they'd dried on
her face, the dampened pillowcase reminded her they'd
existed.

The morning, she told herself as sleep finally came,
would be a new beginning. She'd write the evening at
Culloden House off to experience. After all, it wasn't

often a woman got to meet a Casanova of Matt's apparent prowess and escape with her heart intact. Well...almost intact.

At least she'd learned the truth before things had gone any farther. She still had to work with Matt, but she could handle that. Come morning, she'd be totally professional...and civil...and controlled...and completely unemotional...even if the effort killed her.

IT WAS LATE AFTERNOON by the time they left the *Sea Horse* and returned to the Galloway Guest House.

Mary appeared in the doorway of her room to greet them. "You three have been gone so long I thought you must have drowned. How did it go?"

Jeffery grunted at her. "Sonar's tracking great. But we didn't get anything."

"Nothing?"

Matt shook his head. "Not quite nothing. It was a good run. We covered several of Osborne's routes. We just didn't turn up a Nessie. The sonar tracked several large fish, though. We even had a few promising readings from inside caverns, but they turned out to be eels. They grow to be one hell of a size down there."

"Well, I didn't have any excitement around here, either. If I spend much more time doing environmental tests, I'll have enough data to fill a book. I should have stayed over another day in Edinburgh—done more sight-seeing."

"No, you shouldn't have," Jeffery offered. "I'm glad to get that component."

"Ready to tell us about this secret new invention yet?" Matt asked.

"Not till I'm sure it'll perform. I'll go into Inverness tomorrow and see about having the rest of the mechanism assembled."

"On Saturday?"

"Hopefully the fellows I need will be around. If I'd realized Mary had made it back last night, I'd have gone in today. But Matt didn't mention you were home, Mary, until we'd already gotten under way this morning."

"I was pretty late last night and didn't want to wake anybody up." Mary shot Matt a quick glance.

Stefanie intercepted the look and felt her blood pressure jump. Last night's humiliation came rushing back. She forced herself to smile at Mary. The girl looked disgustingly pretty. She was probably fresh out of the shower. Unlike the rest of them, who were not-so-fresh out of that claustrophobic little sub. Despite its air-conditioning, the interior was so compact it seemed oppressive.

And yet she hadn't felt that yesterday. So what had been bothering her probably wasn't the size of the *Sea Horse* at all. More likely it was being in such close quarters with Matt. But at least she'd made it through the day. And, despite her anger, she'd even managed to be polite to him. She deserved an award for that.

"So," Matt said, "who's for Friday evening at the Highland Shires? We could have pub fare for dinner, enjoy the local color." His glance swept the three of them expectantly.

"Not me, Matt," Mary told him. "I'm..." She paused, her glance darting to Jeffery, then back to Matt. "I have plans for dinner. But I'll probably make it to the pub eventually. Maybe, if you're still there, I'll see you later."

Stefanie muttered an obscenity under her breath. She'd just bet Mary would see Matt later, but she'd bet it wasn't going to be at any pub.

The girl shot them all a quick, nervous-looking grin and darted back into her room.

"And you, Stefanie? Was that a yes you mumbled?" Matt smiled warmly at her.

She bit back a sarcastic reply. What did he think she was? Second fiddle? Backup for Mary? "I'm a little tired. I think I'll pass."

Surprisingly, Jeffery objected. "Oh, come on, Stefanie. Let's go out and celebrate my sonar's performance. I was really pleased with it today. It's only a matter of time till we get what we're after. Besides, you don't want to spend the night sitting in your room."

"Well..." Well, why should she sit in her room? Why should she let Matt ruin her evening? If she went with them, she wouldn't even have to talk to Matt. She could talk to Jeffery. Of course, that prospect wasn't any great selling feature, but she really didn't want to sit home alone, feeling sorry for herself. Soaking up a little local atmosphere sounded like a lot more fun. And she was curious about the Highland Shires Pub, about its Hooray Henries.

"I guess you're right, Jeffery. What time?"

"About six?"

"Six is fine." She turned to her bedroom without a glance in Matt's direction.

Instead of her usual quick fix, Stefanie spent the entire time until six getting ready. The final result wasn't bad at all. She smiled into the mirror, careful not to let the space between her front teeth show. The bulky pink sweater she'd bought for the cool Scottish evenings made her look positively fat... Well, at least not skinny.

She heard Jeffery and Matt talking in the hall, fluffed her hair with her fingers and headed out to join them.

They walked along the cobblestone main street of the tiny village to the Highland Shires. En route Stefanie chattered at Jeffery, studiously ignoring Matt. The pub turned out to be everything she'd expected—an aged collage of stained glass, brass and satiny woods. Except for the air, hanging heavy with the smells of beer and smoke, the place was perfect.

A stand-up bar of dark, gleaming wood stretched across the back wall. Behind it ran a large mirror, reflecting the collection of bottles sitting in front of the glass. Several men stood at the bar. At its far end, a large dog lay curled into a furry heap on the floor.

In front of the bar sat wooden tables and chairs, about half of them occupied. Matt maneuvered her over to an empty table and politely pulled out a chair.

Jeffery plopped down beside her. "You getting the first round, Garrett?"

"Sure. What would you like, Stefanie? Local ale all right?"

"Fine." Stefanie watched Matt wend his way to the bar, suddenly wishing she hadn't come along. She was pushing her luck. Being with Matt hurt. Yet she couldn't take her eyes off him.

He stood at the bar, waiting to be served. She stared at his back, noticing how broad his shoulders were. His dark hair curled down his neck, brushing the top of his creamy sweater. Last night she'd run her fingers through that hair. Last night... last night had been a different world.

Matt started back toward them, carrying three pints of ale. She couldn't help thinking he was a good-looking man. But it wasn't simply that. He was easy to be with...fun...and she'd liked him so much. The fact that she'd completely misjudged him was frightening. How could she not have realized he was a snake?

She turned to Jeffery as Matt reached the table, determined to ignore the snake as much as possible. But Jeffery was paying no attention to her.

He glanced up at Matt, jerking his head in the direction of the entrance. "What are they doing here?"

Stefanie looked across the room. Standing in the doorway, surveying the interior, were Vladimir Chernovsky and two other, equally large, young men. They all wore navy turtlenecks that hugged their muscular chests. The sweaters bore a white insignia of some sort at heart level.

"Looks like the Russian search team's arrived," Matt said.

"But this is our pub!"

Matt grinned down at Jeffery. "I doubt the locals see it that way."

"You know what I mean! We've been coming here almost every night."

"Well," Matt said, sitting down beside Stefanie, "Scotland's a free country."

Vladimir glanced about the room, his gaze pausing on Stefanie. He smiled and gave her an exaggerated salute. Then he and one of his companions sat down at a table near the door. The third man swaggered to the bar, ordered and returned to their table with three pint-sized mugs.

The locals seemed as oblivious to the Russian trio as they were to the Americans. Jeffery, however, continued to stare at them.

Stefanie wished more than ever that she were back at the guest house.

"They're talking about us," Jeffery muttered.

Stefanie glanced in Vladimir's direction. He caught her eye and raised his glass in a toast. She smiled at the improbability of a Chicagoan flirting with a Russian in a Drumnadrochit pub and toasted him back.

"Stefanie! What are you doing?" Jeffery hissed.

She stared at him in amusement. He looked practically apoplectic. "Just saying hello. I know him. He's the fellow who found my suitcase."

"You didn't tell me a Russian found it, Garrett!"

Matt shrugged. "Never occurred to me you'd be interested."

Stefanie looked over at Vladimir again in time to catch one of his friends punch his arm and nod in her direction. She snuck a peek at Matt. He hadn't missed the gesture, either, and he didn't look amused. In fact, he looked a little perturbed. In fact, he looked almost jealous. Well . . . wouldn't that be an interesting twist?

By the time she turned away from Matt, Vladimir was rising. His friend slapped him on the back, grinning encouragement.

Vladimir sauntered over to their table, looking like a self-assured, professional athlete. "Stefanie. Someone tell me your friends come here. I think you maybe come. Is nice to see you."

"It's nice to see you, Vladimir. You've met Matt Garrett. And this is Jeffery Osborne."

Vladimir acknowledged the two men, then smiled back down at her. "You are liking to meet my friends?"

"No," Jeffery snapped. "She is not liking to meet your friends."

Stefanie shot Jeffery what she hoped was a shriveling look and shoved back her chair. "I'd like very much to meet your friends, Vladimir."

"I would, too." Matt stood. "We'll be back in a minute, Osborne."

Stefanie followed Vladimir to his table, with Matt breathing down her neck. The two other Russians rose to greet them.

"Stefanie...Matt...is Boris and Ivan."

As Vladimir spoke, Matt possessively encircled Stefanie's shoulder with his arm. The ticking bomb of anger inside her exploded at his touch. She glared at him, shrugging his arm away, and turned back to Vladimir, trying to concentrate on what he was saying, aware only of how furious she was at Matt. She'd had enough of his tricks. Whatever he was up to at the moment, she didn't intend to be part of it.

"You are joining us for drink now?" Vladimir asked.

Stefanie shook her head. "Thank you, but, no. Actually, I was about to leave. I just wanted to meet your friends first."

"Leave?" Matt asked. "We've barely arrived. What's going on?"

"Nothing—just a headache. It's the smoke, I think. I'll be fine once I'm outside."

"I'll walk you home."

"No, don't be silly, Matt. I know the way. And you can't leave Jeffery sitting there by himself."

"Stefanie, what—"

"You are liking I walk you home?" Vladimir interrupted. He turned and stared evenly at Matt. "You can
be staying with friend."

Stefanie glanced from one man to the other. Vladimir looked hopeful. Matt looked upset . . . extremely
upset . . . wonderfully upset.

She smiled sweetly at Vladimir. "Thank you, Vladimir. That would be nice. Then Matt can stay here
with Jeffery." She resisted the urge to check Matt's
expression, said goodbye to Boris and Ivan and walked
to the door without looking back.

Matt stared at Stefanie's retreating figure, at the big
blond ape with her, feeling his temper heading for the
boiling point. What the hell was going on? He swallowed hard. What was going on was obvious. Stefanie
had just made a complete donkey of him. But why?
What had he done wrong?

He'd realized she was being cool to him all day, but
he'd assumed that was merely an act for Osborne's
benefit. Talk about false assumptions!

From the looks of things, any acting she'd done had
been done last night. How could he have been so stupid? So blind? How could he have finally let down his
guard with a woman, only to have this happen? What
had made him think it was safe to relax with Stefanie?

He had absolutely no idea! All he knew was that
practically the moment she'd arrived, he'd decided she
was something special—the first sincere woman he'd
met in ages.

Sincere? Machiavellian was more like it! What on
earth went wrong with his brain, with his perception,
when it came to women? It had never even occurred to

him she was a game player. And it turned out she was a damned grand master!

So she'd been merrily playing games and he'd been completely oblivious to the fact—had let himself go right ahead and fall for her. That made him the biggest sucker around. Because if Stefanie herself was doing any falling, it was clearly for that muscle-bound Russian. The adoring smile she'd given Vladimir had been a doozy. It was a wonder the creep hadn't begun salivating on the spot.

He glanced at Vladimir's friends. They were eyeing him strangely. Wonderful! He'd probably been muttering out loud. That's what came from years of living with only a dog for company.

He unclenched his fists, wondering fleetingly when they'd become clenched, mumbled goodbye to the Russians and headed back over to Osborne, his mind reeling. Lord, he hated women who played games! He'd been married to one. And one was more than enough.

His ex-wife had definitely left him "once bitten, twice shy." And now, just when he'd thought it was safe to crawl out of his shell, what had he found? Stefanie! Ready and willing to inflict bite number two! He slumped down on the chair across from Osborne, trying to decide whether a hermit or a monk had the preferable life-style.

"What's with Stefanie?" Osborne leaned across the table as he spoke, his voice anxious, his breath hot and beery in Matt's face.

Matt glared at him. "How do I know? She has a headache. Vladimir's walking her home."

"But he's a Russian!"

"Very good, Osborne! Thanks for the news flash!"

"Look, Garrett, we can't have this! First we've got that McFarlane hanging around, out after who knows what. Now you want me to put up with a Russian, as well? What does he do on their search team? He's a sonar engineer, isn't he? That's it, isn't it?"

Matt leaned back in his chair before the urge to take a poke at Osborne's chubby face became overwhelming. "I don't know what Vladimir is. All I know is what I am, and it's not a damn nursemaid! So for pete's sake get off my back about what Stefanie and Mary are doing. They're adults. And they don't know any details about your bloody sonar to tell anybody even if they wanted to!"

"Oh, no! Speak of the other devil! He's with her again." Osborne stared across the pub, apparently oblivious to Matt's outburst.

Matt looked around and groaned. Rob was standing just inside the door, cheerfully greeting the locals, one large arm dwarfing Mary's shoulders. She grimaced an apologetic look at Matt.

He turned back to the table and took a large gulp of beer. This was shaping up to be one hell of a fun evening.

"They're coming over!" Osborne growled.

"Good! This'll give you a chance to ask McFarlane if the Hooray Henries are actually a special branch of the KGB."

"Hi." Mary smiled nervously at them. "We got here a little earlier than I thought we would."

"Aye, I had to catch some of my mates before they went home to dinner."

"Join us," Matt invited them, ignoring Osborne's sullen look. "The more the merrier."

Mary sat down beside Matt. Rob turned the next chair backward and straddled it. "So," he said to Osborne, smoothing his bushy red beard as he spoke, "how's the search going?"

"Fine. Fine."

"Enjoying your stay in Scotland, then, are you?"

"'Enjoying' is hardly the word. We're here to work—not play," he added, glaring pointedly at Mary.

"Aye. Mary's been telling me how hard you've been working. And my dad...he's been telling me about your problems...how worried you've been about things."

Matt eyed Osborne suspiciously. Rob's tone implied he knew something interesting. What else, aside from his new, mysterious invention, could their secretive leader be up to? What had he been talking to Angus McFarlane about?

Osborne shrugged at Rob. "It's been taken care of."

"What's up?" Matt asked. "What's been taken care of?"

"I've hired a night watchman for the *Sea Horse*—I was worried about security. Angus found me someone reliable."

"A watchman? Isn't that a little excessive? The only way anybody would get inside that sub would be with a blowtorch or the help of a master locksmith."

"You can never be too careful!" Osborne snapped defensively.

"Tell me," Rob said, leaning toward Osborne, "don't you think you might be taking this search a mite too seriously? We have teams here every summer. But they generally spend some of their time enjoying the countryside. You can't do better than the river fishing in this area. Hooking a big salmon in a fast current gets very exciting.''

"I don't fish.''

"Well, most of the teams find a lot of different things to do. Sometimes I don't believe they're half as intent on finding Nessie as they are on having a good time.''

"We're not most teams! They undoubtedly realize they don't have much chance of success. But we do. We've got the finest research sub available. And I've revolutionized the science of sonar tracking. If there are Nessies in your lake, we'll find one of them. And you're certain there are, aren't you? You and the rest of your Hooray Henries?''

"Of course Nessie exists. How could anyone but a Cheerless Charlie possibly think otherwise?'' Rob smiled a slow, enigmatic smile that hinted he could as easily be joking as serious.

Mary grinned at him. "I think the whole bunch of you are only in this for the fun.''

"Fun? Mary, my dear, how could you possibly dismiss two groups of serious philosophers as being only in this for the fun?''

"Serious philosophers?'' Mary laughed. "I suspect the only serious thing about any of you is how seriously you enjoy your pints.''

"Not at all! The fact that we meet in the Highland Shires is the purest coincidence. We meet to debate about Nessie. And stimulating meetings they are.

"Now,'' Rob went on, leaning forward conspiratorially, "all of us at this table know she's as real as we are. But those Cheerless Charlies persist in their delusion that she doesn't exist. Mary, it's the duty of the

Hooray Henries, not to mention my duty as a good Scot, to convince them of the truth."

"Rob, you aren't going to make me believe the Hooray Henries and the Cheerless Charlies are anything more than groups you dreamed up to give you an excuse to meet in the pub."

"Mary," Rob said, brushing her cheek affectionately with his fingertips, "no true Scot ever needs an excuse to meet his mates in a pub."

Osborne glared across the table. "Well, if your Nessie's for real, we're going to find her."

Rob nodded slowly, all traces of humor gone. "Perhaps you will. In the meantime, Jeffery, I was wondering if you'd give me a tour of the *Sea Horse*."

"Why?"

"Oh . . . call it professional interest. My bank's financing a research project in the Moray Firth—to do with silt buildup where the River Ness enters the North Sea. I've seen the equipment they're using. If yours is far superior, I might pick up some ideas that would help them."

"Sound Research isn't a nonprofit organization," Osborne snarled. "We're a business. We don't give away our ideas. Or give tours."

Matt took a deep breath, reminding himself Osborne was in charge of their search. "What harm would there be in a tour?" he asked quietly.

"You know we have classified technology aboard!"

"It's not important," Rob said quickly, pushing himself up off the chair. "I've got to get back to Inverness. Do you want me to drop you off at the house, Mary, or are you going to stay here for a bit?"

"You're heading home so early?"

"Sorry. Got to see about something. But tomorrow's Saturday. We'll have the entire day together. You don't," he asked Osborne, "work your team on the weekends, do you?"

"I will if there's work to be done! But not tomorrow. I have business in Inverness."

Matt caught Mary's eye and silently asked her to remain. If he was left alone with Osborne at the moment, homicide wasn't out of the question.

"Well, maybe I'll stay here with Matt and Jeffery for a while."

Rob nodded. "Be seeing you all, then." He bent down, kissed Mary's forehead, then ambled in the direction of the door, pausing to exchange occasional pleasantries as he went.

"He sure doesn't look like an investment banker to me," Osborne muttered at Rob's retreating back.

Matt ignored the comment. Nothing he said to Osborne would come out sounding even close to civil. "Have you eaten?" he asked Mary.

"Yes."

"I'm just going to get something, then."

"Grab me some shepherd's pie, will you?" Osborne asked as Matt rose. "After we eat, I'm going to head down to the *Sea Horse*. I'd better check on the new watchman."

"Good God," Matt muttered, heading for the bar. "First he hires a watchman. Then he decides the watchman needs watching." Mary had been right. Osborne was becoming unhinged.

STEFANIE SAT in the blackness of her bedroom, staring out over the dark front lawn of the Galloway Guest House. In the distance Loch Ness glistened under a half-moon. The setting was pure romance. What an illusion! Romance was obviously the last thing she was going to find in Drumnadrochit.

She forced her thoughts from Matt and concentrated on memorizing what she planned to say to Jeffery when he got back, wishing it were possible to rewrite the past few hours of her life. How could she have been such an idiot? Her brain had only been working on one track.

All she'd been thinking about, when she'd waltzed out of the Highland Shires with Vladimir, was the wonderfully upset look on Matt's face. Leaving with another man had seemed like perfect revenge.

But why hadn't she considered Jeffery's reaction? At best, he was probably furious with her. At worst, he'd send her packing for consorting with the enemy.

And all she could do was apologize for leaving without saying goodbye to him and assure him Vladimir had walked her straight home, then left.

She peered at her watch, wondering how much longer Jeffery and Matt would be. The room was too dark to see the dial. She glanced outside again, just in time to catch a movement. A stray beam of moonlight had been broken momentarily by someone, or something, moving on the lawn.

Stefanie stared at the spot, seeing nothing more—no sign of motion, no shadow to betray a person. Perhaps her imagination was playing tricks.

Another movement caught her eye. Two figures, one short, the other tall, had turned into the driveway, were heading toward the house. Jeffery and Matt. No! A moonbeam highlighted the head of the short person, capturing long, blond hair in its glow. Mary! Matt was with Mary, not Jeffery.

What an incredible operator that man was! He'd left the house earlier with her and Jeffery, but somehow he'd dumped Jeffery and ended up with Mary. And now they were undoubtedly on their way to his room—for a replay of last night's after-hours activities.

Her anger at Matt sizzled. Last night, after all those lies he'd fed her, after those kisses that had left her longing for more, he'd had the gall to make love to Mary in the room right next door. And he was probably about to do it again!

Men like Matt Garrett should be strung up by their thumbs. Well, he probably didn't realize she was onto him, didn't know she'd seen them last night. But she certainly wasn't going to let him off the hook tonight. His Mr. Two-timer routine was disgusting! And insulting to both her and Mary. At the very least, she could put him through a few uncomfortable minutes.

She'd intercept him and Mary in the hall. Maybe she'd make a couple of remarks about the evening at Culloden House—say enough to alert Mary to what Matt was up to. If Mary had any pride, Mr. Two-timer would shortly be Mr. No-timer.

The hall. She needed an excuse to go bursting out into the hall. She flicked on the lights and quickly found her robe and bottles of shampoo and conditioner. She'd have a casual chat with them on her way to shower.

A glance back out into the night told her Matt and Mary must already be inside. She walked quietly over to her door and stood waiting for the sound of footsteps on the stairs.

Moments later, one of the top steps creaked. She took a deep breath and opened the door. Matt was alone.

"Where's your friend, Matt?"

He gave her a hostile look. "Osborne went off to check on the *Sea Horse*."

"Not Jeffery! Mary. I saw her come in with you."

"So? Is that a major surprise? She does live here. But to answer your question, she stopped off downstairs to have tea with Florrie. And since we're speaking of friends, where's your good friend Vladimir? Have a nice evening with him?"

Stefanie glared at Matt. "Lovely. Thank you. And you? Have a nice evening with Mary?"

"Lovely. Thank you."

Stefanie continued to glare, desperately racking her brain for a devastating put-down. Nothing even close to brilliant came to mind. "I'm just going to have a shower," she finally muttered.

Matt nodded curtly and stomped along to his room.

Stefanie walked to the bathroom, disgusted by her failure to manage any cutting repartee. She threw off her clothes, clambered into the old tub and turned on the shower. The warm spray did nothing to improve her mood.

Matt Garrett had more nerve than any man she'd ever met. He'd spent last night sweeping her off her feet, then come home and made love to another woman. And now...now he showed up with Mary and still had the audacity to snarl about Vladimir.

She turned off the hand-held shower while she scrubbed her hair. The air was freezing against her wet skin. How could she be so cold in July? The sooner she got out of this damned country the better. The Sound Research assignment couldn't be finished soon enough. She turned the water back on, rinsed her hair, then scrambled out of the tub, still shivering.

She wrapped a towel around her hair, threw on her robe, gathered her clothes up off the floor and hurried along the hall to her room. There were extra blankets on the shelf in her wardrobe. She'd put them all on the bed and hide her head under the covers until morning.

Her damp hand slipped on the door handle. She tried again, jerking the knob firmly and shoving the door open. She took half a stride forward and froze, staring across the room.

Hunched in front of her open wardrobe, one hand on her gadget bag, a man stared back at her. Stocky build, brown hair, icy blue eyes—Mr. Still Waters!

As her mind identified him, he lunged at her.

She screamed.

CHAPTER SEVEN

MR. STILL WATERS slammed into Stefanie, cutting her off mid-scream. He shoved her roughly to one side, sending everything she was holding flying. She stumbled against the bed and instinctively whirled to one side, expecting him to attack her.

Instead, when she turned, he was disappearing into the hall, tightly clutching her gadget bag. Matt raced past the doorway after him.

Stefanie darted across the room and into the hall in time to see Matt tackle the other man. The two of them crashed in a tangle at the top of the staircase, then seemingly in slow motion began half sliding, half bouncing down it.

Women's voices shouted up from the hall below, yelling words indiscernible above the grunts and thumping.

Stefanie stopped at the top of the stairs. The men were on the landing. Matt's body was heaving, his breathing ragged, but he was sitting astride Still Waters's chest. The man lay motionless beneath him.

A moment later Florrie appeared on the staircase, brandishing a rolling pin. Mary was right behind her.

"I don't think," Matt gasped unevenly, "we'll need your weapon, Florrie. He's out cold. He took the worst of our trip down the stairs. But do you have any rope? He's not going to be unconscious forever."

"Mary," Florrie said, "there's a coil of clothesline hanging on the stairway to the cellar."

"I'm on my way!"

Stefanie stood staring at the scene below, certain she should be doing something to help, not having the foggiest idea what. "Are you all right, Matt?" she asked quietly.

He glanced up at her, nodded curtly, then returned his gaze to Still Waters.

Stefanie noticed her gadget bag lying on the hall floor. She retrieved it and quickly checked inside. Neither her Pentax nor Leica seemed damaged and the rest of the bag's contents were still intact. She put it down again and pulled her robe more tightly around herself.

Mary arrived back on the staircase, the clothesline in her hand.

Matt took it from her. "We shouldn't move him, but I think tying him to the banister will make us all feel safer."

Quickly Matt secured the man's wrists and ankles. "At thirty-five years of age," he muttered, "I finally get to use knots I learned in Boy Scouts."

He checked under Still Waters's jacket and withdrew a gun. "And make use of something I picked up watching TV cop shows," he added, standing up. "Speaking of which, Florrie, you'd better call the police. And where's Angus?"

"At a meeting."

"Can you reach him?"

"Not by phone. I could walk there. Should I?"

"It's probably a good idea. Why don't you call the police and then go. And, Mary, would you keep an eye on our friend here for a minute? I want to talk to Stefanie."

Matt started up the stairs, limping visibly.

Stefanie watched him, feeling incredibly guilty. Somehow what had just happened was her fault. She was the one Still Waters had accosted in Glasgow. It was her room he'd been in tonight and her scream that had brought Matt rushing to help.

"Thanks for the rescue," she murmured as he reached her. "That looked like a professional tackle."

"Not professional. Just college ball. Any idea who your friend is?"

"Yes. He's the man who was in Prestwick Airport and the Auld Highland House."

Matt exhaled slowly. "Once I got a good look at him I suspected that. I'll lay odds he drives a blue sedan."

"What?"

"I'll tell you later. The police will want us to go over all the details, anyway. You okay? There's a bruise forming here." Matt reached out and gently brushed the side of her jaw.

His touch elicited a sudden, overwhelming urge to cry. She quickly turned away, rubbing her eyes. "I'd better go get out of this robe, put on some clothes before the police arrive."

"They'll be a while. They have to drive over from Inverness." Stefanie nodded, a hundred conflicting emotions whirling inside her. Matt had come to her aid. How could she hate someone who'd done that? She didn't. Far from it, she admitted silently. The feelings his merest touch caused were nothing akin to hatred. But how could she not hate someone as two-faced as Matt?

"Well," she said, managing a weak smile, "I'd still better get started. Dressing may take longer than usual.

I'm shaking. Silly, huh? It was you who really might have gotten hurt. Thanks again."

She turned to her door, then paused, glancing back, unable to leave things so strained between them. "Matt, I'm sorry about earlier tonight—about Vladimir. I was acting like a thirteen-year-old."

"I'd have said twelve."

Stefanie shrugged, half wishing she'd left well enough, or in this case, bad enough, alone. "It's just that I misread things between the two of us last night . . . read too much into the evening. I can only blame the magic of Culloden House and the fact that I'm out of practice with men. You were merely passing the time. I realize now that I took things far too seriously."

Matt leaned back against the wall, staring at her. "Stefanie, what are you babbling about?"

"Mary, of course."

"Mary? Are you onto that again? How many times do I have to tell you I have no romantic interest in Mary? Why are you still worrying about it?"

"Matt, I'm trying my best to apologize! And I'm not totally convinced I even owe you an apology! So knock off the innocent act, okay? I saw Mary going into your room last night."

"And?"

"And it was almost two in the morning. And she was wearing a nightgown. And when you wrapped your arms around her you were practically naked. Are those enough 'ands' or should I point out she wasn't carrying a backgammon game at the time?"

Matt shook his head. The half smile on his face was absolutely infuriating. "Stefanie, wasn't there once a hit song that said you should believe none of what you hear and only half of what you see?"

"I'm not up on music trivia!"

"Well, just listen to logic for a minute! It was almost two in the morning because I'd been out so late with you, having—it seems I should remind you—a fantastic time. Mary was wearing a nightgown because she'd gone to bed before we got home. As I recall, she was wearing a robe over the nightgown. I notice you leave out details when it suits you."

Stefanie began to protest.

Matt held up his hand. "Listen to me! As far as my state of dress is concerned, wearing pajama bottoms doesn't count as 'practically naked.' And I was just getting into bed, which makes them eminently appropriate attire.

"And I did *not* wrap my arms around Mary! I opened the door and she blurted out something about being terribly upset. If I put my arm around her, which I don't remember doing, it would merely have been a comforting gesture."

Stefanie eyed Matt doubtfully, wanting so much to believe him but so afraid to. "What was Mary terribly upset about?"

"I'd rather not get into that right now."

His words removed her doubts. She knew what was going on, had known all along. Matt had no answer to her question. But he'd almost managed to sucker her again. Maybe, if he'd carried his story a little farther, she'd have been taken in. But his well of creative lies had apparently run dry.

"All right, Matt. We won't get into the distressing subject of Mary's *terrible upset*. I'll go get dressed." She took a step in the direction of her room.

Matt grabbed her arm. "Wait a minute!

"Mary?" he called.

"Yes?"

"Is our friend still out cold?"

"Hasn't twitched."

He drew Stefanie along to the top of the stairs so they could see the landing.

"Would you come here for a minute? I want you to tell Stefanie what you told me last night."

Mary walked up the stairs, glancing uncertainly from one to the other, finally focusing on Matt. "I thought you didn't want me to say anything. I didn't even tell Rob...or Florrie.... Although I still think I should. Angus should know about it."

"Maybe later. Just tell Stefanie for the moment. Tell her why you were in my room last night."

"Well," Mary began hesitantly, "it was because of Jeffery's invention—more specifically, the component I brought back from Edinburgh for him. When I picked it up, the fellow who'd assembled it made a couple of strange remarks. I started worrying about what Jeffery could be up to. I wanted to talk to Matt about it when I got in, but of course he wasn't here.

"It finally got so late I went to bed. But I couldn't sleep. So, after I heard you two come in, I went to talk with Matt."

"'Talk.'" Matt enunciated the word precisely. "You will notice she said 'talk.'"

Mary looked at him curiously.

"Stefanie saw you going into my room and got the wrong idea."

Mary flashed Stefanie an astonished-looking grin, making her feel two inches tall.

"You thought Matt and I...? Not really!"

"Thanks a lot!" Matt exclaimed. "I just wanted you to get me off the hook, not make me sound as if I'm the Hunchback of Notre Dame!"

"Of course you're not," Mary assured him. "It's just...well, it's just... Well, why don't I finish my story, Stefanie?"

Stefanie nodded, grateful to drop the issue of her own idiocy. She'd been totally, stupidly—wonderfully wrong! No. Only her assumptions had been wrong. Her instincts had been right. To hell with any crystal ball. She didn't need one after all. Her instincts were in fine shape.

Matt wasn't two-faced! He hadn't lied to her. She hadn't simply been backup for an absent Mary. And if that was the case, it must mean... She tried to force the smile from her face, tried to concentrate on what Mary was saying.

"I wanted to talk to Matt because the more I thought about what the component could be for the more worried I got. There must be something in the lake we don't know about—something Jeffery's learned about and wants to salvage. Maybe it's underwater treasure or something."

Mary turned to Matt and continued. "I talked to Rob about Loch Ness searches before we got to the pub tonight. I think that's why he started in on Jeffery for taking our search too seriously. Apparently there aren't many controls on what teams are allowed to do, except for a few laws the local council's gotten around to passing."

"I know," Matt agreed. "We looked into restrictions during our planning stage. There's no trawling allowed. And we couldn't use a nuclear sub. It had to be diesel-electric. But those seemed to be the only major constraints."

"You mean there aren't any environmental controls?" Stefanie asked him.

"Well...environmental, yes. That's where the sub regulations come in. But, as far as the searches go..."

"You aren't saying there are no laws to protect Nessie, are you?"

Matt shrugged. "That gets us back to the question of whether Nessie's real or a myth. The locals aren't about to make themselves look like a bunch of foolish old men in the eyes of the world. As long as there's no definitive proof Nessie exists, she has to be officially considered a myth. And how can you pass laws to protect something that doesn't exist?"

"But that's ridiculous! It—"

"It's the same everywhere, Stefanie. There aren't any laws in North America to protect Bigfoot—or Sasquatch—whatever you want to call him. Could be he exists, too."

"Well, getting back to Jeffery's invention," Mary interrupted, "to that component. I don't know what he's got in mind for it, but I think Angus should be told something's going on. If there's anything valuable on the bottom of Loch Ness, it belongs to the Scots, not to us."

"You've got me so curious it hurts, Mary!" Stefanie exclaimed. "What on earth is this component you picked up?"

"An enormous electromagnet!"

Both Mary and Matt looked at her expectantly, as if *electromagnet* explained everything. It explained nothing.

"You're going to have to back up a few steps for me, Mary. You two and Jeffery are scientists. I'm a photographer. I wouldn't recognize an electromagnet if I saw one, let alone grasp the significance of Jeffery designing one."

"All it basically is," Matt said, "is a core of magnetic material surrounded by an electric coil. Switch it on and it exerts a very powerful magnetic force. To use it underwater, of course, Osborne would have come up with a special housing. But I think the significant factor has to be what he's intending to use the magnet for."

"And that is . . . ?"

"That's a mystery. Obviously, since he told me he's going to use it with the sub's remote manipulator arm, he's expecting to pull something out of the water—something our regular grapplers aren't designed to deal with.

"Mary's guess is as good as any. He might have learned about some treasure down there—maybe artifacts from the Iron Age. Small objects would tend to slip through our grapplers, whereas they'd cling to a magnet. But his *treasure* could be almost anything made of iron or steel—could even be a container with steel support bands on it."

Stefanie nodded. "I understand. But haven't you asked Jeffery what he's up to?"

"Up to? Didn't you hear him yesterday when I asked him what it is he's designed? He wasn't even about to tell us that, let alone what he intends to use it for."

"And Jeffery being Jeffery," Mary added, "he isn't going to let us in on the details a second sooner than he has to."

"The only thing that surprises me about this," Matt said thoughtfully, "is his letting something distract him from the Nessie search. He was so damned hot on it being the ultimate way to demonstrate his sonar."

"But what really got me," Mary interrupted again, "was the fellow in Edinburgh going on about how powerful the magnet was, how he'd never assembled one anywhere near that size. It's so heavy I had to leave it in the trunk last night—must weigh seventy pounds. And there was a second carton that weighed at least twenty. I have no idea what was in it."

"Could we look at it?" Stefanie asked.

"No. Jeffery took both pieces out of my car today just a little after you all got back from the *Sea Horse*. I don't know what he did with them. Maybe—" Mary's words died at the sound of the front door bursting open.

"Garrett! Garrett!" Jeffery sounded hysterical.

Matt quickly headed down the stairs, closely followed by Mary and Stefanie. They stepped gingerly over the motionless body on the landing.

Jeffery stood in the front hall, the door open behind him. His face was red, his breath coming in shallow pants, as if he'd been running for miles. "Call the police! Call the police! There's been a problem at the *Sea Horse*." He stared at Mary for a moment, looking uncomfortable. "Rob's all right, Mary, but I'm afraid I'll have to press charges against him."

"Rob?" Mary whispered, her face growing pale.

"Osborne! What are you talking about?" Matt demanded.

"I'm talking about Mary's fine boyfriend! Rob! He didn't go home to Inverness when he left the Highland Shires. He went to our sub. I found him there. He was trespassing. Lord knows what he was up to! He was practically unconscious when I got there, but I knew he'd been up to no good. Someone had mugged my watchman, too! I had both of them on my hands!''

"Rob? Unconscious?" Mary's face grew even paler. "But you said he was all right. I heard you!"

Jeffery nodded. ''He'd just come to when I found him. Said he didn't know who'd hit him. Said he'd simply stopped off to say hello to my watchman—that they were friends. But he found Ian unconscious and then someone knocked him out, as well.''

"If that's what he told you, that's the truth!" Mary exclaimed. "But where's Rob now? And his friend Ian? You didn't leave them there, did you?"

"Yes. I did offer to drive them back here in Rob's car, though. I didn't take mine, remember?" Jeffery paused, glancing at Stefanie. "It was such a nice night I decided to walk from the pub to the *Sea Horse*. Anyway, I offered to drive Rob's car back, but he wouldn't go for that. In fact, he told me I could... Well, he said no."

"I assume," Matt said dryly, "by that point you'd already told Rob you intended to call the police on him."

"I guess I'd mentioned it by then. He was trespassing! Anyway, Rob wouldn't budge and Ian decided he'd better wait with Rob. I had to run all the way back here—must have been over a mile."

"We've all gotten our exercise tonight," Matt muttered.

"I'll go to the pier," Mary snapped. "I'll take my car and bring them back here. Rob shouldn't drive."

"Do you want me to go with you?" Stefanie asked.

"No. I can manage, thanks. Maybe Florrie has a doctor's number written down by the phone, though. If she does, you could call him."

"And the police," Jeffery added.

Mary glared at him, then turned on her heel.

"We're way ahead of you as far as the police are concerned," Matt said. "And not only do we have them on the way, we just might have taken the mugger prisoner." He gestured at the staircase. "Have a look at what's on the turn at the landing."

Jeffery took a few steps up the stairs, then looked back, his expression confused.

"I'm going to get dressed," Stefanie murmured, certain neither man was the least bit interested. She started up the stairs, not wanting to hear Matt fill Jeffery in on what he'd missed. This evening had already been too long and too full. There should be rules limiting how many things could happen in one person's life in any given length of time.

She'd lived a week—no, a month—in the past few hours. First there'd been her stupid exit scene with Vladimir. Then they'd had the excitement with Mr. Still Waters. She stared at him nervously. He was conscious now, and moaning a little. But he seemed securely tied to the banister and not in any shape to cause more trouble even if he were free.

She pressed herself against the wall, stepped quickly over his feet and hurried on up the stairs, shivering at the recollection of his gun. Their little adventure with him could have gotten them all killed!

Then, hot on the heels of that excitement, she'd learned the truth about Mary going to Matt's room last night and heard the story of Jeffery's giant electromagnet.

Topping things off was Jeffery's news that Rob had been snooping around the *Sea Horse*. Or had he merely been visiting the sub's watchman? A watchman she hadn't known existed.

But whether Rob had been snooping or visiting, someone had conked him over the head for his trouble. Him and the watchman. And had that same someone then come here? Was Still Waters the someone? It was certainly conceivable.

Stefanie mentally raced through her list of the evening's happenings again, wondering if she'd forgotten anything. It was quite possible... maybe even likely. Her mind was well into overload.

And still to go, after all this, was a session with the Inverness police. Well, if she had to face the police, she was at least going to do it wearing something more than a robe.

"'NIGHT, GUYS." Mary flashed a knowing grin at Stefanie and Matt. "We can all sleep tight knowing your Mr. Still Waters is being carted off to an Inverness jail cell." Totally ignoring Jeffery, she opened the door to her room.

She seemed like a different woman from the one who'd gone racing out of the house earlier to fetch Rob. If Stefanie'd had any lingering doubts about who Mary was interested in, they'd have certainly vanished in the past couple of hours.

When she'd returned with Rob and Ian, Mary had looked worried sick. When the doctor had proclaimed both men to be fine, the look had turned to one of relief. Then, when the police had convinced Jeffery not to press trespassing charges against Rob, she'd looked ecstatic.

And just as well the police had been persuasive! As it was, if it hadn't been for Rob's ability to see the humor in Jeffery's rantings, Angus and Florrie would probably have turned the entire team out onto the road. Jeffery had better be on the lookout for poison in his breakfast.

"Yeah, 'night, Stefanie, Garrett," Jeffery muttered. He reached for the door handle, then glared back at Matt. "I still can't understand why you didn't tell me about Still Waters before this! Didn't you think I'd be interested in knowing someone had approached Stefanie? And don't you think I should have been told that she had film stolen along with her suitcase?

"I'm in charge of this damn search, Garrett! I shouldn't learn about things only because the police start asking questions. You made me look like a fool!"

"Osborne, I've apologized for not telling you. There's nothing else I can do, so you may as well knock off the histrionics. Neither thing seemed particularly significant—didn't seem worth bothering you with."

"Next time bother me!" Jeffery opened his door and shot a final, disgusted look at them. "See you whenever I get back from Inverness tomorrow."

Matt waited until Jeffery's door had closed behind him, then took Stefanie's hand in his. "How about a walk in the moonlight? I'd like to talk for a bit."

She smiled tiredly at him. "Aren't you talked out?"

"Not to you."

"Then you've got yourself a walking partner. There's no way I could sleep. My mind is racing at a million miles an hour, trying to process everything that's gone on tonight. And I don't think it has a chance of managing."

They headed back down the stairs in silence and quietly let themselves out. The moon was high in the sky now, bathing the land as well as the lake in its soft light.

"Let's go around the side of the house," Matt suggested, steering Stefanie in that direction. "We can sit on Florrie's lawn swing. I've been wanting to try it out since the first moment I saw it. It looks like something that belongs on the front porch of an old Mickey Rooney movie."

"I thought you wanted to walk."

"Not really. It was just an excuse to keep you with me for a while longer."

They reached the old wooden swing. Matt settled her into it, then sat down himself, putting his arm around her and drawing her to him. His nearness sent a delightful shiver through her.

"Cold, Stefanie?"

"No...it isn't that."

Matt smiled, making her wish the moonlight weren't so bright. Her face must be an open book. Embarrassed by his gaze, by what she knew he was reading in her expression, she rested her head against his shoulder. It seemed the perfect thing to do. Matt shifted his arm slightly and their bodies melded as one.

Beside her, Matt radiated comforting warmth against the coolness of the night air. His masculine scent mingled with the fresh smell of dew-laden grass. The quiet of the moment was in complete antithesis to the frenetic evening they'd just survived.

The swing swung gently back and forth. The night was still except for an occasional insect sound and, in the distance, the barely audible lapping of water against the shore.

"How," Stefanie asked with a sigh, "can things suddenly seem so peaceful when we're actually still in the midst of one big mass of confusion?"

"I suppose it's because the confusion has nothing to do with you and me, Stefanie. The confusion between us has been sorted out. Unless, of course," he added teasingly, "there's more than you're admitting to the Stefanie Taylor-Vladimir Chernovsky relationship."

Stefanie laughed quietly. "What relationship? It turns out Vladimir's a photographer, too. That's his role on the Russian search team. But photography's all we have in common."

"So you haven't made a date to see him again?"

"No. He asked if I'd show him our lighting setup sometime. But I said I didn't think Jeffery'd go for that. And after tonight I'm certain of it."

"Then I have only one more question about other men in your life."

"Which is?"

"Who's Peter and what did you mean earlier about being out of practice with men?"

"That's two questions."

"True. I just didn't want to seem as nosy as I really am."

"Peter . . . where did you get that name?"

"Remember our first day together—when you fell asleep on the way up from Glasgow? You woke up and called me 'Peter.'"

"I did? I don't remember doing that."

"You did. You must have still been half-asleep. Who is he?"

"Well . . . Peter's an old habit. One I've broken. No. To be honest, one he broke. He married someone else. That's also the answer to your second question. I'm out of practice because Peter was around for a long time, and since him . . .''

"Still hurts?"

"I don't think so. Not really. Maybe just a little residual wounded pride over being rejected."

"Join the club. I have an ex-wife who ran off with another man."

"Really?"

"Really."

"I find that difficult to believe."

Matt squeezed her shoulder. "Thanks. I find it difficult to believe there could be such a jerk as Peter in the world."

Stefanie smiled into the night. The smallest thing Matt said or did seemed to affect her with startling intensity. Her reactions to him over the past few days had been bouncing like a rubber ball—bouncing from liking him to hating him and now back to liking again. Actually, it was far more than liking. Each bounce was carrying her to a higher level of emotional intensity.

They sat contentedly together until recollections of the evening began poking at her brain again. "Matt . . . do you really think Rob stopped by the *Sea Horse* to see his friend? Jeffery obviously didn't believe that."

"I don't know what to think. When Rob left the pub he said he had to get straight back to Inverness for something. Stopping off practically in the middle of nowhere seems a little strange. And just before he left us, he asked Osborne for a tour of the sub."

"And Jeffery refused," Stefanie concluded.

"Of course."

"Well . . . I hope Rob's not up to anything—for Mary's sake if nothing else."

"We hope alike, Stefanie."

She snuggled against Matt's chest, wishing her mind would stop racing. It wouldn't. "What about Still Waters? Do you think the police were right? That he was at the sub before he came to the house, that he was the one who mugged Rob and the watchman?"

"It makes sense. Lord knows what he was up to at the *Sea Horse*, but he didn't follow us all the way from Glasgow because he felt like a drive in the country. And the time frame works. He drove his infamous blue sedan from the dock to the house after the mugging. That put him way ahead of Jeffery, who had to make it back on foot."

Stefanie sighed wearily. "I just wish I knew what the man wanted. Why me? Why that message he gave me in Glasgow? Why show up in my room? Why was he after my cameras?"

"Don't forget the rest of the questions. Why follow us from Glasgow and why break into my car to steal your film and suitcase?"

"Do you think the police will come up with answers to all those whys?"

"With any luck. They don't have much to go on, though, do they? They've got a guy who has absolutely no identification on him and who refuses to say a single word. And they couldn't have done more than a cursory search of the dock area. They weren't gone from the house for very long. Probably checking to be sure no one had tampered with the *Sea Horse* was about the extent of it."

"But, Matt, if they don't find out who he is, we'll never know what's been going on."

"Well, they've got his car. That might give them a good lead. And if they manage to identify him, they'll probably learn what he's been up to and why. From what they said, I imagine they'll plug into some international police network—Interpol or something similar.

"But," he added, "that'll all take time. No one's going to consider this a top priority case. A couple of fellows get knocked out but aren't seriously hurt. And someone tries to steal your equipment from the house but doesn't succeed. Those aren't exactly major crimes."

"I guess you're right, Matt. I just wish they didn't seem so major to me. I feel as if I'm a piece of a jigsaw puzzle. But only one piece. And I don't know where I fit into the whole picture. Worse than that, I don't have any idea what the whole picture is."

Matt leaned closer and nuzzled her neck. His nearness banished her worries, replacing them with a feeling of secure warmth.

"Forget about that picture, Stefanie. Still Waters is out of commission. Whatever he was up to is over and done with. Think about a different picture."

Matt moved even closer and captured her lips in a long, loving kiss. A different, incredibly delightful picture zoomed into perfect focus in her mind.

CHAPTER EIGHT

STEFANIE AWOKE TO SUNLIGHT streaming in her window and the sound of Matt's voice. She was no longer merely dreaming about him. He was real. And he was outside her door.

"Come on, Stefanie. It's Saturday. Everyone else is up and gone. I've got plans for us."

Us. What a wonderful word! She rolled out of bed, grabbed her robe and hurried across the room. "I'm barely awake. Give me time to get decent."

Matt chuckled from the other side of the door. "I'd be perfectly happy to see you indecent."

"Trust me—you wouldn't! I'll be down in a few minutes."

"Ten minutes. Maximum. If you aren't in the dining room by then, I'll come back up and take advantage of the lack of locks."

A threat like that, Stefanie answered silently, *is definite encouragement to take my time*.

She began dressing, her mind whirling with recollections of the night before. In the bright light of day, it was easy to push aside thoughts of everything negative that had happened and focus on the positive, on the last hour of the evening, on Matt and her together.

She'd been so miserable the previous day, but in the end everything had turned out fine. Merely fine? Definitely not! *Marvelously terrific* barely even came close.

She'd been wrong about Matt and Mary. And, amazing as it seemed, Matt had fallen for Miss Stefanie Taylor. Maybe even as hard as she'd fallen for him! What a fantastic coincidence!

She finished getting ready and hurried down the stairs.

Matt glanced at his watch as she walked through the dining room doorway. "Just in time. And lucky for you, or your breakfast would be cold."

"What breakfast?"

The question was barely out, when Florrie bustled into the room with two plates of bacon, eggs and toast.

"'Morning, Stefanie. Coffee's right there." She gestured at the sideboard. "Guess I lose the bet, Matt. You were right. She was ready before her breakfast was."

Stefanie grinned across the table as Florrie left. "Are you always time obsessed?"

"No. I just don't want to waste any of the day. So start eating."

Stefanie obediently picked up her fork. "You didn't want to waste any of the day because . . . ?"

"Because I intend to spend every minute of it with you."

"Well, if I'd known you had such a good reason for rushing me, I'd have gotten ready faster!"

Matt laughed, reaching over and covering her free hand with his.

She stared down at it, aware she was smiling like an idiot, not caring in the least. "So what are these plans you have for us?"

"I thought that first of all we could take a little ride in the *Sea Horse*."

"On our day off?"

"It's a chance to be all alone with you. And I've decided I like that."

"I like it, too. But do we have to be alone together in the depths of Loch Ness?"

"Well, anyplace else, you never know when someone might come along and interrupt. That can't happen if we're in the *Sea Horse*. And we won't have Osborne with us. His absence will make a world of difference down there."

"That's certainly true. You know, I have a frightening premonition someone's going to murder Jeffery before this search is over."

Matt nodded. "And you're probably sitting across from the murderer."

"I suspect you'd have to get in line. We may be the last two people in Drumnadrochit who are on speaking terms with him. He's certainly got a well-developed talent for saying the wrong thing at the wrong time."

"Well, it's actually because of Osborne that I'd like to go down in the sub this morning. Not that being alone with you won't add a big bonus to the trip, but if there's any chance of us getting the jump on him, of figuring out what he's up to with his mystery invention, I don't want to miss it.

"He had a lot of nerve last night," Matt went on, "exploding about me not telling him things. He's the most secretive character going. The more time I spend with the man, the less I trust him."

"I'm sure," Stefanie told him with a wry smile, "that says a great deal for your common sense."

"Thanks. And my wonderful common sense tells me we should run a reconnaissance mission. Osborne left his maps in the *Sea Horse*. I thought we could check out a few of the routes we didn't get to yesterday. We just might get lucky and see what he figures on using his giant magnet to retrieve."

"That idea's a little sneaky, isn't it?"

" '*A little sneaky*'? You're being overly kind, Stefanie. *Highly unethical* is more like it. Under normal circumstances I wouldn't consider the plan. But I've got a hunch that whatever Osborne's up to wouldn't get past any ethics committee, either. In my books, that makes him fair game."

Stefanie swallowed the last bite of her toast. "Just give me a minute to get my gear. Then I'm ready when you are, Monsieur Cousteau."

ROB REAPPEARED from the bushes near the dock's storage shed and headed back toward Mary.

"Find anything?"

"This." He showed her a navy knit skullcap. "It was caught in a branch. Could be what we're looking for."

"I still can't imagine why anyone would have wanted to mug Ian," Mary said.

"What about someone mugging me?" Rob teased. "You can imagine that, can you?"

"You know what I mean, Rob! You simply wandered in on the mugger. He had to get rid of you. But what was he up to in the first place? Where did he expect knocking Ian out would get him? According to Matt, the *Sea Horse*'s hatch is tamper proof."

"That might be. But our friend may have had some interesting plans up his sleeve. Who knows? Could be he didn't want to get inside the sub at all. Could be he wanted to plant something on the hull."

"What do you mean, 'something'?"

"I don't know, Mary. I'm only hypothesizing. I have no proof at all. But your Osborne seems certain someone's out to disrupt his search. What if he's right? What if someone wanted to plant a device that would interfere with his sonar's readings? It wouldn't take much. The equipment's supersensitive.''

''Rob, you don't really think that's a likely possibility, do you?''

''I simply don't know. As I said, I'm merely hypothesizing. But there's more going on here than meets the eye. Osborne's such a sneaky fellow. For example...what's he doing in Inverness today?''

''I don't know.''

''You don't know, Mary, or you're not willing to tell me?''

''I...'' Oh, rats! Why was Rob getting on to this? Why was he asking her questions Jeffery would have a fit about?

''I really don't know, Rob. Jeffery's an inventor. He's gone into town to have some work done on something. But I don't know what it is.''

Rob stroked his beard thoughtfully. ''Perhaps we could figure that out. What about your trip to Edinburgh? What was it you picked up for him?''

''Rob...Rob, you've already asked me about that. And I've already said I can't tell you. You've seen the way Jeffery is. He's not giving out any details about his invention—not even to Matt. I don't know much, and what I do know, I just can't talk about with you. You know Jeffery's suspicious of what you're up to.''

''And what about you, Mary? Are you suspicious of what I'm up to, as well? Do you believe what Jeffery's implying—that I'm simply using you?''

''No. No...of course not.''

''But you don't quite trust me...not a hundred percent.''

"Rob, don't do this to me! You're putting me in an impossible position. I do trust you. But I can't talk about something that Jeffery wants kept confidential. Try to understand. Matt had a lot of faith in me to give me this job, to bring me along as part of the team. I have to be loyal to him. If I say or do anything I shouldn't, Jeffery's going to be at Matt's throat."

"Aye . . . I can understand your being loyal to Matt. He seems a nice fellow. But I can't see you worrying about keeping that fat, nasty wee man's secrets."

"Rob, that fat, nasty wee man is running the show. I don't have a whole lot of choice but to do as he says."

Mary heard a noise along the shore and glanced in the direction of its source. Stefanie and Matt were getting out of his car. She sighed with relief at their timely interruption and waved, beckoning them to join her.

"It's a good thing we don't have Osborne along, Mary," Matt teased when they reached her and Rob. "He'd want to have you arrested for associating with his trespasser. What are you two doing here?"

"Rob's been playing supersleuth—searching in the bushes."

"Searching for what?"

"Clues," Rob replied. "I figured the mugger might have left some clue to his identity. The police couldn't have done a very thorough check last night. So it's possible they were jumping to conclusions. Maybe Still Waters and my mugger are different people."

Matt nodded. "You have a point. As far as the police were concerned, we'd already nailed their man for them and solved two crimes with one villain."

"Well, at any rate," Rob said, pulling the knit cap from his pocket, "not only have I been searching, but I found something."

He tossed his find to Matt. "Doesn't look like it's been out in the weather much. Could belong to my mugger."

"Could, all right."

Stefanie peered at the cap as Matt turned it over. He was obviously looking for a label. There wasn't one.

"It's got to be worth passing along to the police," he told Rob. "But these are pretty common among sailors, aren't they? And you're certainly not short of sailors on Loch Ness."

Rob reached to take the cap back. "It's the only potential clue I've turned up. I think I'll search for a while longer. If that guy's still wandering around, I want him caught. I'm not a vindictive man but I do believe in fair play. And sneaking up behind people in the dark, then knocking them out cold, is a far cry from the Queensberry Rules."

Mary shot him a puzzled glance.

"The Marquess of Queensberry," he explained. "He set down the basic rules that govern British boxing."

"Can I assume," Mary teased, "that if you got your mugger alone you could be trusted to remember the Queensberry Rules?"

"Oh, I'd remember them all right," Rob assured her with a grin. "The question would be whether or not I'd be inclined to follow them."

Stefanie smiled at their banter, trying to imagine anyone mugging a man of Rob's size if sneaking up behind him in the dark hadn't been possible.

"Why are you guys here?" Mary asked, turning back to them.

"Just thought Stefanie and I would take a little ride in the sub. I want to check on a couple of things."

"Without Jeffery? I'm amazed he'd go for that."

Matt shrugged. "What he doesn't know..."

"Won't hurt him," Mary concluded. "My lips are sealed."

"Come on." Matt draped his arm over Stefanie's shoulders. "Let's leave these folks to their searching."

When they reached the *Sea Horse*'s hatch, Matt glanced back at the shore one more time, waved good-bye to Mary and Rob, then ran his hand across the lock. "Absolutely no sign of trouble." He unlocked the mechanism, turned the wheel that kept the hatchway watertight and pulled the hatch open. "Ladies first."

Stefanie clambered down the ladder. A few moments later she heard Matt above her, securing the hatch. Then he joined her in the observation chamber.

"I wonder," he said thoughtfully, "if Rob really came here looking for clues, if he actually found that cap in the bushes."

"What do you mean? You think he brought it with him?"

"I think that's possible. There are a lot of things about Ian and Rob being mugged that don't add up very neatly."

"For example?"

"For example, the question you raised yourself when we were talking last night. Did Rob really come by the *Sea Horse* because he wanted to see Ian, or did he have another reason?"

"Matt, last night everything seemed suspicious. Now that I've had a chance to think, it doesn't seem the least bit strange that Rob wanted to see his friend."

"Maybe not. But when he left the Highland Shires, he gave us the impression he was in a rush to get back to Inverness. So why would he have taken time to come by the dock? It's in the opposite direction from the city.

And it isn't only that. His being here today makes no sense to me, either.''

"Why not? Since the police couldn't have done much of a search, looking for evidence strikes me as a perfectly reasonable thing to do. Why else would he be here?''

"I don't know. He wanted a tour of the *Sea Horse*. And at the pub last night, Osborne mentioned he'd be spending today in Inverness. Maybe Rob figured that if he brought Mary here, if they were here alone, she'd show him around.''

"Does she have a key for the sub?''

"No. There are only two keys—mine and Osborne's. But Rob might not have known that. And here's another possibility. What if he came by last night because he hoped to get a tour from his friend Ian?''

"Who didn't have a key, either, if there are only two.''

"True. But again Rob wouldn't have known that.''

"Matt, he may have wanted to look around the sub, but I don't see why you're suspicious about his being here today. If some stranger had mugged me, I'd want to make sure the police had the right fellow.''

"*If* some stranger had mugged you.''

"I'm missing your point.''

"Stefanie, suppose Rob wanted to get inside the sub and figured his friend Ian had a key.''

"All right. I'm supposing.''

"Well, Angus recommended Ian for the watchman's job because he's trustworthy. Now I realize this next bit is pure conjecture, but what if . . . what if Rob figured Ian would never agree to let him into the *Sea Horse*. So he decided to conk Ian over the head, take the key and give himself a quick tour?''

"Matt! You aren't serious! You sound like Jeffery!"

"What a terrible thing to say! I thought you liked me."

"I do like you. But I certainly don't like your train of thought at the moment. It's verging on the insane. If Rob mugged Ian, how did Rob get knocked out? Did he hit himself over the head when Jeffery showed up?"

Matt laughed a halfhearted-sounding laugh. "That does seem a little unlikely, doesn't it? Look, all I'm saying is I'm surprised to see Rob here today, that it strikes me as strange. I guess," he added with a wry smile, "amateur detectives would be better off keeping quiet."

"Amateur detectives would be better off not paying attention to Jeffery's paranoid fantasies!"

"I don't know," Matt said, running his fingers through his hair. "Maybe you have a point. Maybe Osborne's made me overly suspicious. He's been feeding me his 'evidence' about Rob since the first moment the guy started hanging around Mary.

"And he keeps adding things up so convincingly. Look, Stefanie, the locals don't want to take any chances on Nessie actually being found. They're worried that would ruin their tourist trade. So isn't it possible Rob's been assigned to make sure Osborne's wonderful sonar doesn't get a chance to show its stuff?"

"I think it's more likely," Stefanie said firmly, "that Jeffery Osborne has been assigned to drive us all crazy with his suspicions!"

"Maybe you're right, Stefanie. Why don't we just forget about the whole lot of them for the time being and get on with our trip?

"The charts are up here," he said, walking to the front of the sub and opening a drawer in the navigation area. He glanced through a small stack of papers and tossed a few back into the drawer. "Those are the routes we followed yesterday. Now we just have to decide which of the others to try."

Stefanie joined him and peered down at the half-dozen roughly sketched charts he was spreading over the console. On each Jeffery had drawn a trail of figures and arrows indicating routes leading from the pier to various areas of the lake and back.

"I'm not going to be any help at deciding, Matt. Playing eenie, meenie, minee, moe with these would be about as much as I could contribute to decision making."

"In this situation, that's probably as good a method as any. I'll admit it's not very scientific, but go for it."

Stefanie laughed, pointing at the maps in turn. "Eenie, meenie, minee—"

Matt caught her hand and turned her finger to point at herself. "Moe," he said quietly, leaning forward to kiss her.

His lips pressed gently against hers for a moment, then grew demanding. His kiss was incredibly arousing. His tongue sought hers, his arms wrapped tightly about her, hugging her body to his as if he feared she'd vanish if he loosened his hold.

His kiss, the slow caress of his hands on her back, the crush of his body against hers, turned the space where they were standing into a tiny world of their own—a world that could never be shared by anyone else.

Kissing Matt Garrett was like nothing she'd ever known. External reality faded to oblivion, leaving her aware only of internal reality, of the burning desire he ignited inside her. It smoldered at the delicious intimacy of his kiss, leaped into flames as his lips left her mouth to nuzzle her throat. His breath, hot against her skin, fanned the flames until they threatened to consume her.

She clung to him, to the strength of his body, to the exquisite happiness she felt in his arms.

Too soon he drew away. But his words sent another sizzle of delight rushing through her.

"Why is it, Stefanie, that every time you come near me I start thinking I'll die if I don't kiss you?"

"I hope that's a rhetorical question...because I'm in no condition to give you an answer. Every time you kiss me, my brain stops working."

Matt leaned back against the console, encircling her waist with his arms. "Brain stoppage is probably just a temporary reaction. If we expose you to enough of my kissing, it should clear up on its own."

"That's your scientific prognosis?"

"No, that's my not-so-scientific prognosis, aimed at convincing you we should do a lot of kissing."

Stefanie closed her eyes, certain Matt must realize there was no convincing necessary.

He brushed her mouth gently with another kiss. "I'd better decide on one of these routes. If we play another round of eenie, meenie, we're never going to make it away from the pier."

He picked up a couple of the charts. "I'm curious about these ones that lead into underwater caverns."

Matt set the charts to one side and started the sub's engine.

"Does this mean," Stefanie asked, "I have to leave you to your navigating and go man my observation post?"

"Only for a little while."

She took a couple of steps toward the window.

"You know—" Matt's voice stopped her "—I'm awfully tempted to forget about this trip and just keep right on kissing you. I wouldn't need much persuasion." He gazed at her hopefully.

It took all her self-control not to rush back into the warmth of his arms. "Better not, Matt. It's probably the only chance you're going to get—at taking the sub down without Jeffery, I mean...not at kissing me."

He shot her a smile, then turned and began easing the *Sea Horse* away from its dock.

"What about the sonar, Matt? Aren't we going to use it?"

Matt looked back over at her. "I hadn't planned to. I thought we'd concentrate on watching for whatever Osborne's after, not worry about the Nessies today."

"And the sonar's no use for finding Jeffery's treasure?"

"Not likely. It can't be very large. If it were, someone would have spotted it before this. And the sonar will only let us identify a fairly sizable object. Particularly if it's not something that's moving."

"Oh...well...I just thought, since we're going down, anyway..."

Matt shrugged. "If you figure you're strong enough to help me rig the sonar, I guess there's no reason not to."

"If I'm strong enough? That sounds too much like a challenge to ignore! We're going to have to use it now."

Suspending the sonar on its cables was more difficult than it had seemed when she'd watched Matt and
Jeffery do it. But they managed to get the unit into
place, then climbed back down to the observation
chamber.

Matt flicked a couple of small switches on the control console, and the sonar's monitor came alive. A
thin, luminescent green line appeared on the screen,
radiating from the center, swinging in a slow circular
circuit. Occasionally a flash of green, accompanied by
a pinging noise, flared briefly on the thin line.

As the *Sea Horse* made its way out into the lake,
Stefanie turned on the light units around her observa-
tion window and stared at the retreating side of Loch
Ness.

The lake bed, carved out of mountainous terrain by
glaciers aeons ago, didn't drop off gradually. Rather,
its sides plunged almost straight down. They looked
like the sheer mountain cliffs they once were. Rapidly
they disappeared beyond her range of visibility, leaving only black water and, for an instant, a lone lake
trout swimming past the window.

Stefanie glanced toward the front. There was nothing interesting in sight through the navigation window, either. "I wish we had an idea of what we're
looking for, Matt."

"Something stationary. Probably either on the floor
of the lake or inside one of the caverns on the sides. On
the way back we can pick up one of the cavern routes.
But for starters, I'm going to take us down to within
sight of the bottom and along a route leading to the
eastern tip of the lake—to where the water flows into
the Bona Narrows. There's something I want to check
out at the mouth of that channel."

"What?"

Matt glanced back at her for a moment, as if uncertain he should answer her question. "It relates to a theory I have concerning the Nessies. But it's something I haven't told anyone about.

"Even I," he added with a grin, "have the occasional worry over finding myself misquoted in some trashy newspaper. And in this case, it would likely be under a caption reading 'Mad Marine Biologist Reveals the Loch Ness Monster's Secret Sex Life.'"

Stefanie laughed. "Sounds like a fascinating theory you've come up with! You have to tell me about it. I can be trusted. As Mary would say, my lips are sealed."

"Well...let's wait until we get to the narrows, until I've had a look. Then I'll have a better idea if what I've been theorizing is likely or not. There's no point in telling you about it if I see there's no supporting evidence."

Matt increased the sub's speed and stood gazing out the front. Stefanie looked through the observation window, trying to concentrate on watching the lake's bottom. But her thoughts kept wandering to what might lie ahead, to what Matt might be hoping to see.

Eventually he slowed the *Sea Horse* to a crawl and navigated along the steep wall rising from the lake bed. "There's the entry to the Narrows—ahead on the right."

Stefanie hurried to join him by the front window. She could see one edge of an opening in the rocky wall, but the far side of the channel was hidden by dark water.

"I just want to get a little closer," Matt told her. "Hold on to something. There are currents in Loch

Ness that can hit like sudden gusts of wind. And they'll be bad around the channel opening.''

Twenty feet farther along he stopped the sub. "Okay, we seem to be safe enough here." He stepped back and took her hand. "Let's have a look through the observation window. Your lights will be a help."

Matt peered this way and that at the entrance to the Narrows.

"What should I be looking for?" Stefanie asked when he offered nothing.

He pointed to an area of the wall several feet from the channel. "See where the rock's composition changes?"

Stefanie stared intently at the rock, finally making out a barely visible line that reached upward into the blackness. On the channel side, the stone seemed gradually, almost imperceptibly, to grow lighter in color. "Yes. I can see a difference."

"The rock to the left of that demarcation line," Matt explained, "was carved out in the glacial age, when the lake was formed. What you see to the right is actually silt that's been building up ever since. Of course, it's hard as granite now. But originally it was just billions of grains of sand that drifted up the channel."

"And? Is this meaningful as far as your theory is concerned?"

Matt nodded, excitement written across his face. "It's extremely meaningful."

"Well, tell me the theory, then!"

"Look...Stefanie...I will tell you. But it might strike you as pretty wild. If I'm going to confide in you, you have to promise not to laugh. I'm serious about this."

"Okay. My lips are sealed and no laughter will escape them. Promise."

"Then look at this for a minute." Matt pointed to a spot on their topographical chart of the area. "This is where we are—the end of the lake. Now see," he continued, his finger tracing a route, "the water empties into the Bona Narrows, runs into the River Ness and, a few miles along, enters this arm of the North Sea—the Moray Firth."

"All right. I've got the geography straight. But when do we get to the good part you mentioned—the bit about Nessie's sex life?"

"Stefanie! I told you this is serious! Here I am, revealing a scientific theory to you, and you're being flip."

Stefanie tried to look remorseful. "Sorry. Continue."

"All right. Now over the centuries, silt has been building up in the Moray Firth. That's nothing unique, just a natural part of the earth's constant evolution. The sea's motion gradually produces changes in coastlines.

"But there's been a fair amount of recent research on how buildup has been affecting this particular area. I read up on it when we were studying factors relating to our search. And it seemed to me the buildup wouldn't be restricted to the firth, that there'd be a carryover effect as far inland as the narrows. That's what I wanted to see. And that's what's right there in front of us."

"And this silt buildup ties into your theory?"

"Yes. But I'm getting ahead of myself. My theory is based on two basic tenets. The first one is a biological fact, that numerous species of water creatures migrate to their birthplaces to breed."

"Of course. I once did a photo-assignment in British Columbia of salmon scaling horrendous rapids to reach their spawning ground."

Matt smiled. "Good example. But you may not buy my second tenet so easily. It's based on observation, not scientific fact."

"Try me."

"All right. The vast majority of recorded Nessie sightings have taken place in the spring and early summer. They taper off in August, and until the following spring, there are very few—so few, it's reasonable to assume they may not be true sightings at all."

"You mean they could be like my seeing that waterlogged, decaying wood," Stefanie said thoughtfully.

"Exactly."

"So you're saying . . . there are only Nessies in Loch Ness for part of the year?"

Matt leaned forward and kissed her cheek. "Congratulations. I'll make a biologist of you yet. My theory is that the Nessies come into Loch Ness to breed in the relative safety of its confined area. Then, once the newborns are strong enough, the creatures return to the North Sea."

"By swimming," Stefanie concluded, tracing her finger along the route on the map, "through the narrows, up the river and into the sea."

"That's the most likely route."

"All right." Stefanie nodded slowly. "I'll buy your theory so far. But what about the silt buildup?"

"Well, keep in mind we're talking about a period of millions of years—ever since the last ice age. When the glaciers receded, Loch Ness was probably an arm of the sea, the inner tip of the firth. But over all those millenia, passages between the ocean and inland lakes have gradually been closed off by silt washing relentlessly into shore."

"Closed off... Matt, you mean you think that Nessie's route...?"

"I think it's happening. In fact, it's possible it has happened already—within recent history. The first recorded sighting of Nessie dates back well over fourteen hundred years. We have no geographical records showing how much change there's been in the coastline since then."

"Matt, this sounds incredible! What you're saying, what you're theorizing, is that the Nessies have come to Loch Ness every spring to breed. But we're almost at—or past—the point in time where their route becomes impassable. Have I got that right?"

"Pretty well. 'Impassable' may be a little strong. But the route's getting narrower and narrower. At some point the creatures will become aware the passage is more difficult to maneuver in. Then instinct will tell them not to chance coming to Loch Ness again.

"That point in time could be now. Or it could be a thousand years on either side of now. That's no time span at all when the process has taken millions of years."

Stefanie tried to imagine how long a million years was, to envision a million life spans stretching out over the ages. Her imagination refused to cooperate. "It seems inconceivable that there can suddenly be a year, a single breeding season, when the Nessies won't come here anymore."

"It isn't 'suddenly' a year, Stefanie. It's been happening slowly, immeasurably slowly. But at some point, during some winter storm, those final grains of silt were, or will be, washed into the passage, and the

Nessies will decide that the Bona Narrows have become just too narrow. Then they'll stop coming into Loch Ness.''

Stefanie shook her head, realizing what Matt was telling her made sense but unable to accept that the point in time could be this year...or last year...or next year. It was impossible, yet possible.

"But, Matt, if that happens, when that happens, what will become of the Nessies? If this is their birthing ground and they stop coming here . . . ?''

"They'll make out all right. Originally they'd have come in from the sea to bear their young because the lake was a safer place. By now, though, a hundred sheltered areas have probably formed along the coast—coves where they'd be protected. Instinct still brings them back to Loch Ness. But if it becomes too difficult to reach, they'll choose another location.''

Stefanie stared silently out into the deep, dark water. It held more secrets than she'd ever conceived of. And it kept them well.

"You haven't,'' she finally asked, "told anyone else your theory?''

"No. I told the brass at Sound Research I thought it was possible there was a breeding population in the lake. I didn't mention the seasonal migration aspect. Originally I'd intended to tell Osborne the entire theory. But that was before I got to know him. And I almost told Mary. Then I decided to wait and see the narrows first.'' Matt paused, clearly expecting Stefanie to say something more.

She had absolutely no idea what to say.

"Well,'' he prompted, "what do you think?''

"I think I'm incredibly flattered you told me. Aside from that I don't know. I'm overwhelmed. The no-tion's so difficult to deal with. We're talking about something that's been going on virtually forever. And yet its ultimate effect is showing up here and now.''

"I realize it's an amazing concept, Stefanie, that it takes a while for the idea even to seem possible. But how about getting some photographs of the silt buildup? They'll provide concrete proof of what's happening here. Then, once you have your shots, we'd better head back.''

Stefanie reached for her camera and began focusing. "This is an awfully important finding, isn't it Matt?''

"Yes, it is—in some circles at least.''

"But, Matt, what if the narrows have already become too narrow? What if the Nessies have already stopped coming to Loch Ness? Then we're not going to find one, are we?''

"That's true, Stefanie. But I've got a feeling it hasn't happened yet—that the Nessies are still coming to the lake to breed.''

"Another scientific theory?''

"Nope, I just think I'm an incredibly lucky guy—in a lot of ways.''

The look Matt shot her made her knees grow weak.

STEFANIE PERCHED against the navigational console, reloading her camera and watching Matt peer out the front window.

He glanced back at her and grinned, obviously still excited about what they'd seen at Bona Narrows.

"I'm glad you suggested rigging the sonar, Stefanie. After the narrows, I feel as if we're on such a roll we're a shoo-in to find a Nessie.''

"Can you imagine the expression on Jeffery's face if we told him we'd sighted one when he wasn't along?"

Matt laughed. "What a wonderful thought!"

He glanced at the sonar monitor, then down at the chart they were following. "The cave's along here someplace."

They drifted slowly for a few minutes, the silence occasionally broken by a small ping from the monitor as its green line rhythmically swept the screen.

Matt slowed the engine. "Keep an eye out. We have to be getting close."

Stefanie stared into the dark water before them, wishing she had x-ray vision.

"There's something!" Matt exclaimed. "Either it's a mirage or an opening in the rock." He navigated closer to the cliff.

A moment later Stefanie could see the slightly darker area he'd spotted. It was indeed an opening... an extremely tiny opening.

A queasy, anxious feeling settled in her stomach. Her palms were suddenly moist. She wiped them nervously on her jeans as the sub drew nearer to the entrance.

"It doesn't look very big, Matt."

"Hard to tell with the water distortion. Osborne must figure it's large enough to get through safely. Otherwise he wouldn't have marked it. But we won't go inside unless the sonar picks up something worth—"

Suddenly the monitor went wild. A series of large blips danced on its screen. Jarring pings split Stefanie's ears. Her heart jumped. She stared at the screen. After a second the blips disappeared. The sonar fell silent once more; the green line continued its slow sweeping.

"That's something huge!" Matt whispered. "That's one hell of a lot bigger than those eels we tracked yesterday! This may be it, Stefanie. Get your camera ready. I'm taking us in."

Stefanie clutched her Pentax tightly, her stomach turning excited flip-flops. The pictures of a lifetime might be inside that cave!

Slowly the sub moved closer to the rock. The entryway grew magically larger as they neared it. Matt had been right. Water distortion had affected her perception. The sub's nose slid past the opening of the cavern with plenty of room to spare.

Matt grinned at her again. "See? Piece of cake! Now—"

A gut-wrenching noise erupted, a sickening, ear-shattering, metallic scraping. The *Sea Horse* shuddered convulsively, its motion slamming Stefanie forward against the console, then sending her stumbling wildly to one side.

Her knees and palms slammed simultaneously against the floor and she began sliding across its smooth surface. Matt grabbed her, jerking her back onto her feet, hugging her to him.

Her camera swung violently against her chest. She clutched at it with one hand, at the edge of the console with her other, as fresh vibrations, accompanied by further, terrifying sounds of crunching and banging metal, shook the sub.

Then with one final, deathly moan the *Sea Horse* shivered to a halt.

CHAPTER NINE

STEFANIE CLUNG TO MATT, intensely aware of his arm about her. She waited, not breathing, expecting further vibrations. But there was nothing...no motion at all. They were dead in the water.

"Oh, jeez! Don't let me have holed the sub!"

She barely heard Matt's words, but there was no missing the depth of his alarm. She stood tensely, her heart ringed with fear, waiting for him to tell her what had gone wrong, wanting him to assure her everything would be fine.

He slowly released his hold. "You all right, Stefanie?"

"Yes...but what...?"

"Just a minute. I'll see if I can tell." He looked down at the control panel for a moment, then flicked a switch. "Reverse," he whispered. The engine continued to hum quietly; the sub didn't move.

He hit a second switch. "Forward." The word sounded like a prayer. There was still no motion.

He glanced at Stefanie, not quite meeting her eyes. "She's jammed somehow—won't budge either way. I don't want to force anything, don't want to make the problem worse." He gazed back down at the console.

Stefanie could see the artery in his neck pulsing furiously. Sweat was forming beneath his hairline.

"Let me think. We'll be fine. I simply need to think for a minute."

His voice sounded so strained that she wished he hadn't spoken. She stared at him, certain she could smell fear—a mingling of her own and Matt's. The *Sea Horse* seemed suddenly smaller...the observation chamber claustrophobic. The air felt heavier than it had; her breathing was becoming labored. Was that a sign their oxygen supply was low, or had her nerves gone into overload?

Stefanie swallowed hard, telling herself not to panic. Her stomach continued churning, ignoring the order. She took a long, slow breath. She was overreacting. Nothing incredibly serious had happened...at least not yet. There was no water pouring in, seemed to be no immediate threat to their lives. She'd been in more frightening situations than this and come through them unscathed.

She tried to calmly recall the list of her photosession misadventures—the charging rhino in Africa, the rock slide in Spain, the grizzly in Oregon whose cub she'd inadvertently cornered. But each time safety had been close at hand. And each time she'd been with experts, with people who'd known precisely what to do.

This time there were only her and Matt. She looked at him anxiously. It was clear he didn't know precisely what to do. And there was no safe place close by. All there was, in every direction, was the frigid, black water of Loch Ness.

Her and Matt...her eyes were riveted on him. His were riveted on the control panel. The only sounds were occasional, ominous creaks that sent shivers up her spine, and must be doing the same to him. She couldn't stand the silence between them another second.

"What do you think, Matt?" Good. Her voice was still working. Not too steady, but functional.

He exhaled slowly before replying, as if he weren't at all certain his voice was in working order, either. "Given that abrupt, initial impact, I'd say we ran into a wall of the cave, that it's hung us up. We must be wedged somehow. But I don't know how I could have done it! I can't see anything wrong out front. Let's try the side."

Stefanie followed him to one of the observation windows. He turned on the lighting banks and they peered out. Behind the sub, just a few yards back of the glass, the cavern entrance was clearly visible. Its rocky edge appeared to be a good ten feet from the *Sea Horse*.

"I don't think we were too close on the other side, either, Matt. I was watching out that way as we were coming through."

"You're right. I'm sure we had lots of room." Matt leaned forward as he spoke, his gaze slowly sweeping along the top of the window toward the back of the sub. "I don't know what—"

Stefanie saw his body tense, heard him catch his breath. "Oh, Lord! I see what happened! I didn't bring her in low enough. The sail structure caught on the top of the cave's mouth. It's jammed into a crevice in the rock. I didn't even think about that fin sticking up back there! What a jackass! What an idiotic thing to do!"

Stefanie tried to look reassuring, certain she looked every bit as frightened as she felt. "We were moving awfully slowly, Matt. Surely we can't have done much damage, can't be wedged very tightly. We just have to figure out how to get free.

"Except," she added, fighting back tears, "this half of the 'we' isn't going to be much help. I know almost nothing about subs."

Matt gave her a look of pure relief and wrapped his arms around her. "Thanks, Stefanie. Thanks for not falling apart and thanks for not pointing out how stupid I am. That more than takes care of your half of the help." He hugged her so tightly she could scarcely breathe.

His body felt warm and strong against her, but even his nearness didn't ease the terror. It engulfed her like a tightly wrapped shroud.

She'd seen wild animals caught in cruel, steel traps. But the horror she felt now struck her with even more force than the horror of those sights. Now she was in the trap. Trapped with Matt in the steel confines of this little chamber.

When Matt released her and headed back to the console, she began to tremble. Stop this! she ordered silently, forcing herself to concentrate on what he was up to. He stared intently down at the controls.

"All I have to do," he muttered, "is my half of the job—figure out how the hell to get us free."

All he had to do. And what was going to happen if his half of the job turned out to be impossible?

Stefanie moved away from the observation window, uncertain if it was her fear or the heat radiating from the lighting banks that was making her perspire. She joined Matt at the control panel and gazed down, breathing deeply, willing herself to be calm, trying to make even the slightest sense of the confusion of levers, buttons and switches.

"When I tried the reverse and forward controls," Matt explained, "I had the power set as low as I could. That wasn't enough to move her in either direction. I might be able to free us by increasing power, but I'm afraid to force her, afraid of damaging the sail structure."

"What about straight down?" Stefanie asked tentatively. "Maybe...if we aren't trapped too tightly..."

"No. That can't be done. Subs use diving planes to descend and surface. And the planes need horizontal propulsion."

"Matt, you aren't talking to Jeffery! Speak English."

"Sorry." He shot her a grin that came off more like a grimace. "Diving planes are small, rotating wings attached to the stern and bow. But they act in conjunction with forward motion. No forward motion, no ability to dive."

"Then..." The word caught in Stefanie's throat; she tried again. "Then there's no way out?"

"No! I didn't mean to suggest that! There are other ways." He reached across and gave her hand a quick, reassuring squeeze.

"I could try," he continued hesitantly, "increasing the level of flooding in the water-ballast tanks. Keeping neutral buoyancy is a computer-programmed function. But if I override the program and draw excess water into the tanks, it's possible the sub would drop a little."

"Possible? Very possible?"

"I'm not certain—depends how badly we're jammed."

"Go for it, Matt!"

Matt gave her another sick-looking smile and moved one of the levers forward slightly.

The sound of rushing water filled the chamber.

Stefanie swallowed hard, wishing she hadn't been so quick with her encouragement.

A second passed...another. Matt pulled the lever back. The rushing sound became a gurgle, then there was silence.

"I can't chance letting any more water in. The structure's jammed too tight. If the sub tears itself apart dropping loose, we'll be in real trouble!"

Real trouble? Stefanie stared at Matt, feeling desperately ill. How much more real could trouble be than this?

He thrust his hands into his jeans pockets, his expression a mixture of frustration and anxiety.

"Damn it, Stefanie! This is all my fault. I'm not the engineer, not the submarine expert on our team. Osborne is. I should never have tried exploring this cavern without him along. Clear sailing in open water is one thing. Navigating in a confined space is another!"

The ring of fear closed a little tighter around Stefanie's heart. She resolved not to let herself cry. Everything would turn out fine. Matt knew a hundred times more about subs than she did...except he'd said himself he wasn't the expert. What if he didn't know enough?

He had to! They couldn't die down here! They simply couldn't! Not when they'd barely found each other. Not when they'd never made love to each other.

She placed her hand on his arm, wondering why that thought had popped into her mind at a moment like this. "We both wanted to come down without Jeffery. Me as well as you, Matt. Remember? We wanted to be alone together... And I was as excited about coming in here, about possibly seeing a Nessie, as you were."

Her gaze flickered to the monitor. It wasn't even emitting an occasional bleep. Whatever had been inside the cavern was obviously long gone.

Her throat was so constricted that she could scarcely speak. Yet she had to continue, had to know if this problem was really as serious as she feared. "Matt, I don't understand the technology—don't know anything about water-ballast tanks or buoyancy or diving planes—but if we can't descend without moving forward and we can't move forward..."

Matt brushed his fingertips gently beneath the corners of her eyes.

Damn! So much for holding back her tears. Bad enough she was scared spitless. She'd even failed at *looking* brave.

"Don't worry, Stefanie. We have several hours of oxygen. We're not in any imminent danger. It's simply a matter of coming up with a viable plan."

He gazed at the controls again—for another silent eternity. "There's always the diving equipment," he finally said. "I'm an experienced diver."

Matt going outside? The thought was terrifying! "But you said we probably wouldn't use the diving equipment at all, that Sound Research just figured we should have it along. And you can't go out from down here, Matt, can you? Isn't there a problem with pressurization?"

"Not really. The inside pressure has been adjusting automatically as we've changed depths. That," he added wryly, "is all that prevents the sides of a sub from caving in. I'd only need a couple of minutes in the compression chamber, just time to get the pressure in it high enough to keep water from rushing in when I opened the trap.

"It's worth a shot, Stefanie. I could suit up and go outside—take something to use as a pry bar and try shoving us free. At minimum, I could see precisely what the problem is."

"Matt! Don't go getting suicidal on me, okay? The lake's practically freezing. And you said yourself it has treacherous currents. And one man could never free the sub, not when the engine couldn't budge it."

"I could try. We have to try something. The dry suit would protect me against the cold. And there shouldn't be strong currents inside the cavern."

"No! Look, Matt, don't be selfish. What if you go out there and drown? I'd be left here all alone! What on earth would I do then?" She tried a grin. It must have worked, because Matt grinned back.

"Well, if you're going to lay a guilt trip on me, I guess I'll have to come up with another idea." He paused, taking her hands in his. "We'll be okay, Stefanie. Worst comes to worst, we'll both suit up and get ourselves to the surface."

"I certainly hope it doesn't come to that! I'm far from the world's greatest diver."

Matt chuckled a hollow-sounding chuckle. "If we get to that point, braving the diving will be the least of our worries. Braving Osborne, after we've abandoned his sub and his precious sonar, will be far worse." He stared back down at the controls for a moment. "I wonder if..."

"What? You wonder if what?"

"The remote manipulator arm. It's strong—able to retrieve over a thousand pounds. What if I try pushing the end of the arm against the top of the cavern? It would provide more force than several men could exert. If we aren't wedged too tightly, it might be enough to free us.''

Stefanie nodded her encouragement. That idea sounded far preferable to the thought of Matt going out into the lake. ''I'd forgotten all about us having an arm. You know, I haven't even seen it.''

''That's because it isn't visible when it's not in use. It tucks neatly in along the side of the sub—just a little beneath the observation windows and tight against the hull. But once it's activated, it can reach out over thirty feet in any direction, including straight up.''

''And you've operated it, Matt?''

''A few times. Osborne and I worked with it during our trial runs. And Sound Research has a simulator. I got a lot of practice on that before we left New England.''

''And you really think it'll push us free?''

Matt nodded slowly. ''In theory the idea makes sense. It's a different application from those I've played around with, but I can't see why it wouldn't work. The only unknown is whether the arm is strong enough to do the job.''

''Let's find out!'' Stefanie crossed her fingers, forcing her mind into a positive mode. This plan was going to work. It *had* to work!

''Right!'' Matt leaned over the console. ''Here goes.''

He flicked a switch, then grasped a large lever on the right-hand side of the control panel. ''This is the hand controller that activates the arm.''

''It looks like a joystick for playing computer games.''

"Actually, the principle is similar. This lever is attached to a gear box containing electronic sensors. I simulate the way I want the arm to move by moving the control. The motion is translated into electronic signals and those signals make the motor, clutch and brakes work inside the arm."

Matt clicked a button on the top of the lever, then, ever so slowly, began to shift it.

Stefanie felt a slight vibration, heard a dull thud. She looked anxiously at him.

"Nothing to worry about. That's just the arm being unstowed. See the image on this screen? See that red line moving away from the side of the sub? That shows me the arm's precise motion so I can see if it's doing exactly what I want it to. But watch outside. You'll see the real thing."

Stefanie glanced forward.

"No. Not out there—out on the right-hand side. In a minute the manipulator will move past the observation window."

Moments later, a long, fragile-looking appendage sheathed in white moved slowly into view. It seemed to be floating in the water, its free end gradually rising, the motion creating a tiny stream of bubbles that trailed behind. The effect was eerie—a white, ghostlike arm in the darkness, moving effortlessly, as if no force was needed to push it through the water.

Stefanie raced over to the observation window, snapping the lens cover off her camera. Shots of the manipulator in action would be great . . . assuming she and Matt ever got out of here so she'd have a chance to develop them.

She shoved that thought aside and shot the entire roll of film, clicking off the final few frames as the arm reached the cavern ceiling and tentatively nudged the rock.

Quickly she removed the exposed roll, reached into her gadget bag and pulled out another. It was her last one, the last of the dozen films she'd packed into her bag back in Chicago.

She reloaded the Pentax, making a mental note to refill her bag with film from the sub's storage locker. If... No! Not if. *When* they were free of the cave.

"We're halfway there, Stefanie. I've got the end of the arm tight against the roof of the cavern."

She hurried back to the navigation area and gazed out. Now that the manipulator had stopped moving, it looked even more fragile. "The arm's so slender, Matt. Do you really think this will work?"

"Let's hope so. The manipulator isn't anywhere near as delicate as you'd think. See that elbow?" Matt pointed at an angled joint partway along its length.

"Yes."

"There are motor-driven gears inside the joint. I'm going to activate them and straighten the elbow out. With any luck, the pressure against the roof will push us down a bit. We don't need much. From what I can see, an inch or two will clear us."

Stefanie nodded. "I'll just get the sail fin in focus— see if I can manage a good series of shots as we push free. I wish we had lights on this front window."

"Sorry, Stefanie. That's one series you're going to miss. I need your help. As soon as we unjam, I'll have to control both the steering and the arm. I can't manage those and the engine speed, as well."

"And you expect me to give helping save our lives priority over taking photographs?" she teased, removing the camera from around her neck. "I'm probably going to miss some fantastic shots, but what do you want me to do?"

"Aside from praying?" Matt's expression teased her back. His voice, though, was tense. "Aside from that, put your finger on this reverse switch. Once we're free, I'm going to try backing out the way we came in. The moment I feel us moving down, I'll say *go*. Flick that switch straight up the instant I do."

"And then?"

"And then just keep your finger on it. When I say *stop*, flick it right back down again. We want to free the sail structure, but we don't want to back up too far. We don't want to risk ramming our stern into something else!"

Stefanie poised her finger above the switch, praying Matt's plan would work. His right hand was on the control lever. He was staring intently at the monitor, at the thin red line that represented the arm. Perspiration had stained his face. His sweatshirt clung to his back, a damp, darker gray streak up its center.

He looked over and gave her a nervous smile. "All right, Stefanie. I'm going to begin straightening the joint out. Remember, at the word *go*, hit reverse."

"Got it." Stefanie stared down at her own hand, at her finger now on the switch, assuring herself she wouldn't screw up, wondering how an action as simple as this could have taken on such gargantuan importance.

She could hear her heart pounding, could hear Matt breathing. Then those sounds were broken by a series of clunks and scrapes. The *Sea Horse* quivered a little and jerked beneath her feet.

"Go!"

Stefanie snapped the switch up and stood frozen to the spot, aware of the engine beginning to pulse. She gazed at the switch, waiting for Matt's next command, trying to decide whether she was actually feeling backward motion beneath her feet or if her imagination was playing tricks.

"Stop!"

She shoved the switch down. The engine's hum died. The sub gradually stopped moving. It sat motionless in the water. But its movement had been real! She glanced out the side. The back half of *Sea Horse* had cleared the entrance. They were almost outside the cave. They were free!

She looked over at Matt, adrenaline racing through her system. His hand was on the arm's control lever; his eyes were focused on the monitor. On the screen, the red line was inching its way down.

Through the observation window, the arm itself came into view, slowly descending, finally disappearing from sight again. A minute or two later, it locked back into its housing with a muffled thump.

"That's it," Matt whispered. "We did it!"

"I knew you could, Matt!"

"I'm glad to hear one of us was confident. I was shaking in my sneakers."

"And all for nothing. You ended up being a hero."

"Only with your help."

Matt closed the space between them and wrapped his arms around Stefanie, hugging her tightly, making her feel safe and warm and sexy. A minute later, he released her and stepped to the instrument panel. A flood of disappointment washed over her.

He glanced back and smiled. "Don't look as if I'd just rejected you. This is only a momentary break." He started the engine. "I'm going to try surfacing. I want to make sure we can ascend all right, that we haven't done any serious damage.

"In the meantime," he added, leaning across and giving her nose a quick kiss, "we'll put things on hold until we get up top. Unless, of course, you're still intent on looking around down here for interesting shots."

"No way!"

"In that case, let me get us completely clear of the cave. Then it'll be full speed ahead. We'll be safe and sound in no time.

"I'm going to expel that water I added to the ballast tanks. Don't worry about the noise."

Despite his warning, Stefanie flinched at the sudden roar of water.

The noise ceased. Slowly Matt navigated the *Sea Horse* backward, turned its nose around and started them moving forward. They stared out into the darkness as the sub gradually rose through the water. After a few minutes, stray shafts of light began to appear.

Matt switched the motor off. The *Sea Horse* drifted to a halt. "That's it. We've surfaced."

"The top of the sub may have," Stefanie said, grinning with relief, "but you and I are still underwater in this awful observation chamber. How about a breath of fresh air? Let me see with my own eyes that it's really dry above us."

"Sounds like a wonderful idea. Let me go ahead and open the hatch."

Matt climbed the ladder and unscrewed the seal, then shoved the hatch open. Stefanie sighed with relief as sunlight poured in.

Matt scrambled through the opening and leaned back to help her up onto the smooth main deck.

"This," she said, clutching the handrail and taking a deep breath of fresh air, "is almost as good as being on dry land again."

Matt smiled, reaching as if to touch her arm. Then he pulled his hand back and shrugged ruefully. "Look, I have to talk to you for a minute. And I find it difficult to talk when I'm too close to you. In fact, whenever I'm touching you, I can't even think straight. All I can think about is how good you feel."

Stefanie felt every last trace of her anxiety disappearing as he spoke.

"First off, I'm more sorry than I can say about what just happened. I was a damned imbecile to get us into such a dangerous situation. But you were terrific. Now that we're out of it, I'm glad it was you down there with me."

"Not Jeffery? Not the expert?" Stefanie teased.

"No, not Jeffery. Jeffery would have gone into hysterics. You're far more stable...and better natured...not to mention a million times prettier."

"Ah! A man who appreciates tall, skinny women. What more could I ask for?"

"You aren't tall and skinny. You're...just right."

Matt leaned toward her once more, resting his hand on her arm, sending a ripple of arousal through her.

"Just right," he repeated softly. "Maybe even perfect."

Stefanie swallowed hard, anticipating Matt's kiss.

He merely stood gazing at her, his hand drifting up her arm, gently caressing her shoulder, causing her heart to pound with excitement.

"Well, not quite perfect," she finally said, breaking the tension before it became unbearable. "There's this major gap between my front teeth."

"Where?"

"Right here." She smiled self-consciously, feeling like an idiot. Would she ever learn to keep quiet instead of filling silences with incredibly inane remarks?

"That? You call that tiny space a gap?" Matt brushed his fingers gently along her bottom lip.

Another, stronger ripple of desire raced through her.

"That little space is barely enough to add character to your smile, Stefanie. I never even noticed it before."

"Really?"

"Really."

"Well...that doesn't say much for your powers of observation. In the mirror it's at least an inch wide. But you're in luck. I've always had a weakness for men with perceptual problems." Stefanie paused, determined not to say anything more. Why didn't Matt kiss her? The air between them was so charged it was practically crackling.

She waited, her entire body alive with longing. How could Matt not notice? How could he stand there, caressing her shoulder, driving her insane, and not realize she desperately needed to be held?

"Stefanie, what I want to tell you is...when we were trapped, when I should have been concentrating entirely on getting us out, I kept thinking about what I'd be missing, what we'd be missing, if we didn't get out. Until just then, I hadn't quite realized what I was feeling for you...how strong it was. I...it isn't something I'm used to feeling."

Matt stroked the side of her neck gently as he spoke. He had to be aware she was trembling at his touch, at his words.

"Funny," she managed, "for some reason, I was thinking about what we'd be missing, too."

"I'm glad," Matt whispered, his hand cradling the back of her neck, drawing her closer.

Suddenly, wondrously, she was in his arms once more, being smothered against the strength of his body, enveloped by his earthy, sweaty scent. It excited her senses more than any after-shave possibly could.

His mouth closed hotly over hers, possessing her, kissing her into a state of breathless longing. She was vaguely aware of his five-o'clock shadow bristling against her face, was incredibly aware of his body pressing against hers.

His hands ranged down her back, crushing her breasts to his chest, coming to rest on her behind, drawing her against his hardness. The length of his body against her own started a deep throbbing inside her.

She ran her hands under his sweatshirt, across his cool, damp skin, hugging him even more closely. Her entire body craved to be touched, to be kissed.

Matt caressed her hips, making her squirm against him with exquisite longing. His breathing had become heavier, his tongue more demanding, and his hands...his hands were searching over her body, making it tingle in response to their touch, making her want him so badly she ached.

He slid his hands under her sweater, slipped her breasts free from the lace of her bra and fondled them gently, stroking her nipples to taut, eager arousal. His touch, feather-light yet incredibly provocative, sent quivers of delight through her.

Then his kiss subsided and his hands moved from her breasts to draw her head into the hollow of his shoulder. "Stefanie...Stefanie, you drive me absolutely crazy. If we don't stop right now I'm going to be making love to you on the deck of the sub."

"Would that be bad?" she whispered.

"Bad? I doubt there's a chance in a million of that. I expect making love to you anywhere on earth will be wonderful. But I think, just to be safe, we should get back to shore while my mind is still marginally in control."

"I hate your mind." Stefanie nibbled on his neck.

"Don't worry. It's only in charge temporarily—only long enough to get us home. And believe me, the first thing I intend to do once we're on dry land is pick up exactly where we're leaving off."

"Promise?"

"Promise."

Matt draped one arm securely across her shoulders. "Come on back down. You can help me navigate—as long as you promise not to be too distracting."

Stefanie followed Matt down into the *Sea Horse* again and across to the navigation area. She wound her arms around his waist, slid her hands under his sweatshirt and ran her fingers up his chest, tangling them in its wiry hair.

His body felt absolutely wonderful against her. She nudged her hip suggestively against his. "Is this too distracting?"

"Only about three thousand and twenty percent."

She laughed, reluctantly pulling away.

Matt caught her hands in his. "Stay where you are. I may as well enjoy your touching me, because being anywhere within ten feet of you is too distracting."

"Honestly?"

"You haven't noticed? And you have the nerve to criticize my powers of observation? I think my blood pressure increases five points every time you look at me."

"So I shouldn't look at you?"

"Mmm. You should look at me all you want to. I'll practice controlling my reaction."

"Spoilsport!"

Matt grinned, starting the engine. "Let's go, Stefanie. The sooner we make it back the better. My blood pressure's liable to get high enough to bring on a stroke before I have a chance at enjoying what you're promising."

Stefanie stood silently, her arms resting about Matt's waist, as he navigated the sub. "Do you think," she finally asked, "that was a Nessie we tracked in the cavern?"

"Whatever it was, it was one hell of a size—and definitely worth a second look. At least when I tell Osborne about our accident I'll have some promising news to give him, as well." Matt lapsed into silence once more.

"It's strange how fate works, isn't it?" he murmured after a few minutes. "Something as awful as Nancy being murdered results in something as wonderful as us being here like this."

"Oh, Matt, I wish you hadn't reminded me of Nancy."

"Sorry. I guess I can't quite believe this is real, that you aren't a dream."

Stefanie gently pinched his arm.

"Ouch!"

"Just thought that might help you believe I'm real."

"Very funny. Bad enough you distract me. Don't start inflicting serious pain!"

"It's retaliation for the whisker burn you gave me."

Matt looked at her. "You're right! Your face is red. I'll have to start walking around with a razor. Maybe we could pack one into your gadget bag."

"That's not a bad idea. And it reminds me, I'm out of film. I'll just get some out of the locker now."

Matt wrapped his arm tightly around her. "We're almost home. It can wait till we've docked." He cut the engine speed. "We should be seeing the pier any second."

Moments later the pilings became visible. Matt brought the *Sea Horse* up against them and switched the engine off once more.

"Certain you want to take the time to dig that film out?" he asked with an exaggerated leer.

"Certain."

"Now who's being a spoilsport?"

Stefanie laughed, heading across to the locker. "It'll take three seconds. I just need to grab a few boxes from the top carton. Whoever initially stacked them must have been psychic. When I checked out the supply my first time down, I noticed that the cartons of film I'll want to use most of the time ended up on top of the piles."

She opened the door and reached inside for the top carton, realizing, her arms in midair, that the locker was empty.

CHAPTER TEN

STEFANIE STARED into the empty locker, her mind first reeling crazily, then clicking into gear and correcting her initial impression. The locker wasn't empty. The diving equipment was still there, seemingly untouched. Only the right-hand side, where the cartons of film had been stacked, was bare.

"Let's go, Stefanie."

She looked over at Matt.

He was standing, hands on hips, watching her with obvious impatience. "Need any help?"

She pulled the door farther to let him see inside. "Matt . . . Matt, it's gone."

"What's gone?"

"The film. It's gone. Every single carton."

Matt stepped quickly to her side. "What the hell . . . ?"

"It was in here the first day I was down, Matt. Remember Jeffery moving the sonar to let me check it?"

Matt nodded. "I remember."

"There were a dozen cartons! Right here!" She stared at Matt, desperately hoping he had an explanation.

"Someone's been in here." His whisper rang with disbelief.

"How could anyone get in, Matt? You said there are only two keys. You said the lock hadn't been forced."

"I know what I said! What I said obviously wasn't worth diddly! Someone's been in here. Unless Osborne moved the film for some reason."

Matt glanced around the interior. "I'll just check the compression chamber. That's the only possible place there's room for a stack of cartons."

He strode over to the chamber's hatch, opened it and peered in. "Nothing," he muttered. "It's not here. It's gone."

"You don't think Jeffery might have taken it out of the sub?"

"No. What possible reason would he have?"

"I don't know." Stefanie shrugged, clutching for straws. "A practical joke, maybe?"

"Osborne? Mr. Total-lack-of-humor playing a joke? Get serious, Stefanie!"

"Don't snap at me, Matt! I'm as upset as you are!"

Matt jammed his hands into his pockets. "Sorry. Didn't mean to snap. But Osborne would never have taken the film out of the sub when he knew this was where you'd be needing it. That would make no sense at all. Lord! He'd have been chancing missing his precious shots of the Loch Ness Monster."

Matt stared back into the half-empty locker, apparently thinking out loud as much as talking to her. "The police checked on the *Sea Horse* after the excitement last night and assured us the hatch was secure.

"Of course," he added slowly, "it was secure when we got here this morning, too. So what the hell's happened?"

Stefanie merely shrugged once more. Any other idea she came up with was likely to be as absurd as the thought of Jeffery having a sense of humor. "The only obvious thing that's happened is I have no film."

"Don't worry about your film, Stefanie. We can buy more.

"Let's try to figure this out," he suggested after a moment. "Someone got in here without a key and without forcing the lock. Then, once he was inside, all he seems to have taken is your film." Matt paused, running his fingers through his hair.

"Why the hell take that, Stefanie? Look at everything that's in here! Not only was Osborne's state-of-the-art sonar sitting right out in the open, but there's a fortune in electronics. And there's all this expensive diving gear—in the same locker. Somebody left an entire sub full of valuable equipment and took a dozen cartons of lousy film? Why?"

Stefanie's thoughts whirled in ten different directions, suddenly coming together in a frightening answer to Matt's questions.

"Still Waters has got to be the *somebody*, Matt! He was more of a thief than we realized. He must have gotten in here last night, as well as into my room. And he must have been after something he thought was in with my film."

"What?"

"I don't know. But it's all adding up. First he followed us from Glasgow and stole those two cartons of film I brought from Chicago. Then he took the film Nancy shipped.

"Still Waters thinks I have something I don't. That would explain it all—his approaching me in the restaurant, why he tried to steal my gadget bag last night and why he broke into the sub."

Matt stared at her for a second, then nodded. "You're right. That's the only logical explanation."

"Matt..." Stefanie's voice cracked at the horror of her next realization.

"Matt, there's nothing he'd want to steal that I know anything about. But if the mystery has something to do with the photography on this search project...then what if it has something to do with Nancy Goitano...with her murder?"

She looked fearfully at Matt, aware her heart was racing, feeling the pulse in her temple throbbing.

His expression said he thought she could be right. He reached for her, putting his arms around her waist, drawing her to him.

She pressed against his chest, aware she was trembling, unable to stop.

"Listen to me," he ordered. "Whatever has been going on is over. You've probably got it figured. Still Waters was likely behind this. But the police have him in custody—he's out of commission. And once we talk to them again, tell them there may be a connection between him and Nancy's murder, they'll be sure to keep him locked up until they get to the bottom of things.

"Nothing's going to happen to you," he whispered, burying his face in her hair. "God, Stefanie, I won't let anything happen to you."

Stefanie took a deep breath, forcing herself to think rationally. Still Waters was in jail. So she was safe...unless he wasn't working alone. A sick, sinking feeling began churning inside her stomach.

"Matt, what if Still Waters has a friend?"

"Oh, Lord," Matt murmured. "That's possible. Heaven knows who's still wandering around loose! Let's get out of here. We'll go into Inverness, to the police—tell them about the film, about Nancy. Maybe they've identified Still Waters already. We'll go straight into the city and find out where things stand.''

"What about Jeffery? It's past two o'clock. He may be back at the house by now. After his outburst last night, shouldn't we stop off and check? Fill him in on what's been happening?"

"Later! We can tell him later. Right now your safety gets priority, Stefanie. If Still Waters *does* have a friend, we have no idea who he is or where he is. I don't want anyone to know we've discovered the film's gone, or that we're going to the police, before we have a chance to talk to them.

"Come on. With any luck the answer to our puzzle is waiting in Inverness."

THEY STOPPED OUTSIDE Jeffery's closed bedroom door. Matt glanced anxiously at Stefanie and squeezed her hand. "You had to do enough talking at the police station, Stefanie. You look beat. Why don't you try to get some rest? I'd really just as soon deal with Osborne alone.''

"No. I'm all right. He's going to insist on talking to me anyway, so we may as well get it over with all at once." *Besides,* she added silently, *I don't want to let you out of my sight.*

Their session with the police had done nothing to reassure her. Quite the opposite. Still Waters had yet to utter a single word. The police had no idea who the man was or what he'd been up to, but they thought it highly likely he had an accomplice. And they had no idea who that accomplice might be. It could as easily be a local as a stranger.

Matt was the only person she felt certain she could trust, the only person she felt safe with.

Officer McKay's logic echoed in her ears. "'Tis the time frame that makes me certain there was more than one of them, lass," he'd explained. "It would be an incredible coincidence if the muggings weren't related to the theft. So, most likely the same person who mugged McFarlane and the watchman took the film from your submarine.

"But if it was your Mr. Still Waters, and he was acting alone, what happened to that film? It wasn't in his car when we impounded it. And he'd hardly have had time, between the mugging and when you found him in your room, to load twelve cartons into his car, take them somewhere and unload and conceal them.

"And he certainly wouldn't have gone to all the trouble of getting the film and then have simply dumped it. So where did it go?

"My guess," McKay had said, answering his own question, "is that there was at least one other person involved. Either someone else took the film from the *Sea Horse* or, if Still Waters was the thief, he proceeded to the guest house while his accomplice made off with the cartons.

"Aye, I'd say there's more than one of them, Miss Taylor. So you be careful until we sort this out. We're working on identifying your Mr. Still Waters. And now that you've told us about that murder, we'll be contacting New York to see what they've put together," McKay had concluded.

Matt tapped on Jeffery's door, jerking Stefanie's thoughts back to the present.

"Come in," Jeffery called out.

Stefanie tightened her grip on Matt's hand. "I feel as if I'm ten years old and standing outside the principal's office," she whispered.

"And I feel as if I'm about to deliver a very tasteless good-news-bad-news joke. With any luck," Matt murmured, turning the doorknob, "Principal Osborne will expel both of us from this damn project and we can get the hell out of Scotland."

Jeffery was sitting at his desk. He looked up at them expectantly.

Matt closed the door. "Mind if we sit?"

Jeffery gestured to the bed, shifting his chair around to face it.

Stefanie followed Matt across the room and perched anxiously beside him.

"So? What's up?"

Matt cleared his throat. "Osborne, you're not going to like much of this, but try to keep a lid on your reaction, okay? With any luck, things aren't as bad as they're going to sound."

Jeffery's face paled perceptibly. He straightened in the chair and leaned forward, watching Matt intently. "Okay...what things may not be as bad as they sound?"

"The *Sea Horse* was broken into."

"My sonar!"

"No!" Matt cut him off. "Your sonar's fine. Everything seems to be fine. All that was taken was film—the cartons of film in the storage locker."

Jeffery stared at them, his hands clutching the arms of the chair. "My sonar. You're certain about my sonar?"

"Your sonar's fine. We used it today."

"What?"

"Stefanie and I took the *Sea Horse* out. We followed one of your routes and we tracked something. It could have been a Nessie, Osborne. It was something awfully big.''

''You didn't see it?'' Jeffery was practically bouncing in his chair.

''No . . . we ran into a little trouble.''

''Trouble?'' Jeffery sank back, eyeing Matt suspiciously.

Matt briefly told Jeffery about their accident in the cave. He didn't, Stefanie noted fleetingly, mention they'd explored the Bona Narrows area.

She watched Jeffery closely. An entire series of expressions crossed his face. Shock was replaced by dismay, concern, anger. She should get her camera out and capture his reactions. No. Stupid idea. Aside from the fact that Jeffery would have a fit, there was no film in her camera.

Her thoughts flashed to the supply of film they'd stopped to pick up in Inverness. They'd left it locked inside Matt's car. Maybe they should have taken the time to unload it. Was it safe where it was? More important, were they safe where they were?

Jeffery stood. ''I'm going to check out the *Sea Horse*. I want to see for myself that you didn't cause any serious damage.''

Matt rose quickly, stopping Jeffery with a raised hand. ''Take it easy. We can't get onto the sub at the moment. The police are there.''

''The police? What's going on now? Why wasn't I told?''

''You are being told! So listen! We went to the police about the break-in. The fact that only the damn film was taken didn't make much sense until we started putting everything together—Nancy's murder, Still

Waters coming after Stefanie's gadget bag last night and all the other strange things that have happened.

"At any rate, we went into Inverness to talk to the police. We've just gotten back. They've gone to the sub to dust for prints and see if they can figure out how the thief got inside."

"Well, we should go there—see what they've found!"

"Osborne, we're not wanted there. We'd be in the way. They told us to come back here and wait. They'll be by shortly. They want to take all of the team's fingerprints to see if any of those in the *Sea Horse* don't belong. So just sit down and I'll tell you the rest of the details."

Jeffery slumped back into the chair, his distress apparent.

By the time Matt finished recounting their session with the police, Jeffery was wearing firmly etched worry lines. When he spoke, he was making an apparent effort to control his temper.

"How could anyone have gotten on board, Garrett? Someone must have taken your key! Taken it and had a copy made. How else could they have gotten into the sub?"

"I don't know how. But I doubt it was with the help of my key. When I'm dressed, I always keep my keys in my pocket. And I'm an awfully light sleeper. Maybe someone took *your* key!"

Jeffery waved his hand, clearly dismissing that idea as absurd. "This is far worse than we thought! The police convinced me it wasn't worth replacing Ian—not since they had Still Waters in custody. But I'll have to now. I'll have to hire a new watchman. How am I going to find someone at this time on a Saturday?"

"What's the point of bothering? Whoever wanted inside the sub has already been—and has already gotten what he wanted."

Jeffery glared at Matt, clearly frustrated by his logic. "I don't understand why you took the sub down in the first place!" he finally snapped. "Why go without me? You aren't that good a pilot, damn it! What if you've done serious damage to the craft? It'll delay our search!"

"Our search isn't the issue, Osborne. But just to set your mind at ease, I had a quick look at the *Sea Horse* before we left the dock. Aside from scrapes and dents on the top of the sail structure, she seems fine. And we got back from the cave without a hitch—no operational problems."

"But you shouldn't have taken her out at all! If there *were* fingerprints, you two undoubtedly messed them up!"

Matt exhaled slowly, his patience obviously wearing thin. "You're probably right. I'm sorry if we did. But that isn't the issue, either. With or without fingerprints, we can be pretty damn sure it was Still Waters—or an accomplice—who was in the sub after that film. And pretty damn sure this is all somehow connected to Nancy, to the photographic equipment.

"Everything points to it—even our strobes going astray way back when we first arrived in Scotland. Put it all together and what's happened starts to make sense. Someone probably intercepted those strobes and checked them out."

"Checked them out for what?"

"How should I know? Nancy must have shipped something in the equipment or the film cartons. At least, somebody must think she did."

"Then why steal the film Stefanie brought from Chicago? Why try to steal her gadget bag?"

"Osborne, I'm not Sherlock Holmes! They must have figured Stefanie might be involved—might be linked to whatever Nancy was up to. Beyond that, I don't know."

"I'll call Sound Research," Jeffery said. "I'll talk to Finch, find out if there've been any developments as far as Nancy's murder is concerned. With any luck, you're right. With any luck, this is all related to some foolish plot of Nancy's. As long as that's the case, we're fine."

"Fine?" Matt spit the word out. "Fine? What the hell are you talking about? I said things might not be as bad as they sound. Not that everything was hunky-dory! If Still Waters has an accomplice walking around loose out there, things may not be the least bit fine, especially not for Stefanie.

"Look, I've asked Florrie to search out the keys for our rooms and to make certain the front door's kept locked. But I'm not at all sure Stefanie shouldn't be taking the next plane out of the country."

"No! No, we can't have that. The search must go on!"

"Osborne! Get real! The search must go on? As in the show must go on? Have you overdosed on late movies? Who the hell cares if the search goes on? I don't! Not any longer!"

"Wait . . . wait, Garrett."

Stefanie stared at Jeffery. His tone actually sounded cajoling.

"Look, Garrett. If you think the police are right, that Still Waters has an accomplice, we'll figure out who it could be. There just can't be that many possibilities. And Stefanie's probably not in any real danger, anyway. No one's actually tried to harm her. Not even Still Waters.

"I need you to stay," he continued, turning to Stefanie. "Shots of a lifetime. Remember? You can't pass that up. Especially not when we're so close, when you think you may actually have tracked a Nessie!

"And I've had a fantastic new idea—that's where my invention comes in. It's all ready. My prototype's being delivered to the dock on Monday."

Jeffery paused, frowning. "I just couldn't convince them to deliver it tomorrow—to work on Sunday. But come Monday, we'll get everything set up. We may have a chance at an incredible series of action shots. The search has to proceed. It's more important than ever, now."

"Why?" Matt snapped, clearly at the end of his rope.

"Because I've figured out a way to..." Jeffery's expression grew cautious, as if he'd just realized they'd been watching his face.

"We're all bright people," he rushed on. "Between the three of us and the police, how hard can it be to determine who could have gotten into the *Sea Horse*? We've got one awfully likely suspect already.

"I've been assuming Rob McFarlane's interest lay in disrupting our search, in the stupid Loch Ness tourist industry. But maybe his loveydovey act with Mary has been in aid of something else entirely. You just told me the police admitted it could easily be a local who's involved with Still Waters."

Matt nodded thoughtfully. "That's true. And the only local who's been hanging around is McFarlane. All right. We can't take any chances, not with Stefanie's safety at risk. Regardless of what the police have to say about Rob, I'll talk to Mary, tell her he's completely off-limits from here on in.''

Stefanie stared at Matt, taken aback by his snap decision, imagining how she'd feel if someone ordered her to stay away from him. Mary would be devastated. Besides, he and Jeffery were wrong about Rob. She'd stake her life on that.

''Who made you two fellows judge and jury?'' Damn! She'd meant that to sound like a joke. Matt's irritated look told her it hadn't. She plunged ahead, realizing she was treading on thin ice, that Jeffery had gotten Matt extremely angry. But this was too important to let pass.

''Matt, you aren't being fair to Mary. Rob isn't putting on any *act* as far as his feelings for her are concerned. You're both completely out to lunch on that angle.''

''Don't be so damn sure about who's out to lunch!'' Matt snapped. ''Let's not forget Rob was nosing around the *Sea Horse* last night . . . and this morning.''

''What?'' Jeffery exploded.

''This morning,'' Matt repeated. ''When Stefanie and I arrived at the sub, McFarlane and Mary were there. He said he was looking for clues about his mugger—even had a knit cap he claimed he'd found in the bushes.''

''That cinches it, then! We've got our accomplice, Garrett. See, Stefanie? I told you we could figure this out. Once we talk to the police, they'll arrest McFarlane and you'll be perfectly safe.''

''No one—'' Stefanie began, uncertain which of the two men she was becoming more upset with ''—no one is going to arrest Rob McFarlane for trying to identify his mugger. Rob's no criminal. I can tell that simply by looking at him.''

"Oh?" Matt muttered sarcastically. "I suppose that's another example of your famous photographer's powers of observation, is it? Forgive me for throwing cold water on your self-confidence, but aren't you the same photographer who was dead certain Mary and I were an item? The same photographer who jumped to a whole lot of wrong conclusions based on what you saw?''

Stefanie glared at Matt. There was no longer any contest as far as who was upsetting her went.

He pressed annoyingly on. "Let's go with the facts, Stefanie. Not with your dubious talent for *seeing* things. And the facts are that McFarlane's been lurking around since the moment we arrived. A couple of strange things happened before you got here, but I won't even bother getting into those.

"Let's just think about what's gone on over the past few days. Rob walked out of the house after you arrived, and a few minutes later, we found your things had been stolen from my car.

"Rob asked for a tour of the *Sea Horse*. Osborne said no dice. The next thing we knew, our watchman had been mugged. And who was on the scene? The same joker who was skulking around the sub this morning!''

"I suppose," Stefanie said, jumping in when Matt paused for breath, "you intend to ignore the fact that Rob was mugged, as well!''

Matt shrugged. "There are muggings and muggings.''

Stefanie could feel her face growing red. Matt could be absolutely infuriating! How had she missed that up to now?

"And what about this morning?" he asked in an obnoxiously logical tone. "Do you really think Rob was at the dock looking for clues? I don't. I think he was looking for something he lost there last night—something that might tie him in to the break-in."

Stefanie opened her mouth, then closed it again, realizing she was so upset that if she said anything more she'd undoubtedly come to regret it. She took a couple of deep breaths, ordering herself to speak calmly.

"Your evidence is circumstantial, Mr. Amateur Detective," she finally managed, staring evenly at Matt. "And all of it can be easily explained away. We're staying in Rob's parents' house. He happened to come by, met Mary, fell for her and proceeded to hang around. In my books that's romantic, not suspicious."

"What about his being at the sub last night?" Matt snapped.

"What about it? Ian's his friend. He could have had a hundred different reasons for wanting to see him."

"And this morning?"

"I buy his story. He was looking for clues. Think about Rob himself, Matt! He's a known entity, a respectable investment banker who's lived around here all his life. How on earth... why on earth... would he get mixed up in a scheme to murder someone in New York and steal my film in Glasgow, or in Drumnadrochit, or wherever it happened to be up for grabs?"

"I don't know, Stefanie. All I know is that someone's been messing with your equipment. I sure as hell don't want him deciding to mess with you. And there's too much suspicion around Rob to simply ignore.''

"Matt, you're wrong about him! I can't believe for a minute he's interested in my film, or Jeffery's sonar, or anything else related to this damned search. But he's definitely interested in Mary. That's as plain as the nose on your face.''

"Maybe to you, Stefanie, but not to Osborne or me. And what's plain to you isn't exactly gospel. First you had *me* pegged as being in love with Mary. Now you're convinced Rob is. Maybe you should consider taking your eyes in for an overhaul. What you see through them doesn't seem to be reality!''

"You...you...pompous ass!'' Stefanie whirled around, flung the door open and slammed it soundly behind herself.

Rob and Mary were standing across the hall outside Mary's open door, eyeing Stefanie anxiously.

"I couldn't make out the words,'' Mary said hesitantly, "but things sounded pretty rowdy in there. Any problems the junior member of the team should know about?''

"Stick around! Any minute now you're going to know more than you want to! The police will be here shortly—to take our fingerprints! Once they've arrived, I'm sure you'll hear the entire story—Jeffery and Matt's version of the entire story, at least.''

Stefanie focused on Rob. "I want you to know I'm not party to their deluded belief system. Of course, I'm just a photographer who can't see what's in front of her eyes, so what I believe doesn't matter!''

Mary glanced at Rob, then stepped across the hall and placed one hand gently on Stefanie's arm. "Would you like me to talk to them? I'm sure they didn't mean to get you so upset. Jeffery doesn't always think before he speaks.''

''Jeffery's boorishness I can deal with! I just hadn't realized Matt was so completely unreasonable! It turns out they make quite a pair. The two of them think—''

From below, the sound of knocking on the front door interrupted her.

A few moments later, Florrie bustled up the stairs. ''There are two police officers here, asking for Matthew.''

''He's in Jeffery's room. I'll get him,'' Mary offered.

Florrie nodded, turning back to the stairs. ''I'll just have them wait in the parlor.''

Mary knocked tentatively on Jeffery's door. Matt opened it, his glance taking in the three of them.

Stefanie thought he looked at Rob guiltily, at her sheepishly. But what did she know? Apparently she didn't see things as they actually were.

Mary spoke quietly to Matt. He called Jeffery, and a second later, there were five of them in the hallway.

''Well, let's all go down,'' Jeffery muttered. ''We're all involved in this . . . one way or another.''

ROB PACED the length of Florrie's kitchen and back. Mary watched him anxiously, stealing the occasional glance across the table at his mother. It was impossible to decide which of the two were angrier.

She swallowed hard, trying to calm her own temper, glad she'd managed to escape into the kitchen. After the police had left, as the rest of the team had headed back up to the second floor, Matt had muttered something about wanting to talk to her.

But she was better off staying where she was until she cooled down. At the moment, saying her allegiance was torn would be a major understatement. That could make talking to Matt dangerous. She might have trouble keeping in mind he was her boss—never mind her thesis adviser to boot!

The hour the four of them had spent with the police had been unreal. *Bizarre* was probably closer to it! She hadn't felt the least bit like part of the team—certainly not part of the witch-hunt Jeffery had tried to mount after Rob. That Jeffery and Matt could have seriously suggested . . . could seriously believe . . . Well, Jeffery, maybe. But Matt?

"How could they think that?" Rob muttered, voicing her thoughts. "How could they possibly believe I'd be party to any of that? When Officer McKay told me what they'd said, I felt like killing them!"

"Stefanie doesn't believe it, Rob. And the police obviously didn't. And I'm sure Matt doesn't, not really. Jeffery just got him going."

Rob glared at her. "From what Officer McKay said, your Matthew Garrett is every bit as suspicious of me as that nasty wee man who's in charge."

"Rob . . . why don't you simply tell Matt why you stopped by to see Ian. Not knowing your reason for that is what's really bothering him. If he knew the truth, I'm sure he'd think differently."

"No. I don't intend to tell him. It's none of his damn business!"

"But it is, Rob. In a way, it is."

"Not yet it isn't. Not at this stage. I won't be saying anything to him about the matter until things are more definite."

"Well, maybe you're right. But at least the police know the idea of you being the mugger is crazy. McKay didn't even want to take your fingerprints. He only took them because you insisted."

"Aye. Well, they won't be finding my prints in Osborne's precious submarine. That I can guarantee." Rob slumped into the chair next to Mary's.

She covered his hand with her own for a moment. "I know they won't, Rob. And when they don't, I'm sure Matt and Jeffery will come to their senses. At least Matt will. I'm surprised at him. He's acting completely out of character. I suppose it's because he's so worried about something happening to Stefanie. You've got to admit things have been pretty weird for her."

"What about that cap you found?" Florrie asked. "What did Officer McKay think of that?"

"Hard to say. He took it along with him, said it might provide a lead. But it's probably not very important. I gather the critical thing is to establish Still Waters's identity—that and to figure out how someone got into the *Sea Horse*."

Florrie frowned thoughtfully. "Do they have any idea, son?"

"Either the thief had a key or he picked the lock. Apparently those are the only possible answers. And only an expert could have picked that lock. So, if Still Waters's prints are in the sub or if he turns out to be a locksmith, they've undoubtedly got their man."

"Then we'd be safe." Mary sighed, wishing they weren't in the midst of this mystery, wishing she didn't feel her emotions were being pulled in two entirely different directions.

Rob rested his arm across her shoulders. "You'll be safe. I'll be making sure of that. If it's all right with you, Mom," he said, glancing at Florrie, "I'll stay in the spare room for the next little while. There's still that accomplice they figure is hanging around. The accomplice," he added blackly, "that Mary's friends believe is me!"

Florrie cleared her throat. "Speaking of staying here...has it occurred to you what your father will have to say about all of this? He'll not brook those men in his house after today, not after their accusations. They'll have to be moving out. I've half a mind to go upstairs right now and start them packing."

"But Mary will stay, Mom."

"Why... of course. Mary is welcome to stay."

"Rob, I can't. I may be mad as hell at them, but I'm still part of the team. I still have to work with them. If they go, I'll have to go with them."

Rob stared at her for a second, stroking his beard thoughtfully. He looked over at Florrie. "She's right. They'll all have to stay. They probably aren't going to like it any more than we will, but none of us has much choice. With the Highland Festival starting in Inverness next week, they'll never find accommodation in the city. And I want Mary here with us. Whatever's going on, this is the safest place for her."

"But your father—"

"You can handle him. Play this down. Don't tell him any more than you have to. Mary has got to stay here."

Florrie looked at them doubtfully. "I'll try."

"Thanks, Mom!" Rob grinned at her. "And I'll be around if you need help convincing him."

Rob pushed away from the table and stood. "Come on, Mary. We'll try to forget this incident. Forgive and forget. Let your friends sulk in their rooms if they like, but you and I should go out and have a little fun.''

Mary felt a rush of guilt. She probably shouldn't be going off with Rob. Angry as she was at Matt and Jeffery, she probably should spend the evening with the rest of the team. Maybe if she spoke to Matt, she could talk some sense into him. Maybe she could enlist Stefanie's help. Except that Stefanie was still seething mad at both men.

She smiled hesitantly at Rob and took his hand. It might be best simply to leave the other team members alone—give them, and herself, time to calm down. ''Just let me run upstairs and get a sweater, Rob.''

Rob nodded, gesturing her ahead of him toward the kitchen door.

''Oh, Mary,'' Florrie called. ''Wait a minute, dear. In all the excitement I forgot about something.''

Mary looked back.

Florrie hurried over to the refrigerator, reached up to the top and retrieved a small, beige mailing pouch.

''This was delivered earlier today. None of you were here, so I put it aside. I recognized the name from your reservations, but I didn't know who should get it now...your Mr. Osborne, I imagine. I'll just give it to you and you can take it along upstairs with you.''

Mary reached for the package, glanced down at the handwritten address and froze. She forced her eyes to the postmark. New York City...mailed over a week ago. She stared at the handwriting once more, rereading the designated destination in silent disbelief: Nancy Goitano, c/o The Galloway Guest House, Drumnadrochit, Scotland.

CHAPTER ELEVEN

MARY STOOD in Jeffery's doorway, anxiously watching as he ripped the mail pouch open.

He thrust his stubby fingers inside, pulled out a little metal film canister and fumbled with the screw cap, swearing to himself when it wouldn't open. Finally he twisted the top off and tapped the open end against his palm.

Mary leaned closer, watching intently, as a film cassette slid out.

Jeffery stared at it for an instant. "It's been exposed. We'll have to get it developed—see what the hell this is all about."

He pushed rudely past Mary, hurried across to Stefanie's door and pounded loudly on it.

"What?" Stefanie snapped from inside the room.

"Open up! Something's happened! I need your help."

The door flew open and Stefanie appeared, glaring at Jeffery, clearly still as angry as she'd been during their session with the police.

Almost simultaneously Matt opened his door. The look Stefanie shot him was as black as the one she'd given Jeffery.

The two men, Mary thought fleetingly, were lucky looks couldn't kill.

Jeffery waved the film cassette in Stefanie's face. "This came. Addressed to Nancy Goitano!"

Stefanie's angry expression faded to worried curiosity. She took the film from him and examined it.

"Can you develop it?" he demanded.

"Well, I can. But it's ASA 1600."

"Which means?"

"Which means it's about as fast a film as you can get. And that means the quality of my prints is going to be far from great. They'll come out awfully grainy."

"I don't care about quality—only content. I want to know what the hell is on this film."

"That's no problem. Everything I need to do the job is sitting right on the floor of my wardrobe." Stefanie slipped the cassette into her shirt pocket, turned away, then looked back through her doorway at Jeffery. "I'll need the bathroom for the next hour or so."

A few minutes later she hurried out into the hall, carrying a stack of metal trays. The top one, full of processing materials, was propped precariously against her chest.

Matt stepped forward, reaching to help her.

Her eyes shot daggers at him and she headed toward the bathroom.

He froze, his arms gradually dropping to his sides.

Mary peered at the contents of the top tray, deciding the film developing process must be at least as complex as the analytic procedures she'd been carrying out for the past week.

Jammed onto the tray were a steel canister, five dark brown chemical bottles, a large steel spool, a roll of twine, clips and a red light.

Stefanie maneuvered through the bathroom doorway. "One developed film coming up," she muttered, kicking the door closed behind her. A few moments later the lock snapped soundly into place.

"So now we wait and wonder," Jeffery said.

Mary glanced uncertainly from the bathroom door to the stairway. Rob was waiting for her downstairs. But she couldn't go out with him now. She wasn't about to miss seeing those prints the instant they were ready. "I'm just going downstairs again for a second. I'll be right back."

"Mary?" Jeffery's voice stopped her. "You heading down to see McFarlane?"

She nodded, feeling guilty, then feeling annoyed over that guilt. She wasn't the one who was wrong about Rob.

"I think," Jeffery muttered to Matt, "this would be an ideal time for that little talk."

Mary glanced at Matt. He looked incredibly uncomfortable. It wasn't hard to figure out what the "little talk" was going to be about. She backed a few steps farther away. "I'll only be a minute. I was going out with Rob, but I'll just let him know I can't, that I'm staying up here."

"Don't tell him about the film," Matt said quietly.

"But, Matt, he'll wonder—"

"Don't tell him."

"All right . . . I won't." Mary turned and headed for the stairs before either man had a chance to issue more orders. Terrific position she was in! No doubt the first question Rob would ask her would be about the contents of that package. And she couldn't tell him. And he'd be annoyed when she didn't. And he'd conclude she didn't trust him.

This simply wasn't fair! She couldn't keep her balancing act up any longer. Much as she didn't like the idea of a "little talk" with Matt, it might be a good idea. The air had to be cleared somehow. All the free-floating suspicion was driving her insane.

Matt waited until the sound of Mary's footsteps reached the downstairs hall before turning to Osborne. "Look, I've been thinking. I was a little hasty earlier. The police obviously don't believe there's a chance in hell McFarlane is our thief. They're the experts. We have to assume they're right. And in that case, ordering Mary to stay clear of him seems pretty draconian."

"Better safe than sorry!"

"Well . . . I'll remind her not to talk about anything relating to the search. But as far as telling her she can't even see him goes, there's no way."

"Garrett, this isn't up for discussion. I'm in charge here and I'm not taking any chances. I don't want Mary within a country mile of McFarlane. Now either you can tell her that or I will, but when she comes back upstairs, she's going to be told. Your choice. You or me?"

Matt swore silently. Talk about a lose-lose situation. He could subject Mary to a session with their "beloved" leader or be the villain himself.

He'd have to do it himself, of course. Lord! Both Stefanie and Mary were fuming at him already. And Osborne's temper was mercurial. By the time this expedition was over, it would be miraculous if a single member of the team was on speaking terms with another.

Damn! He had to straighten things out with Stefanie—admit he'd gotten carried away about Rob. He'd do that the moment she finished developing the film. Hopefully she'd understand why he still had to talk to

Mary. He'd remind Stefanie he didn't make the final decisions. He'd make her understand! But there wasn't a prayer Mary would. Ordering her to stay away from McFarlane was going to ice the cake as far as she was concerned.

"WHY DON'T YOU sit down, Mary?" Matt closed his bedroom door and leaned back against it, trying to appear casual, trying not to look even half the bastard he felt like, determined not to mention Mary had been downstairs almost an hour instead of the minute she'd promised.

Mary settled lightly on the arm of the stuffed chair, eyeing him suspiciously.

"Look, I'll get straight to the point. I don't want you spending any more time with Rob. Not until the police have established precisely who's been playing games around here."

"You, Matt? You don't want me spending any more time with Rob? Or Jeffery wants it and you get to play bad guy?"

Matt jammed his hands into his pockets, wishing he were sitting in his office at Rossmuir, wishing he'd never heard of this damned project. He glanced across at Mary. She was staring at him defiantly.

Well, what had he expected? That she was going to say "Yes, sir, yes sir, three bags full," and skip merrily off to her own room?

"Do you really think Rob's guilty of anything, Matt?"

Hell! How had she managed to make him feel a foot tall in less than sixty seconds? "I don't know, Mary. That's the problem. None of us knows. Not Osborne, not me and not you, even though I realize you can't admit that fact."

"It isn't a fact at all, Matt. I do know. Your suspicions are way out of line. I know why Rob stopped by the *Sea Horse* to see Ian. And it had absolutely nothing to do with the theft or the mugging."

"Then what?"

"I can't tell you."

"Mary! For pete's sake give me a break! After our session with the police, I'm ready to believe Rob's innocent. I can't think they'd be so certain if it wasn't true. Just tell me what he was doing at the dock, just so I won't have any nagging doubts, just so I can tell Osborne what was going on so that I can get him off my back."

Mary shook her head. "Rob's asking me questions you've told me not to answer and you're asking me questions he's told me not to answer. I'm sick of it! Matt, you've always trusted my judgment. Trust it now. All I can tell you is that I know Rob is an honest, law-abiding man. Just take that on faith. Okay? Have I ever misled you about anyone before?"

Matt exhaled slowly. Had she? Certainly not that he could recall. Mary had been his student for three years, had worked as his teaching assistant for two. And she had an uncanny knack for reading people—students who dredged up lame excuses for late assignments, faculty members with hidden agendas. She could peg a phony a mile away.

And she was assuring him McFarlane was no phony. That was the way the police saw things, as well. Which had to mean Osborne's suspicions were off base. He silently met her gaze, hating to think about what a schmuck he'd been.

"Matt," she added, taking a visibly deep breath and pushing herself up, "I don't have the slightest intention of not spending my free time with Rob simply because of Jeffery Osborne's delusions. I'm sorry if that causes you a problem with Jeffery, but this has gone far enough. We're living in the twentieth century. The civilized world has recognized that women have brains and rights."

"Mary, it isn't that. It's—"

"Of course," she interrupted sarcastically, "I realize Jeffery exists on—or maybe beyond—the outermost fringe of the civilized world. So I can almost excuse him on the basis of ignorance. But I'm disappointed in you, Matt. I think associating with that man must be warping you. When you start yelling at Stefanie because of Jeffery's craziness, you've lost your sense of perspective. When she came storming out of Jeffery's room earlier, she was livid with both of you. Whatever you said to her," Mary added icily, "you should be ashamed of yourself."

She walked across to the door. "If you'll excuse me now," she said, reaching past him for the doorknob, "I'm going out with Rob. I'd intended to wait until Stefanie had finished developing that film. But Jeffery probably wouldn't let a spy like me look at the prints, anyway."

Matt barely had time to step out of the way before Mary jerked the door open. She closed it behind herself, ever so gently, leaving him feeling like two cents.

Mary was right. He'd lost his sense of perspective. He'd behaved like a total and complete jerk!

How could he possibly have sided with Osborne against Stefanie? Why hadn't he kept in mind that Osborne was a few bricks short of a load? Why was the phrase, *mad scientist*? Why not *mad engineer—mad sonar engineer*, to be specific. Yes, Mary had hit the nail on the head. He should be ashamed of himself... He was!

All right. Things would have to change. They'd all put up with far too many of Osborne's fascist tactics. He'd go across the hall right now and lay down the law. They were members of a team, not subjects in a dictatorship. They each had their jobs to do. And they were doing it. That should be Osborne's only concern. Matt opened his door and started across to Osborne's room. A sound at the end of the hall stopped him. He glanced to his left. Stefanie stood in the bathroom doorway, holding a stack of prints.

He changed direction and strode toward her. "What did you get?"

She looked at him uncertainly for a moment, as if seeing him had reminded her of her anger.

"Stefanie...I'm sorry about earlier. Really sorry. I'll apologize properly later. We'll talk. Okay?"

She hesitated, then cast him a half smile that said she'd give him the benefit of the doubt for the moment. "Fine. We'll talk about it later. I got pretty steamed myself."

She glanced down at the prints, clearly all business again. "I don't know exactly what we've got here. Some sort of underwater installation. It looks like a series of satellite dishes on the floor of a body of water." She held the pictures out to him.

He took them and began skimming through the stack. The first shots were of circular screens that indeed looked like a row of eight large communications dishes, spaced at regular intervals on a rocky, underwater base.

"See that structure in the background?" Stefanie pointed at a dark shape on the print he'd just reached. "Farther down in the pile are close-ups of it—even several interior shots. It's an operations center, sort of like the navigation area of the *Sea Horse*."

Matt quickly flipped through the prints until he reached the ones of the interior. They showed a tiny underwater room crammed with electronic devices. He paused at a shot of an incredibly complex-looking instrument panel. "This makes the *Sea Horse*'s controls look like child's play."

He sorted through the rest of the photographs, trying to make sense of what he was seeing.

"What do you think, Matt?"

"With all those dishes, it must be part of an underwater communication system. Beyond that I haven't got a clue. Maybe our engineer will have a better idea."

Matt turned back along the hall. He was just reaching out to knock on Osborne's door, when it opened.

"I thought I heard you out here." Osborne stared at the prints in Matt's hand, then glanced up at his face with an expression of horror. "You've looked at them!"

"Of course I've looked at them! You think you're the only one with a sense of curiosity?"

Osborne snatched the prints and gazed at the top one. He thrust it to the bottom of the pile, glanced at the next shot and sucked his breath in so loudly it sounded like the beginning of an asthma attack. His face turned white. Then without a word he wheeled around and strode into his room, slamming the door behind him.

A surge of anger swept through Matt. He threw Osborne's door open again and stormed inside, vaguely aware Stefanie was on his heels. "What the hell do you think you're doing? I want to know what those are pictures of. I want to know what's going on here!"

The engineer slumped into his desk chair as if he hadn't even heard Matt's outburst.

"Osborne! What the hell are those pictures all about?"

Osborne turned to stare up at him. "I can't tell you," he whispered. "It's classified."

Matt glared down, his fists clenched at his sides, and ordered himself to control his temper. "Don't give me your damned 'classified' garbage! We've already decided there's something going on here that's all mixed up with Nancy Goitano—something that's been causing problems for Stefanie. So don't think for a second I'm going to be brushed off with 'classified'!"

"You're going to have to be!"

"That film," Matt snarled, "was addressed to a dead woman. And you look as if you've just seen a ghost! What the hell are the pictures of?"

"I can't tell you anything! I can't!"

"Fine! Fine! Don't you tell us a damned thing. We'll just take these prints into Inverness to Officer McKay. Now that he's got Interpol trying to identify Still Waters, now that he's got that connection set up, maybe he'd like to show Interpol these pictures."

Osborne dived for his desk drawer, yanked it open, threw the prints inside and snapped the key in the lock. He pulled it out and thrust it into his shirt pocket.

"Those prints stay where they are!" He gave Matt an infuriatingly smug smile.

Matt glowered at him. "Well...I suppose I could turn you upside down and take that key away from you. But since Stefanie has the negatives, I guess it would be easier for us just to take them to McKay."

Osborne's gaze flashed to Stefanie.

Matt snuck a sidelong peak at her. She was staring down at Osborne, looking cool as a cucumber.

"Give those negatives to me!" Osborne hissed.

"Matt?" She glanced at him.

He shook his head.

"Sorry, Jeffery. I report to Matt."

Osborne glared back at Matt. "And you report to me!"

"I've got news for you! All the rules are off! I was hired as a marine biologist, not as some party to a *classified* mystery. From here on in, Stefanie's safety is my priority—not your orders."

"Garrett, I've got to have the negatives! You have to listen to reason! You don't understand the significance of these pictures."

"I might understand the significance if you were to explain it. I might even be willing to listen to reason. So why don't you pull those prints back out of your desk and tell us what they're all about. You can tell us...or, if you'd rather, maybe Interpol can." Matt held his breath while Osborne ran his fingers through his thinning hair.

"This is blackmail! You're trying to make me break all the rules! I won't!"

"All right." Matt turned to the door. "Let's go, Stefanie."

"Wait! You can't go to the police."

Matt paused, looking back. "It's up to you."

Osborne scowled at them, then slowly pulled the key from his pocket, unlocked the drawer and withdrew the prints. He held them tightly to his chest. "If I tell you, nothing I say goes out of this room. You can't breathe a word of it."

Matt and Stefanie both nodded.

Osborne selected a few prints and spread them across the top of his desk. "What we have here," he began hesitantly, "are shots of a communications relay system for submarines. I recognize this installation. I've been to the site. Sound Research had a contract with the navy. We produced the communication dishes. And I did a little consulting on the sonar system they're using."

"And what's the story about the installation being classified?"

Osborne shrugged wearily. "Underwater communication with submarines is a difficult, tricky business. This particular system was designed to utilize long radio waves. It's a technology that enables the communication range to be extended almost a hundred miles farther than standard systems."

"So the design is secret...classified," Stefanie murmured.

Osborne nodded. His eye twitched.

"And what else?" Matt held his breath. That twitch had to mean there was more.

"Not only is the design classified...so is the location of the installation. If it could be proved the navy has an underwater installation like this...where it is..." Osborne's words trailed off for a moment.

"The location I absolutely can't tell you, Garrett. We're dealing with national security here! You've got to trust me on that. And for heaven's sake, forget the idea of turning these prints over to anyone!"

"What about Nancy?" Matt pressed. "Where does she fit into all this? Why did a top secret film show up here, addressed to her?"

"She must have sent it to herself. It has to have been her own film. She took these shots."

"What?"

"Nancy was working for Sound Research on this installation—doing the underwater photography for our files. But from the looks of this, she took an extra roll of shots...and they didn't end up in the company's vaults.

"I just can't figure how she got such a wide range of pictures on this one roll," Jeffery muttered. "Sound Research got everything it expected from her. And naval security would have observed Nancy, wouldn't have allowed her to go around the site more than once, shooting the same shots a second time around."

"She wouldn't have had to," Stefanie explained. "On a shoot like that she'd have been carrying more than one camera. Ninety-nine percent of the time I use my Pentax, but I generally carry my Leica, as well—for special situations.

"Nancy could easily have been switching back and forth from one camera to another. And she could have replaced the films in one camera several times and just taken selected shots on this roll. Would anyone have kept count of how many films she used, of which cameras she shot with?"

"Maybe not," Osborne replied. "Nancy needed the highest level security clearance just to get down to the site. Once she was there, people would have taken her for legit."

"But then," Matt said thoughtfully, trying to piece the puzzle together, "she sent the film here? Mailed it to herself?"

Osborne nodded. "I thought the writing on the package looked like hers. But I wasn't certain. I haven't worked with her all that much."

"Why would she send the film here?" Stefanie asked, her tone nervous.

Matt turned to her, taking her hand in his, drawing her closer. They were coming nearer to unraveling the mystery...hopefully coming nearer to ensuring Stefanie's safety. He looked back at Osborne, waiting for an answer to her question.

"The likely reason Nancy wanted the film here," he said slowly, "was that she intended to give it to someone."

"Still Waters!" Matt exclaimed.

"That would be my guess," Osborne agreed. "Nancy expected to be here now...didn't expect to be dead. But she didn't want to chance bringing the film with her. Espionage and treason are incredibly serious offenses."

"Espionage? Treason?" Stefanie whispered.

Osborne shot her a derisive look. "What do you think Still Waters is, Stefanie? A Boy Scout?" Osborne stared down at the prints once more, flipping through them slowly, occasionally shaking his head.

Matt tried to think. He didn't know all the facts. And he didn't know anything about espionage or treason. Osborne obviously did. And he knew about naval secrets and had a high level security clearance. And Osborne was saying *no police*. But was he right?

"Look, Osborne, if we're talking spies and treason, we're not out of the woods yet. If this is as serious as you're making it out, it's even more likely Still Waters has an accomplice. We'd be fools not to call in the police—for our own safety. What's the problem with that? Nancy's the criminal. She'd be the one in trouble. And she's beyond caring.''

"No! Nancy's not the problem. It's American government security that's at stake.

"Finch," Osborne muttered. "That's what I have to do now. I have to call Finch, tell him what a potential hornet's nest we've got here, see how he wants us to proceed."

Osborne glanced at his watch. "Five hours' difference. It's only a little after two in New England. I'll head into Inverness. Thank heavens Finch isn't a golfer. With any luck, he spends his Saturday afternoons at home. Just give me time to talk to him. He'll know what to do."

"Why don't you call from here?" Stefanie asked.

Osborne shot her a withering glance. "From the one phone in the house? The one sitting in the McFarlane kitchen? Which reminds me, Garrett. You did talk to Mary about McFarlane, didn't you?"

"We talked."

Stefanie looked at Matt questioningly. He caught her eye and grinned before turning back to Osborne. "We talked, but Mary will still be seeing Rob. There's no way he's working with Still Waters. And you have to accept there's a limit to your rule setting, Osborne."

The engineer glared at him.

Matt merely shrugged. "That's just a fact you're going to have to live with for the rest of our stay here."

He looked back at Stefanie. Her warm smile made up for Osborne's glare a hundred times over.

"I'll tell you what. Stefanie and I will give you time to go into Inverness and call Finch, as long as you agree to come straight back and let us know where things stand, what he has to say. Once we hear that, we'll decide what to do about the police."

Osborne muttered something unintelligible, grabbed his jacket and stomped out of the room.

Stefanie smiled at Matt again. He looked at her closely, still unable to see why she thought that tiny space between her front teeth was so big. She had an absolutely perfect smile...a perfect mouth. Just looking at it aroused him. Just recalling how soft her lips felt against his made it impossible to stand here without—

"Did you want to go out and grab some dinner, Matt? While Jeffery's gone?"

"Oh...right...nothing I'd rather do."

THEY WALKED hand in hand back from their dinner at the Highland Shires. Hazy moonlight had begun dusting the calm surface of Loch Ness. The cool evening air was laced with a sweet scent of heather.

Stefanie glanced at Matt, barely aware of the surrounding beauty. Instead her senses were captivated by his nearness. The twilight softened his chiseled features, muted his five-o'clock shadow. She moved a little closer...just an inch...just close enough so she could smell his maleness.

He looked over, caught her watching him, smiled and squeezed her hand. A tiny series of delicious shivers raced through her.

How could the mere pressure of his hand on hers cause a reaction like that? All it took was a simple touch or a single glance to flood her with recollections of how wonderful his arms felt around her, the way his hands gently caressed her . . . how easily his kisses took her breath away.

But why were those recollections crystal clear when she could barely remember what they'd just had for dinner? The food had been irrelevant. All that had mattered was the way they'd sat in a quiet corner of the pub, unable to take their eyes off each other.

Their fight this afternoon was long forgotten—the memory of it brushed away by a few soft words. But the earlier part of the day, their time in the *Sea Horse*, the promises of being alone together again, were etched in her mind.

They were almost back to the guest house. Stefanie felt a tiny throb of anticipation begin pulsing deep within. She'd be all alone with Matt and then—

"Osborne's back from Inverness. There's his car in the drive."

Stefanie stared ahead at Jeffery's car, wondering when she'd begun hating it.

Matt picked up the pace, turning their leisurely walk into a race up the driveway. They were stopped short at the door.

Matt began searching through his pockets. "I should have put the front door key in my case right away. At least Florrie's keeping the house locked. That makes me feel better."

He located the key and unlocked the door. They hurried up the stairs to the second floor.

Jeffery's door was ajar. He appeared in the doorway before they were halfway along the hall. "Where've you been?" he demanded anxiously.

"Just getting something to eat," Matt told him. "What did Finch have to say?"

"He's on his way." Jeffery glanced at his watch. "He'll be leaving Logan shortly—be here in the morning."

"What? He's coming to Scotland?"

Jeffery nodded. "I told you how important that film is. He wants to see the shots for himself."

"I'm sure we could have faxed him copies of the prints from Inverness," Stefanie said.

"Right! Great idea! Facsimile transmission across half the world would do a lot to preserve national security."

"Knock off the sarcasm!" Matt snarled. "Stefanie and I aren't part of the damned secret service. She was simply being practical. I can't believe Finch is actually going to spend his Saturday night on a plane just to confirm what you've already told him."

"Believe it. I'll be off to Glasgow first thing in the morning to pick him up. In the meantime, give me the negatives, Stefanie. Finch's orders."

Stefanie glanced at Matt. She could almost see his mind working. He shook his head slowly.

"I don't think so. You keep those prints safe and Stefanie and I will keep the negatives safe. Look on it as an example of teamwork."

"Garrett! That was an order!"

Matt shrugged. "I told you earlier—there are limits to your rule setting. We'll talk to Finch about what happens to the negatives. I'm still not convinced they shouldn't be going to the FBI or the CIA or whoever looks after this sort of thing. If Sound Research just sits on them... What if Nancy was involved in other capers like this one?"

"That's none of your damn business!"

"Maybe not. But maybe it is. I'll have to think about that a little. At least until Finch gets here."

Jeffery swore under his breath, opened his mouth as if to speak, then quickly shut it again. They all turned to look down the hall, their attention drawn by the sound of footsteps hurrying up the stairs.

Mary rounded the corner and stopped short, glancing anxiously at each of them in turn, finally focusing on Matt. "I was looking for you...wanted to talk to you for a minute...but I guess this isn't a good time." She glanced meaningfully at Jeffery for an instant.

"Damn it!" he exploded. "I'm in charge here! What the hell is going on? There shouldn't be any talking that can't be done in front of me!"

"I...well, I...I was just wondering if we'd be working tomorrow...if you'd need me around?"

"Why?" Jeffery snapped.

Mary glanced at Matt with a helpless look, then swallowed visibly. "I have a chance to tour a research site in the Moray Firth. Some of the work that's going on there is closely related to my thesis topic. I thought...if you wouldn't need me for anything...if there wasn't going to be any testing for me to do tomorrow...?"

"Who's offered you a tour? Who'd be taking you?" Jeffery demanded.

Mary looked like someone had snapped a trap shut on her. "Rob knows someone working on the project. He'd take me." Her voice broke nervously.

"Well, I don't see any problem. Do you, Matt?"

Stefanie stared at Jeffery in amazement. He was almost smiling at Mary. She looked at Matt in time to catch him recovering from apparent surprise.

"No," he agreed. "I don't see any problem. I still want to get some sedimentary rock samples from the lake bottom. Once we have those there'll be optical analysis and preliminary radiometric dating analysis to do. But I doubt we'll have a chance to collect the samples until Monday."

"Right!" This time Jeffery shot Mary a smile that actually seemed authentic. "So you can take both tomorrow and Monday off, if you like. You might want to see a bit of that festival that's starting in Inverness."

Mary glanced at Matt with a look of pure disbelief. He gave an almost imperceptible shrug.

"Well, then," she said hesitantly, taking a couple of steps backward, "that's great. I'll just go and tell Rob we're all set. We'll leave first thing in the morning. And...as long as you're sure it's all right...I probably won't be back until Monday night." She continued backing until she reached the end of the hall, then turned and quickly fled down the stairs.

"Want to explain that?" Matt asked Jeffery.

"What's to explain? Regardless of what you or Stefanie or Mary or the local police think about McFarlane, almost nothing in the world would make me happier than to know he wasn't around Drumnadrochit. I especially don't want him around when Finch arrives. If Mary has to be with McFarlane, the farther away from here she's with him, the better.

"If we've finished our discussion," he added, turning back to his room, "it would make sense for me to go to bed now. I could use an early night. Be sure both you two and the negatives are here when Finch and I arrive from Glasgow tomorrow."

Jeffery's final order was barely out before he slammed his door soundly in their faces.

Matt grinned at Stefanie. "He didn't even wish us good-night."

She managed a weak smile. "I don't know how you can joke about this, Matt. I'll be glad to get rid of those negatives."

"Well, so will I. I just want to be certain we're getting rid of them to the right people. I . . . Oh, hell, Stefanie, let's forget about them for the moment." He gazed longingly at her. "Just because Jeffery didn't wish you a proper good-night doesn't mean I don't intend to."

Matt encircled her waist with his arms, drawing her against him. There was no mistaking his desire, his arousal.

Stefanie could feel the mounting excitement within her own body—the rapid beating of her heart, the aching throb deep within her.

"I think," Matt whispered, nuzzling her ear, "it would make sense for us to go to bed now, too."

CHAPTER TWELVE

MATT CLOSED THE DOOR of his room behind them and stood fumbling with the lock.

Stefanie watched him in nervous anticipation, certain he could hear the pounding of her heart, wanting him so much it frightened her.

The lock clicked and he turned, smiling across the few feet between them. He was, she suddenly realized, as nervous as she. Funny that he was... that either of them was. They were so clearly right together.

Matt was the most wonderful man she'd ever known. And he was here, alone with her, his eyes saying loving things. The entire room was filled with longing... his... hers.

He stepped toward her and folded her into his arms, into the aura of his musky maleness. His hands smoothed down her back, drawing her fully against him, then rested on her hips, fitting her body to the hardness of his own, causing a warm rush within her.

His lips urgently sought hers, claiming her mouth in a deeply passionate kiss. It lasted an eternity, his tongue intimately searching, exploring, heightening her desire until she was breathless.

"How," she whispered when he finally released her from his kiss, "can you possibly be so hungry when we've just eaten?"

"It's a different hunger, Stefanie. I want you so badly it hurts."

"Well . . . we can't have you in pain."

Matt smiled, brushing a stray tangle of hair from her cheek, then reached to pull the covers down on the bed. "Let's get out of these clothes before I starve to death."

He began unbuttoning her shirt, brushing the soft cotton aside as he went, his lips following his fingers down to the swell of her breasts.

"Matt . . . turn out the light."

"Why?"

"I'm skinny."

"Oh, Stefanie," he whispered, nuzzling her breast, his tongue probing beneath the lace of her bra, "you aren't skinny . . . and you don't have a huge gap between your front teeth, either. You must have had a mirror from a fun house while you were growing up. Only one that distorts images could make you see yourself the way you do. In reality you're absolutely beautiful!"

He pulled back for a moment and flicked the wall switch, leaving only night shadows for light. "Happier?"

"Happier," she murmured. The understatement of her life! She was beautiful! In Matt's eyes she was beautiful! And no other eyes mattered.

Matt quickly removed the rest of her clothes, his hands sliding smoothly and warmly over her skin, making her quiver with excitement.

A second later he was naked himself, was drawing her to him, skin against skin, softness against hardness, desire against desire. Her body melted against his heat. Standing was almost impossible.

Matt pulled her gently onto the bed, cradling her closely to him, stroking her hair in the darkness, kissing her neck with tiny, moist kisses that slowly began to drive her mad.

"Happy...happier...happiest." She ran her hand slowly, lightly down his chest, smiling at the tremor her touch induced.

His hand caught hers as it reached his waist.

"Matt? Your hand's trembling."

"Sorry. It's because I've never wanted to make love to anyone so badly before."

"Oh...I guess that's all right, then. I could get used to you trembling. Or wouldn't it last?"

"I think it would last for a long, long time." Matt's kiss ended his words. His hands detailed her face, her shoulders, her breasts. His mouth followed their lead, intensifying her desire to an impossible level, leaving her nipples moist against the cool air when his kisses trailed lower.

She moaned, quivering involuntarily.

"Okay?" Matt whispered.

"Yes...just a little cold."

He covered her entire body with his own, his hands still caressing her, warming her, arousing her, making her want him, stroking her hips, her stomach, her thighs, moving slowly, gently, making her lower body throb faster than her heart was pounding.

Stefanie smoothed her hand across the muscles of his chest until she could feel his heartbeat beneath her palm. Its rhythm was synchronized with the rapid pulsing of her own heart. They were perfectly attuned...as one.

Her body was turning to liquid at Matt's touch, becoming a deep, wet pool that was growing hotter with each movement of his body on hers.

She was all liquid . . . liquid fire . . . and she was pulling him closer, arching into him, needing him to stop the burning ache inside her.

Slowly he nudged her legs apart and filled her. They were one. She was complete. His body had no beginning...hers had no end. She could no longer tell where one stopped and the other began. She was only aware of the fire in the dark . . . a fire of excitement that was melting her, dissolving her.

Matt was moving tantalizingly within her. She silently begged time to stand still, to let that motion last for infinity. But already she was losing herself in its primitive pulse, in an onrushing tide that was dragging her ever farther from the shores of conscious thought.

Suddenly she was trembling out of control. For an instant time did stand still. Then it exploded into a series of instinctive shudders that consumed her body... her mind. Vaguely she was aware of Matt's body exploding with hers. And then they both collapsed amid the scent of sweat and passion.

They lay motionless until, gradually, reality poked its way back into her mind. Matt was beside her in the darkness, his arms still enfolding her.

Their bodies were slickly damp—warm where their skin touched, cool where air found tiny spaces to sneak between them. The silence was broken only by ragged breathing that slowly began to subside.

"I don't know what you do to me," Matt finally whispered, stroking her shoulder, "but I think I'm reduced to 'wow' again. I just can't find words to describe how you make me feel.''

Stefanie snuggled against his warmth, tangling her little finger in his chest hair. ''What I do to you? How about what you do to me? Every time you hold me or kiss me or touch me or...Matt, everything you do feels so right I can't believe it.''

''Well...I *am* a biologist...and this *is* sex we're talking about.''

She thought she could hear a smile in his voice, but slid her fingers gently across his lips to be sure. ''So it's just biology, is it...just sex?'' she teased back.

'''Just'? Don't put words in my mouth. I never said *just*. I've got no doubt at all that sex with love beats the hell out of sex without love.''

Love. The magic word! Stefanie smiled into the darkness, glad Matt couldn't see precisely how broad her smile was. She took his hand from her waist to hold between both her own.

''It's the strangest thing, Matt. Here I am in a foreign country, in a house sitting by a lake that's supposedly inhabited by a monster, and someplace out there a spy's accomplice is probably walking around loose, plotting to get my cameras or those negatives of Nancy's or something else I have.

''But instead of worrying about all of that, I'm lying in a strange bed with a man I've known for hardly any time at all, feeling perfectly content. All I need is you holding me and everything seems fine.''

Matt gently pushed her hair back from her face with his free hand. ''Sometimes I wish you got as tongue-tied as I do, Stefanie. I don't want to be reminded there's a world outside this room. Everything may seem fine right now, here in this bed, but I can't help worrying that it isn't. I can't help worrying about you, and I don't want to let you out of my sight.''

''Well, sooner or later you're bound to close your eyes. So would you settle for me not being out of your arms—at least not until daylight?''

''Sounds like a pretty good settlement to me.'' Matt freed his hand from hers and slid it down to stroke her inner thigh.

She moaned softly in anticipation.

''Now let's see...where were we?'' The smile was in his voice again.

THUNDER WOKE STEFANIE. She sat bolt upright in bed, naked, uncertain where she was. Matt's arm reached for her and the present came flooding back. She was in Matt's bedroom, in Matt's bed. It was morning...very late morning. Sunlight streamed in through the window. So how could there be thunder?

The noise erupted again. Oh, Lord! It wasn't thunder. It was someone pounding on Matt's door.

''Garrett! Garrett!'' Jeffery's voice was sharp with annoyance. ''I thought you said you were a light sleeper!''

Matt groaned her name and pulled her down on top of him, his hands fondling her breasts, his lips seeking hers.

''Matt!'' She pushed firmly against his shoulders.

He opened his eyes. ''What's wrong?''

''Garrett! Garrett! Are you in there?'' A rattling of the door handle accompanied the question.

Stefanie breathed a silent prayer of thanks that Florrie had found room keys for each of them.

''Yeah! Yeah, I'm here,'' Matt shouted at the door. He glanced at his watch. ''Good grief,'' he whispered.

"That'll teach us to make love until dawn. It's practically noon."

"Well, open up! Finch is with me! We want to talk to you. And where the hell is Stefanie?"

Matt grinned at her. "Want to try a bluff, or should we just 'fess up?"

"Bluff! By all means bluff!" Her face felt so hot it must be crimson.

"How should I know?" Matt yelled. "Probably went out for a walk. Give me a minute to get dressed. I'll meet you downstairs for coffee...okay?"

"No. We'll meet in my room. We don't want Florrie hovering around us. Finch and I will go outside and have a quick look around for Stefanie. See you in ten minutes.

"I specifically told both of them not to go anywhere until you got here," Jeffery muttered, his voice gradually fading down the hall.

Matt kissed her quickly. "I think we may have snookered them. All you have to do is say you came in from your walk while they were out looking for you."

"That's all, huh? I'll bet the odds on them buying that explanation are about one in a hundred."

"Well, then, I guess you'll just have to go through the rest of the month with a tarnished reputation. At least you can get back to your room and put on clothes that aren't the ones you were wearing last night."

Stefanie rolled out of bed, threw on yesterday's clothes and unlocked the door. She peered cautiously into the hall. "Coast's clear. But I feel like a fugitive."

"If you don't get going, you'll be feeling like a trapped fugitive."

Stefanie shot him a rueful grin. "Matt...if I do have to go through the rest of the month with a tarnished reputation . . . last night was worth it!'' She opened the door and raced to her own room.

"SO, YOU SEE," Finch concluded, "the worst thing we could possibly do would be involve anyone who doesn't absolutely have to be involved. I'll take these prints . . . and the negatives . . . back with me, see that they're delivered to the appropriate person.

"Then Nancy's activities for the past while will be discreetly but thoroughly investigated. Believe me when I tell you that any other action would prove embarrassing—most embarrassing—for our government."

Stefanie glanced at Matt. What David Finch was saying made perfect sense to her.

"What about this accomplice of Still Waters's the police figure is around?" he asked. "I'm worried about Stefanie's safety."

"Matt, Sound Research works closely with the government. I have contacts in extremely high places . . . extremely high. Everything is already being taken care of. The CIA has contacted MI-5." He paused, glancing at Stefanie. "MI-5 is the CIA's British counterpart. They're looking after liaison with the local police."

He focused on Matt again. "Our concerns about this possible accomplice have been couched in terms of what Still Waters was up to. There was no need to mention either Nancy's name or the existence of her film. But by later this afternoon, MI-5 will have so many agents around Stefanie she won't be able to see her own shadow.

"And our people are already working to find out what game Nancy was playing—without alerting anyone outside our own government to a possible security leak.''

Finch turned back to Stefanie, eyeing her intently. "You've made no other prints of that film?''

She shook her head.

"And you both understand how important it is that I have the negatives...and that nothing is ever said about what's happened here?''

She looked over at Matt again. He shrugged.

"You guarantee,'' he said to Finch, "that Stefanie will have protection.''

"I guarantee it. The agents should be in Drumnadrochit already.''

Matt nodded. "Then I guess we'll go along with you.''

Stefanie reached down to the gadget bag at her side, pulled out the negatives and handed them to Finch.

He flashed her a relieved-looking smile, checked the negatives, then tucked the envelope into his breast pocket and turned to Jeffery.

"Well, I have a few hours before my return flight. There's no point in heading back to Glasgow just yet. How about lending me your car and giving me the keys to the *Sea Horse*? I'd like to poke around it a bit—see what we got for all that money we spent equipping her.''

"Sure. But you don't have to go on your own. I'll drive you to the dock.''

"No. The three of you should stick around the guest house until MI-5 has its security firmly in place. No sense taking any chances. Give me the keys and I'll scout around on my own. The dock's just down the road, isn't it?''

"Yeah." Jeffery fished in his pocket, then tossed Finch a key ring. "There's a large ruin—Urquhart Castle—about a mile along. You'll see a road leading to the lake just before you reach that."

Finch nodded. "Well...you three sit tight. I'll be back shortly." He headed out of Jeffery's room; the sound of his footsteps trailed along the hall, started down the stairs.

"There's something about this I don't like," Matt muttered.

"What's not to like?" Jeffery snapped. "Finch has everything under control. And we should be damned glad this little episode didn't bring an end to our entire project.

"Lord, I wish we could get out on the lake today! Wish I didn't have to putz around driving Finch back to Glasgow. I'm dying to get to that cavern where you tracked something big.

"At least tomorrow my invention will be delivered. Once it's here we can really get underway...get on with the serious part of our search."

Stefanie thought fleetingly of asking Jeffery about his invention again, then brushed the impulse aside. She wouldn't give him the satisfaction of knowing she was still curious.

STEFANIE SAT CLUTCHING Matt's hand, wishing her mind would stop reeling. She glanced across the corridor at Jeffery. His face was still white with shock. Only a few hours ago, the three of them had been sitting in the Galloway Guest House, quietly talking about tomorrow's search route, waiting for Finch to return from the *Sea Horse*.

Now they were sitting in the Inverness police station, waiting for an FBI agent to explain what had happened—why what seemed like a hundred Scottish police officers had descended on the house, why FBI agents had been there, asking them a million questions about Sound Research and their project, about Finch, Still Waters and Vladimir Chernovsky.

Matt put his arm around her shoulder and silently drew her against him.

There was no point in talking, no point in asking Matt any more questions. He had the same number of answers she had—none. They simply waited.

Finally the heavily scarred door marked Conference Room opened and FBI agent Rutherford appeared. "Mr. Osborne, Mr. Garrett, Miss Taylor...would you please come in now."

Matt squeezed her shoulder reassuringly, then rose. The three of them trailed silently into the conference room.

Inside, two men sat at a long, wooden table. Both had been among the throng of law enforcement officers at the guest house—Officer McKay, of the Inverness Police, and a man who'd been introduced to them as Agent Hacking of MI-5.

"Please sit down." Rutherford gestured to one side of the table, then walked around to sit on the other, next to Hacking.

Stefanie settled nervously into a chair beside Matt. Jeffery sat down a couple of seats along from them.

Rutherford glanced at Hacking. The older man nodded. The FBI agent turned back to the team. "We're in MI-5's jurisdiction. But since this is a United States security matter, since I've been involved with the investigation, Agent Hacking has asked me to fill you in on what I can of what's been going on.

"And I will tell you as much as I can . . . but you appreciate we're dealing with classified matters . . . that I won't be able to elaborate on many details . . . and that anything I do tell you can never be repeated."

"We understand that," Matt assured him.

Rutherford almost smiled. "It hardly seems fair—after all you've been through—but I'll do my best to clear up the mystery."

Stefanie leaned forward, anxious to hear whatever explaining Rutherford was allowed to do.

"The FBI has been involved in this case since Nancy Goitano's body was discovered. The New York police found a bug on her phone, suspected there was more to her murder than was evident on the surface, and called us in."

"Who'd bugged her?" Jeffery asked.

Rutherford frowned, as if deciding whether to answer. "KGB," he finally said.

"The Russians!" Stefanie whispered. "Does that explain all those questions your men asked about Vladimir?"

"Yes. Vladimir Chernovsky was Nancy's contact in Drumnadrochit. But we'll talk about that in a minute. I don't want to get ahead of myself or none of this will make sense to you.

"When the NYPD contacted us, we searched Nancy's apartment and turned up her links to Finch. We've had him under surveillance since then—alerted MI-5 the moment he boarded the plane for Glasgow last night."

"Finch." Jeffery shook his head. "I still can't believe that everything he told us about having contacted you people was a pack of lies."

"It was. He may have talked a good story, but we're the last people he wanted involved—the last people he expected or wanted to see here.

"Your David Finch is a greedy man," Rutherford continued. "It turns out he's been doing a little business on the side for some time now. But Nancy was greedy, too. That's what tripped them up.

"According to Finch's plan, Nancy was to shoot one extra film of the naval installation. Instead she shot two—figured if Finch could make deals, she could, as well.

"Only, when she made her own, private deal to sell the second film, the KGB was listening in."

"And the second extra film is the one that arrived for her yesterday?" Matt asked.

Rutherford nodded. "She gave one of her unauthorized films to Finch as planned. He concealed it in the equipment that was shipped. The arrangements with Chernovsky were that Nancy would retrieve it from the sub for him."

"And that," Stefanie concluded, "is why the cartons of film were stolen from the *Sea Horse*...why the strobes went astray. Vladimir knew Nancy's film was someplace in the equipment."

"Right," Rutherford agreed. "The KGB doesn't mess around with double-crossers. When they learned Nancy was making deals on the side, they took her out before she could follow through with her plans. That left them knowing the film was someplace in the equipment but not precisely where."

"How did Vladimir get into the sub?" Jeffery demanded. "And did he get that film? Where was it?"

"One question at a time. He got into the sub very easily. His photographer identity was simply a cover. As a spy, he's been trained as a master locksmith. Nancy would have known where the film was hidden, but she wouldn't have had a key to the sub. So the plan required Vladimir to gain access so Nancy could retrieve the film.

"To answer your second question, no, Vladimir didn't get the film. It was still on board when Finch went to the *Sea Horse* today. In fact, he'd taken it from the sub and was delivering it to Vladimir when MI-5 grabbed them both."

"Where was it hidden?" Matt asked.

"In the housing of one of the light fixtures."

"But what about the second film?" Stefanie asked. "The one she sent here."

"That's where your Mr. Still Waters came in. Nancy had arranged to sell him the second film, without telling him one was already going to the Russians, of course. She told him she'd bring it with her, make the drop in Glasgow. But then she must have changed her mind for some reason and mailed it to herself, instead."

"And who *is* Still Waters?" Stefanie asked.

Rutherford shrugged. "He's a free-lancer. We think he may be working for the Chinese on this one, but there are plenty of other possibilities."

"But was he here alone?" Matt asked. "Now that you have both him and Chernovsky in custody, are you sure there aren't others lurking around?"

"No, there are no others. Officer McKay assumed Still Waters had an accomplice because there wasn't enough time to steal the film from the sub and make it to the guest house as fast as he did. That was a reasonable conclusion. As we know now, though, the two incidents were independent. It was Chernovsky who mugged the watchman and stole the film. But we're certain there's no one left on the loose to bother you. And we'll be extraditing these fellows to the States in short order.''

"But why was Still Waters after *my* things?'' Stefanie asked. "What made him think *I* might have Nancy's film?''

"He still isn't talking, so I don't know if he actually thought you had it or was grasping at straws. As far as he knew, Nancy was bringing the film with her. When she didn't arrive with the rest of the team, he assumed she was coming later and kept the airport under surveillance. When you showed up, he initially thought you were Nancy and delivered the password to you in that restaurant.''

"Still waters run deep...''

"That's right. Then, when he realized you weren't Nancy, his only hope was that she'd sent the film with you, possibly without your knowledge. So he followed you, stole your suitcase and the cartons of film you'd brought from Chicago, then tried to steal the rest of your equipment the other night.''

"He had no idea at all there was a film in the *Sea Horse*,'' Jeffery concluded.

"Right. The Russians had that tap on Nancy's phone, so they knew all about her deal with Still Waters. But he knew nothing of them, nothing of another film.'' Rutherford paused. "That's about all I can say. I hope it's clarified things for you.''

"You're absolutely certain there's no one else involved," Matt said slowly, "that there'll be no further problems?"

Rutherford nodded. "Even the other members of the Russian search team are legit. Chernovsky's an amateur photographer. The KGB had him planted on the team and he was obviously good enough to fool everyone."

"So they were never after my sonar at all," Jeffery muttered.

Stefanie glanced at him and smiled in amusement. He clearly found that fact insulting.

"And our search?" he continued hesitantly. "What's its status now?"

"I can't see a problem with it continuing. Sound Research itself is clean. Finch's activities were all his own."

Rutherford looked across at Matt and Stefanie. "I wonder if you'd mind waiting outside for a few minutes? Osborne here has security clearance. There are a few things I need to talk with him about that I can't really . . ."

"Of course." Matt stood and extended his hand to Rutherford. "Thanks for telling us as much as you did."

Stefanie smiled her thanks to the three men and followed Matt from the room. They crossed the hall to sit on the same bench they'd waited on earlier.

Stefanie felt a blanket of relief gradually enveloping her. Their mystery had been solved.

"David Finch involved in a plot with Nancy," she finally murmured. "That explains his panic call to the airport . . . why he was so upset about her death. But never in a million years would it have occurred to me that either Finch or Vladimir were up to what they were."

Matt laughed quietly. "That makes two of us."

"We'd never make it as detectives, would we? Because when you think back, we passed over some little clues that fit right in."

"Such as?" Matt asked, putting one arm around her shoulders.

"Such as that cap Rob found by the sub—that navy knit cap. I'll bet it goes with those navy knit sweaters the Russian team had on the other night—the night the *Sea Horse* was broken into."

"You're probably right . . . and that reminds me, I owe you an apology."

"For?"

"Over Rob. You were right about him."

"Well, it isn't really me you owe the apology to. It's Rob and Mary. And I'm not one for saying 'I told you so,' but next time," she added with a grin, "you might think twice before suggesting I take my eyes in for an overhaul. I quite often do know what I'm talking about."

"Ouch! Next time I don't listen to you, just remind me of that."

Stefanie smiled, leaning comfortably against Matt, still trying to believe their adventure was over, that they'd made it through safely. "Things are going to seem awfully tame from here on in, aren't they, Matt? I feel as if we've been in the midst of a spy film since the moment I arrived."

"Well, we have one little mystery left," Matt said teasingly. "We still don't know what Osborne's wonderful new invention is or what he intends to do with it. That gives us something exciting to look forward to."

"Somehow I just can't imagine it'll be quite as exciting as being overrun by a horde of FBI and MI-5 agents, not to mention the entire Inverness police force.

"Matt," she continued hesitantly after a moment, "are you sure you think I'm beautiful?"

"Of course. I told you I did. Why?"

"Just checking. I must admit to having been flattered when Vladimir was so taken with me...but it turns out it wasn't me he was interested in at all. That kind of revelation doesn't do much for a woman's ego."

Matt grinned at her. "What do you care about Vladimir? You've got me."

"Do I?"

"Damn right you do! And don't even think about letting me go."

"Is that a threat?"

Matt leaned closer. "Just think of it as—"

The door of the conference room opened and Jeffery darted out, wearing a mile-wide grin. "I just phoned the president of Sound Research. It's all systems go as far as the search is concerned! They're hoping to keep the Finch incident hush-hush, of course, but he said he'd like to see all the positive publicity we can get, just in case.

"I ran the concept of my new invention by him and he was really enthusiastic—gave me the go-ahead. Doesn't have a lot of faith that I can really pull this off, of course, but we'll show him. We'll show them all! We'll be as famous as the Three Musketeers by the time our search is done."

Stefanie watched Jeffery in amazement. She'd never seen him this excited, never seen a trace of the animation he was displaying at the moment. He looked as if he were about to do a jig right there in the police station.

"Jeffery," she said, unable to resist a try, "isn't it about time you shared your new invention with us— told us what we're going to show everyone, what's going to make us all famous?"

Jeffery nodded enthusiastically. "I think it is, Stefanie."

"Well?" Matt pressed after a moment's pause.

Jeffery grinned gleefully. "Garrett...Stefanie... we're no longer simply going to track a Nessie...no longer simply out after photographs. It's far more exciting.... I've got the go-ahead. We're going to take a specimen!"

CHAPTER THIRTEEN

"'TAKE A SPECIMEN'?" Stefanie whispered, certain she must have misheard. "What do you mean...'take a specimen'?"

"Which word," Jeffery snapped sarcastically, "didn't you understand?"

Stefanie glared at him. She'd understood his words perfectly. It was believing he was serious that was giving her trouble.

"You've both been so curious about my invention," Jeffery continued smugly. "Well, I'm finally ready to tell you what it is. It's an enormous trap. It extends to over thirty feet in length."

Thirty feet? Stefanie's mind raced. That was the frequent estimate of Nessie's length. She stared at Jeffery, certain that if she tried to speak, no words would come out. Surely this must be a bad joke.

"The trap design incorporates a huge magnet," Jeffery continued proudly. "We attach a second electromagnet to our manipulator arm and we've got the capability to transport the trap out into the lake and position it on the floor. Then we simply raise it to the surface once there's a Nessie inside."

"A Nessie?" Stefanie managed to sputter. "Jeffery! You aren't serious!"

"Of course I am."

Of course he is, a little voice whispered inside Stefanie's head. *He isn't capable of humor.*

"It's a huge long box," Jeffery went on, apparently oblivious to her expression of horror. "The shape is formed by steel bars and each side is covered with closely woven rope webbing.

"It works on the principle of a lobster trap. It has a funneled net entrance. Once a creature goes inside, the funnel backs up on itself, preventing the animal from escaping until we open the one side that's hinged. Of course, we'll only do that when we're ready to put Nessie into a more permanent cage."

"This just may be the most ridiculous thing I've ever heard!" Stefanie exploded. "You can't do that! You know you can't!"

"Why not? My design is excellent. The trap is partially collapsible—makes it easily portable and prevents problems with weight and stress. I expect both the trap and the arm to work perfectly."

"Jeffery! I don't mean you can't physically do it! I mean you can't *do* it! You can't trap a Nessie!"

"Says who? I'm within my legal rights. I've checked. There are absolutely no laws about trapping Nessies. The only relevant law prohibits trawling in Loch Ness. But we won't be trawling. We'll be using a stationary trap."

"But that's not—"

"Look, Stefanie, forget the litany of objections, will you? We'd be quite within the law to trap a fish in the lake. We could even take it back to the States if we wanted to. What's the difference between a fish and a Nessie?"

"What's the difference? That question doesn't even warrant an answer! And take it back to the States?

You're out of your mind! The Scottish authorities would never allow that."

"Don't be so sure. A Nessie would be worth a lot of money to Sound Research. And I'm certain money talks in Scotland the same as it does elsewhere."

"This whole idea is insane!" Stefanie snapped, trying to keep some semblance of control over her temper. "And you can forget about *us* taking a Nessie anywhere! I'm not having any part of this craziness. And neither is Matt! Right, Matt?"

She turned to Matt, suddenly realizing he'd been silent throughout her harangue.

His expression wasn't even close to the one of outraged anger she'd expected to see. He gazed back at her with apparent discomfort. Her heart sank.

"Stefanie...let's not reject this idea right off the top. There may be some merit to it."

"Merit? Merit?" She paused, ordering herself to stop shrieking, realizing that might not be possible. She was instantly almost as angry with Matt as with Jeffery.

"Matt . . . why aren't you backing me up? What possible merit could there be? You're sounding as absurd as Jeffery! How could you even consider what he's suggesting? If Nessies do exist, saying they're an endangered species would be the understatement of the millenium! We can't go merrily trying to trap one. That wasn't the plan! The plan was to photograph one. You two are nuts! I'm not getting involved in this nonsense!"

"Read your contract!" Jeffery snarled. "It's completely airtight, so you'll damn well get involved in any 'nonsense' I say you'll get involved in! Break that contract, and I swear to God, Sound Research will break

you. Your professional reputation will be mud! If
you—"

"Take it easy, Osborne," Matt interrupted sharply.
"You're just getting Stefanie more upset."

Pictures of history's dictators whirled through Stefanie's mind. Napoleon had been short . . . Hitler, too.
Overcompensation—that's what at least part of Jeffery's problem was!

"Don't threaten me, Jeffery!" she snapped when
Matt paused. "Why should you even care whether I'm
involved or not? If you're going to end up with your
very own Nessie in a stupid trap, you sure as hell don't
need me! You'll be able to take all the pictures you
want to . . . yourself . . . with a damned Polaroid!"

"I want," Jeffery said icily, "pictures of the Nessie
being trapped . . . of her in the trap . . . of our raising the
trap. Action shots. Get the idea?"

Stefanie shook her head in frustration. "This isn't
only insane, it's completely immoral! What if you did
trap a Nessie? What if the Scottish authorities did let
you take it out of the country—although I can't believe for a minute they would. What then? Would you
put it on display like a circus animal?"

Jeffery shrugged. "Perhaps. Or perhaps it would be
more feasible to sacrifice it for extensive study."

"Sacrifice? Sacrifice?" She was shrieking again; she
didn't care. "What a nice clinical term for murder!
This is ludicrous! Matt! For heaven's sake tell him it's
ludicrous!"

Matt's gaze didn't meet hers. She was seized by an
almost uncontrollable urge to try shaking him out of
whatever trance he must be in.

"Matt...Matt, just a few minutes ago you were telling me to remind you that I quite often know what I'm talking about. So why aren't you listening to me?"

"Stefanie, calm down," he said quietly. "I've been listening to you. And I understand why you're upset. I realize you're into preserving wildlife, that the idea of doing anything more to an animal than photographing it is against your principles.

"But," Matt continued, "we're obviously not talking about an average situation here. This is the chance of a lifetime. If Osborne can pull it off, if we could actually take a specimen, the scientific ramifications would be incredible."

"Ramifications? Don't try to razzle-dazzle me with five-syllable words! Scientific ramifications, my foot! What you mean is Matt Garrett would be famous—the marine biologist who had a part in capturing the Loch Ness Monster. That's what you mean, isn't it?"

"No! That's not it at all! Well...of course...we *would* be famous...all our names would be famous. But that isn't the—"

"Not my name! Not Stefanie Taylor's name! You two butchers aren't dragging me into this. If you're serious about going along with Jeffery, I'll be on a plane first thing in the morning!"

"Damn it, Stefanie, just listen to me for a minute. I understand how you're feeling. Try to understand me. At least listen to what I think."

Stefanie took a deep breath, ordering herself to calm down. If she could swing Matt to her side, maybe they could overrule Jeffery. But to do that she had to know what Matt saw in Jeffery's plan.

"All right. I'm listening."

"Okay." Matt eyed her closely. "Do you have any idea how important marine animals are to medical research?"

"I don't believe in animal research!"

"Well...I don't believe in all of it, either. But much of it's been useful, Stefanie. Be reasonable. You can't honestly tell me it wasn't worth experimental surgery on dogs to perfect the heart bypass operation."

"No, of course I won't tell you that. But you're talking apples and oranges—giving me an example that has absolutely nothing to do with Nessies."

"That's true. But you can't begin to imagine what a close look at even one Nessie might tell science. If the creatures are truly what I think they are—prehistoric beings that have evolved so successfully they've managed to survive all this time—just think of what we could learn from them."

"What?" Stefanie challenged.

"I don't know *exactly* what. But marine animals share fundamental processes with humans—processes like metabolism and immunity. And they offer a simpler, clearer model of biological phenomena than mammals do.

"Stefanie, sharks almost never develop cancerous tumors. They may have some as yet undetected protective mechanism that would benefit human cancer victims. And ice fish totally lack red blood cells. Think about the potential importance of that to human anemics.

"If we have a chance to examine a previously unknown species," Matt went on, "one that's adapted over millions of years, we can't pass up the opportunity."

"Examine? As in 'sacrifice,' to use Jeffery's ridiculous euphemism? As in 'kill and dissect'? Matt...that isn't right!"

Matt shrugged slowly. "Stefanie, right or wrong, it isn't something that could be passed up—not simply because you have qualms about animal research. This chance is too important. Every ounce of my scientific training tells me that. Who knows what a Nessie could teach us about aquaculture or pollution or pathology?"

Stefanie stared at Matt with a sick, sinking feeling. He was seeing this issue from a purely scientific point of view. And she knew she was seeing it from a purely emotional one. And Jeffery...Lord knows where Jeffery was coming from...but it was all too clear where he was heading.

It didn't look as if she had a hope in hell of convincing either man to drop the idea of trapping a Nessie. So she could pack up and get out—wash her hands of the entire project—or she could stick around and work on them, could try to wear them down, to convince them this idea was immoral. Because they couldn't take a Nessie. They just couldn't. She wouldn't let them! And that meant she had to stay.

"I gather from your silence, Stefanie," Jeffery finally said, "that you've seen reason. That's good. So we'll take the *Sea Horse* down first thing in the morning and head across to that cavern where you two spotted something.

"If we get a strong sonar reading again tomorrow, we'll come back to shore for my trap, take it out, set it up and bait it. If Garrett's right about the creatures' eating habits, a trap full of live salmon or trout will attract them. I've already arranged for a fisherman to supply the bait. Once that's in place," Jeffery concluded with a self-satisfied smile, "it'll merely be a matter of waiting."

Stefanie barely listened to Jeffery's insane babbling. She stood looking at Matt in total disillusionment, wondering how she'd ever believed he was wonderful, how she'd ever believed she was in love with him.

He wasn't at all the sensitive man she'd thought him to be. Deep down, hidden by surface warmth, was a cold, clinical, scientific mind...a mind that lacked the emotional depth to realize they weren't dealing with a scientific question.

They were dealing with a moral question, an issue of right and wrong. And Matt was wrong. And she couldn't possibly love a man who was wrong about something that mattered to her as much as this did.

STEFANIE GLANCED ANXIOUSLY about the interior of the *Sea Horse*. After the mishap she and Matt had experienced in the cavern, she wasn't the least bit eager to go down in the sub again. But she didn't have much choice.

If Jeffery and Matt succeeded in tracking a Nessie today, she wanted to know about it. Whatever happened, she intended to be right there with them. At the very least, she could act as a voice of sanity, a voice of conscience. Maybe at some point her words would get through to one of them.

She rubbed her eyes, trying to focus on a lake trout that was tentatively bumping its nose against one of the observation windows. Her eyes wouldn't or couldn't cooperate—not on the little sleep she'd had. She'd spent half of the previous night arguing with Matt and

Jeffery, vainly trying to convince them to scrap the idea of trapping a Nessie.

All she'd succeeded in doing was working herself into a state of exhausted frustration. Then, when she'd eventually gotten to bed, she'd tossed and turned, only nodding off as dawn had begun creeping through her window. And what sleep she had managed to get had ended abruptly in a nightmare.

A Nessie had been trapped, had been fighting for its freedom, for its life. And she'd been unable to help it, unable to convince either Matt or Jeffery to set it free. She'd awakened in a cold sweat.

She heard the two men coming back into the sub...heard the hatch's lock being turned into place...heard their footsteps on the ladder.

"We've got the sonar all set," Matt announced cheerily. He was still ignoring, or pretending to ignore, her sullen silence.

She didn't look at him. She couldn't. Every time she inadvertently glanced in his direction a lump formed in her throat. How could he be so unfeeling? How could he be so unlike what she'd thought him to be? How could life be so unfair? How could she have fallen in love with Matt only to have things turn out so terribly? How could Matthew Garrett...Mr. Wonderful...have turned out to be Mr. Horrible?

Jeffery marched across to the control console and turned his sonar on. Its monitor lit up.

Stefanie stared at the screen...at Jeffery's sonar... Nessie's enemy.

"Connection's good," he muttered. "Sonar's tracking fine. So let's get this show on the road." He started the engine.

It throbbed to life, then settled into a quiet hum. Jeffery began whistling tunelessly under his breath, flipped a lever and navigated the *Sea Horse* slowly away from the dock.

Stefanie stared out into the blackness. Her nightmare was becoming reality.

The sub glided quietly through the water. Matt made a few attempts at conversation. Stefanie didn't respond. Jeffery was so immersed in what he was doing that he seemed not even to hear. He simply stood at the controls, making that infernal noise, his head moving in a pattern from the chart to the navigation window before him, to the screen, then back to the chart.

Eventually Stefanie glanced at her watch. They'd been under way for almost half an hour. It seemed like an eternity. The *Sea Horse* had become a torture chamber, and Jeffery was chief torturer. His breathless whistle grated on her ears. Maybe she should start talking. Maybe he'd stop whistling to listen.

But she had nothing left to say. She'd already brought up every reasonable argument—and a whole lot of unreasonable ones—and they'd gotten her nowhere.

Matt and Jeffery were two of the most pigheaded men she'd ever met. She hated them both! There was no point in discussing their plan further. They wouldn't listen to her. And she'd talked so much last night her throat was raw.

All she could do at the moment was hope there were no Nessies in that cavern...hope there were no Nessies in the whole damned lake! Or if there were, that Jeffery's sonar didn't locate one.

She thought once again about Matt's silt buildup theory. Maybe the Nessies hadn't been able to reach

Loch Ness this year. Perhaps what she and Matt had tracked on Saturday had been something else. In that case, all her fears would prove groundless.

But her mind's eye pictured Jeffery's trap sitting back on the dock, and she shuddered. If they did locate a Nessie's lair, that enormous contraption of cold steel bars and rope netting would come into use. Just looking at the monstrosity had made her feel ill. But Jeffery had been so pleased with it he'd practically danced along the pier.

Why were things going right for him? Talk about life being unfair! If the world were just, his insane plot would be crumbling around him. Instead a moving van had delivered his creation first thing this morning, right on schedule. And before they'd left shore, a fisherman had arrived with two huge barrels full of live bait.

She looked toward the front of the sub at the sonar screen, trying to banish the image of that enormous awful trap. The circular sweep of the sonar's green line was hypnotic. Each time a blip flashed, each time a ping sounded, her breath caught and she stared at the screen. But each time the blip was small, probably just indicating a large fish. She prayed that was all they'd track.

Jeffery's whistling ceased.

Stefanie thanked heaven for small mercies.

He waved his hand across the chart on the console. "We're nearing your cavern now."

Matt moved closer to the navigation controls and glanced down at the chart.

"From what you've said about the Nessies," Jeffery told him, "I figure this would be an ideal refuge for them. They could breed in the safety of the caves, where their young would be protected from currents.

"Of course, if the creatures are in there, the adults will come out for food intermittently. And that," Jeffery added, glancing back at Stefanie with a malicious grin, "will be when we get one."

Stefanie glared at him, an angry, nauseous feeling swirling in her stomach. The man was revolting. What had Mary told her that Rob called Jeffery? "A nasty wee man!" That was it. The description fit perfectly. He positively relished the idea of trapping a Nessie. As a child he'd pulled wings off flies. She just knew he had.

"Stefanie, switch on those observation lights," Jeffery ordered, gesturing at a window. "We're near enough that we should be able to see something."

She hesitated, then headed across the sub. She wouldn't gain anything by angering Jeffery further. And if worst came to worst, if he did trap a Nessie, she intended to try reasoning with him again. Unlikely as he'd be to listen, the likelihood would be even less if she'd been uncooperative.

She turned on the lights. At the outermost range of visibility, through the heavy veil of peat particles that hung suspended in the water, she was able to make out the rocky side of the lake.

Jeffery had slowed the sub to a crawl and they drifted along parallel to the wall, about twenty-five feet from it.

"The cavern should be right around here," Jeffery muttered. "Once we spot the entrance, I'll move in closer...see what the sonar can pick up through the opening." He finished speaking and gazed through the observation window.

Stefanie peered into the dark water once more. She realized her nails were digging into her palms and un-clenched her fists.

The sub's interior had become so quiet that she could hear her own breathing above the almost inaudible hum of the engine. The silence continued, stretching into minutes. The *Sea Horse* drifted slowly along.

And then the sonar erupted in a blaze of light, a se-ries of jarring pings.

Stefanie didn't breathe... stood stark still... willed the sonar's thin line to sweep smoothly, quietly around its course again.

It did... for a moment. Then it reached the three o'clock position once more and all hell broke loose for a second time.

"That's it!" Jeffery pointed through the observa-tion window. "See that shadow on the wall? That's an opening! That's your cavern. And my sonar's picking up something moving inside! I'm going to take us closer. Get your camera ready, Stefanie!

"Hot damn, Garrett! I think we've done it! This one's no fish! There's something enormous moving around in that cave!"

"Get your camera ready." Stefanie had heard the order but stood rooted to the spot.

"Your camera!" Jeffery screamed. "Get your damned camera out! That's what we're paying you for, for God's sake."

Stefanie fumbled with her gadget bag, not knowing what else to do. The sonar erupted in another flurry of light and sound as she managed to get the bag open.

She pulled her Pentax out, quickly screwed in the telephoto lens, snapped its cap off and aimed at the window. Automatically she tried to focus, then realized she couldn't see. Tears were forming, blinding her. She kept the camera to her eye, hoping Jeffery wouldn't realize she was faking.

Jeffery maneuvered the sub closer to the wall and brought it to a halt about ten feet from the opening. Each time the sonar line reached three o'clock the pings blasted louder, the flashes seemed more intense.

Stefanie chanced moving her camera so she could rub the tears from her eyes. She had to see what it was they'd tracked. She prayed it wasn't a Nessie.

She stared into the black water, at the murky opening of the cave. And then, as she watched, a long, graceful, dark shadow glided into view. Stefanie held her breath. The large, hazy shape was visible in the entrance for a mere second. The screen exploded into a cacophony of light and sound. Then the shadow vanished as suddenly as it had appeared. For a moment deathly quiet reigned in the *Sea Horse*.

"That was it!" Jeffery's hiss, sharp with excitement, cut the air. "That was a Nessie! We've found one! Did you get her, Stefanie? Did you get a picture?"

"I'm not certain," she lied. "She disappeared so fast I'm not certain. I may have just gotten the entrance."

Jeffery swore.

Stefanie guiltily clicked off a couple of shots. She'd better have something on this film.

"What are you doing?" Jeffery snapped. "If you missed her, you missed her!" He revved the engine. "Well... this isn't going to be our last chance. This is merely the beginning. Now that we know where one is, we'll get my trap and come directly back here. In an hour or so we'll have things set up. We'll get her! We can't miss!"

STEFANIE WATCHED in silent agony as Jeffery and Matt worked the controls of the remote manipulator arm, setting the huge trap gently onto the floor of the lake. They were about forty feet from the side wall. They'd passed the cavern's entrance, pinpointing its location before continuing down to the bottom. The Nessie's lair couldn't be more than twenty feet above them. And a creature was inside it. At least, one had been an hour ago.

"That's it!" Jeffery exclaimed gleefully. "That's positioned perfectly. I'll just switch off the electromagnet. Then we can get into our diving gear and bait the trap."

Stefanie had never felt more helpless in her life. She watched the two men remove the dry suits and scuba equipment from the storage locker and disappear into the compression chamber. Neither of them spoke to her. She was certain they didn't even remember she existed.

How could Matt possibly be taking part in this? She swallowed over the lump in her throat, wishing she were anywhere but there, were doing anything except staring out at the patch of illumination the sub's lighting equipment was casting into the lake.

After a few minutes, Matt and Jeffery appeared outside the *Sea Horse*. As if in a trance, as if imagining the scene, she watched the two figures in diving equipment—one tall and lean, the other short and chubby.

They moved in slow motion toward the trap, towing one of the barrels of live fish between them, clinging first to the remote arm for support and then, once they'd reached the trap, to its netting.

They were clearly fighting strong currents as they walked. With each exhaled breath, air bubbles swept away from them, rushing off in streams almost parallel to the lake's floor.

Once the first container of bait was positioned outside the trap's opening, the men returned to the *Sea Horse* for the second, then repeated the slow trip out.

The near side of the trap, its hinged end, was by an observation window, but its entrance was at the far end—at the outer range of Stefanie's visibility. The haziness that enveloped detail made the scene seem even more unreal.

When both containers of bait were in place, the two men upended one barrel, pried off its top and guided the fish into the cage. Stefanie cheered silently when a few salmon escaped into the darkness of the surrounding water.

The second barrel yielded half a dozen more renegades. But the majority of the bait swam willingly through the opening. Once inside, a few turned back the way they'd come. Too late. As Jeffery had explained, his design was like a lobster trap. Large as the entrance was, its funnel of rope allowed only one-way passage.

Matt and Jeffery started back to the *Sea Horse*, still carefully holding on to supports, each sliding one of the barrels through the water. They disappeared from her sight, and moments later, Jeffery walked in through the doorway of the compression chamber. He stood dripping water onto the floor, grinning at her.

"Were you watching? Easy as pie, huh? Just like I said."

"You forgot to change back into your clothes," Stefanie pointed out sarcastically.

"I didn't forget! Matt's changing, but I'm leaving my dry suit on. Once Nessie's in the trap, I'm going back out. I want my photograph taken on the floor of Loch Ness—a photograph of me and my trophy!"

Stefanie glared at the nasty wee man. *"Once Nessie's in the trap."* Jeffery had no doubt that would be the outcome of their venture. And thus far today, he'd been batting a thousand.

Matt came out of the compression chamber and glanced at her. "Those currents are strong as hell out there."

She turned away. There was nothing to say to him . . . nothing to say to either man . . . not unless the worst happened, not unless they did trap a Nessie. Then she'd give her arguments one final try.

She stared out at the trap, watching the bait swimming inside. The cage seemed such a simple design . . . but so effective. Like the fish before her, Nessie would swim in and be unable to swim out again. Her only exit would be through the hinged side at the near end. And that side was held closed by a solid metal wheel turned securely into place.

Stefanie had listened carefully to Jeffery's explanation of how he'd transfer Nessie into a more permanent container. Opening the cage was merely a matter of rotating that circular closing device with the manipulator arm and pulling the side of the trap ajar.

She'd watched Jeffery gesturing at the controls as he'd talked, wondering, if the worst materialized, whether she could manage to open the cage.

She'd realized that wasn't a possibility. Not only didn't she have any idea of how to work the arm, but before she'd ever get a chance to try, she'd have to overpower Matt and Jeffery. If she were Superwoman, maybe. But she wasn't. She was merely a photographer who was in the last place on earth she wanted to be, with the last two people she wanted to be with.

"I guess we wait and watch," Matt murmured.

"What about these lights?" Jeffery asked. "Are they likely to bother the Nessie?"

"Not as long as they're constant. They just become part of the environment. Same as the *Sea Horse* and the trap. As long as nothing moves, fish won't even notice there's anything unusual."

"Then we'll leave the lights on—all the better to see her with." Jeffery perched his bulky frame on one corner of the console and peered intently out.

Stefanie realized her back was sore from standing and sank onto the floor, propping her camera on her knees. *"All the better to see her with."* That sounded like a line from Little Red Riding Hood. *All the better to see you with, my dear.* Jeffery a wolf and Nessie his unsuspecting victim... how fitting.

They waited forever. Stefanie's leg went to sleep and she pushed herself backward across the floor to lean against the far wall.

"Stay alert!" Jeffery snapped.

"I am alert! But I'm not going to be any good to you if my leg's paralyzed! I just—"

"Look!"

Matt's excited whisper riveted all their eyes to the window. At the far end of the trap, barely visible, was a huge, dark shadow.

Stefanie stared through the water, feeling her heart sinking. That couldn't be a Nessie... and yet... Gradually the shadow swam nearer, the distorted object became a little clearer. Gradually Stefanie's eyes began to make out details—a long, sleek body, an elongated neck, a small head poking curiously about the trap. The creature was moving nearer to the entrance. It was a Nessie!

Half of Stefanie watched in breathless excitement, fascinated by the sight. The other half wanted to shout, to cry out a warning. But that would be pointless. Her voice wouldn't carry through the walls of the sub. Her effort wouldn't save Nessie, would only anger Jeffery.

"Your camera!" Jeffery yelled. "Get to the window! Start shooting!"

Stefanie shoved herself up off the floor and raced to the window, pulling the cap from her telephoto lens. She aimed the camera at the far side of the trap and began shooting, praying Nessie would stay outside the trap. That could happen... with any luck. If it did, Nessie would escape, but they'd have photographs of her. That would be the perfect ending...the only bearable ending.

Her camera whirred as Nessie grew closer, came into better focus. The shots were wonderful! But she'd taken enough of them! The creature had to turn away before it was too late. *Now, Nessie!* she screamed silently. Then she watched in horror as Nessie poked her slim head into the trap and began swimming toward the bait.

CHAPTER FOURTEEN

"COME ON, NESSIE," Jeffery whispered, his voice feverish with excitement.

Stefanie closed her eyes, unable to watch any longer.

"Come on, baby. Just a couple of more feet and I've got you. That's it! She's mine!"

Stefanie's breath caught at Jeffery's cry. Without looking, she knew Nessie was inside the trap. He'd won...and she'd lost.

"Action shots!" Jeffery screamed. "I want action shots. In a second she'll realize she's caught! Lord knows what she'll do then! Probably try to fight the netting. Come on, Stefanie, move it!"

Blindly Stefanie gazed out at the trap, trying to blink away her tears, wanting but not wanting to see. The Loch Ness Monster was real! Was here! And Stefanie Taylor was one of only three people ever to get this close...to know for certain...would be the one to take the definitive photograph.

Yet her feelings were an ambivalent confusion of excitement and guilt. She'd wanted to see Nessie...to photograph her. But not like this! They were going too far!

"Stefanie! Get it together! I don't want to miss anything good!"

She began shooting again—automatically, paying no attention to what she was doing. It was clearly the only thing that would shut Jeffery up, and she couldn't stand the sound of his voice a second longer.

Vision blurred, she stared through her viewfinder at the creature, terrified of what might become of it if Jeffery and Matt had their way.

Nessie's interest in the fish seemed to have been replaced by curiosity about her surroundings. She began nosing at the rope netting, moving slowly about the walls of the cage, clearly searching for an exit.

But her movements were gentle and cautious, not at all the frantic activities Jeffery had expected. Of course, she'd never been inside a trap before, would have no idea what was happening.

Stefanie gazed into the cage, her throat tight, her eyes welling over with tears. She adjusted the camera and wiped at her eyes, clearing her vision a little.

She watched Nessie in morbid fascination, hating herself for being there, for being part of it, yet totally enthralled by what she saw.

In front of her was a Loch Ness Monster. But no one who'd actually seen this creature would ever call it a "monster." Nessie looked much as Matt had expected her to—like a gigantic, elongated seal, or perhaps an enormous otter.

The thirty-foot-size estimate had been accurate. Stretched out, Nessie's slim body would extend almost the full length of the trap. Despite her length, though, she seemed surprisingly delicate—her body so slender that she appeared fragile.

The creature was undoubtedly no match for Jeffery's cage—not when he'd been bragging that the netting was strong enough to keep a whale from escaping.

Through the almost opaque water, Stefanie could make out the deft movements of Nessie's flippers as she swam into the sphere of light thrown by the sub. They cut the water smoothly, guiding her progress.

She circled gracefully around the cramped confines of the trap, moving with the peculiar S-shaped motion several eyewitnesses had described. Each time she swam into the near end of the cage, where the illumination from the sub's lights was strongest, her short, dark fur glistened with highlights.

Stefanie stared through the observation window, spellbound. She hadn't expected the emotions she was feeling... hadn't anticipated being caught up in the excitement of seeing Nessie up close. She could almost understand... almost, but not completely... not nearly enough to go along with Matt and Jeffery.

Nessie paused, arched her long neck and peered tentatively toward the source of light. She was a proud-looking creature with dark, expressive eyes that seemed almost too large for her delicate head. Her gaze was eerily human... puzzled and uncertain.

She stared directly at the observation window and Stefanie felt a tug on her heartstrings. Her Pentax stopped whirring.

Instantly Jeffery wheeled around. "Keep shooting, damn it! And what the hell are you looking so upset about? It's just a dumb animal!"

"The film's done! Haven't you got enough? Can't you let her go now?"

"Reload! You've only shot one roll of film, haven't you?"

Stefanie nodded guiltily.

"Well, put another one in! And don't stop shooting again till I tell you to. And for God's sake stop babbling about letting her go. That was settled long ago.

It's not on my list of things to do today—or any other day.

"What *is* on my list," Jeffery continued, "is having my picture taken with the Loch Ness Monster—underwater, at the site of her capture. I'm going back out. And you, Stefanie, you make damn sure you get some good pictures of me at the cage—shots with both me and Nessie in them."

"Don't be an idiot, Osborne!" Matt snapped. "We were lucky to get the bait in place without being swept away by those currents. Let's raise the cage to the surface. You can get all the pictures you want to later."

"They won't be the same. I want some taken here and now on the floor of Loch Ness."

Matt muttered something under his breath, then threw up his hands. "All right. Just hold your horses for a minute and I'll get back into my dry suit. If you're going to behave like a lunatic you can't be allowed out without a keeper."

"No. Don't bother changing. I don't need you, don't want you out there. I can manage perfectly without your help."

"Don't be a jerk! Wasn't the buddy system lesson number one when you learned to dive? Or are you just out after individual glory?"

Jeffery didn't reply. He merely turned and marched across to the compression chamber.

"Fine!" Matt shouted at the other man's retreating back. "Have it your own way. Just don't go getting yourself drowned. I can live without having to explain that one to Sound Research."

The hatch clanged behind Jeffery.

Matt muttered something indecipherable. Stefanie's glance flickered to his face.

He was staring straight at her, caught her gaze and looked at her evenly for a moment, his expression tense. But when he spoke, his words were quiet, his tone conciliatory.

"Stefanie, that icy shoulder of yours is driving me crazy. Let's get things settled between us while Osborne's playing around out there, okay?

"Look, I'm sorry he's been so rough on you. And I'm sorry you're upset. But none of this is my doing, so I wish you'd stop taking your anger out on me. Life isn't perfect. You know that. Some things hurt."

Stefanie swallowed hard, trying to regain control of her emotions, trying to imagine how Matt must be feeling about capturing Nessie. If seeing the creature up close had excited her, how must a biologist feel about the prospect of studying it?

She tried to understand how much he must want that opportunity.

Yet all she could think about was freeing Nessie. Matt was her last chance. Jeffery was a lost cause, but possibly, just possibly, she could change Matt's mind. She simply had to convince him to let the creature go.

She couldn't quite believe—or perhaps she simply didn't want to believe—that Matt could be so unresponsive when Nessie's freedom mattered so terribly much to her. The other night, when they'd been making love, he'd seemed so incredibly... but what was it he'd said?

Something about his being a biologist and their dealing with sex. Maybe what they'd shared had just been sex to him, after all. Maybe he really didn't care about her. Maybe "love" had merely been the word he'd used because it fit the situation.

Well, it no longer mattered. Then was then and this was now. Circumstances had changed completely. And their relationship had changed with them. Now they stood on opposite sides of the issue facing them.

Or was it only an issue in her mind? Neither Matt nor Jeffery thought there was any question about Nessie's fate. They clearly believed the creature was theirs... to do with as they wished.

But Matt had to possess *some* feelings. And surely any compassionate man who simply looked at Nessie would realize that what Jeffery intended doing couldn't be done. Surely the cold eye of science couldn't completely overwhelm Matt's emotional responses.

"Matt... Matt, you aren't really going to let Jeffery go through with this, are you?"

He shook his head slowly. "Let's not get into that one again, Stefanie. Osborne was right about the issue being settled. Look..." He paused, reached across the space between them and gently touched her arm.

She jerked away. So much for hoping Matt had any compassion. "Matt, that issue you don't want to get into is the entire cause of my cold shoulder, the entire problem between us! I simply can't go along with this lunacy. Matt, can't you see that? Just think about what Jeffery's proposing!"

"Stefanie... be reasonable. Just because I love you doesn't mean I can agree with you a hundred percent of the time. In this instance I have to side with Osborne."

"Love me? Love me? Ha! You don't know the meaning of love. Or sensitivity. Or simple right and wrong. If you did, we wouldn't be here now. There wouldn't be a Nessie in that trap. There wouldn't even be a damn trap!

"Matt, if you hadn't gone along with Jeffery in the first place, if you'd sided with me when he suggested his crazy plan, we'd have tracked a Nessie, taken her picture and gone on our way. That was what we were supposed to do. That was *all* we were supposed to do!

"Instead of that..." She tried to hold back her tears. It was impossible. "Instead of that," she repeated between sobs, "we're here and Nessie's doomed and you're lying about loving me. Matt... if you really do love me... let Nessie go. Argue with Jeffery. He won't listen to me, but he'll listen to you. If he has a mutiny on his hands, he'll have to listen to reason."

"Stefanie, I do love you. I love you more than I've ever loved anyone in my life. But trapping a Nessie and loving you are two completely unrelated things. Can't you see that? Can't you see you're being every bit as unreasonable as you believe Osborne is?

"It's only one Nessie we're talking about. Taking one specimen won't wipe the species out forever. None of your so-called arguments are the least bit rational. They're purely and simply emotional. What you're using on me isn't logic. It's emotional blackmail.

"Don't ask me to prove my love in a way that I can't, Stefanie—in a way that has nothing to do with whether or not I love you. Nessie has to do with science... not with you and me.

"I'm fascinated by her, Stefanie. Now that we've got her we have to study her...to learn...to widen the scope of human knowledge. I just *can't* let her go. I love you. The person in me loves you. But the scientist in me can't set Nessie free."

Stefanie closed her eyes, not wanting Matt to do or say anything else. He wasn't going to argue Nessie's case with Jeffery, wasn't going to listen to her pleas.

"I'm sorry you're two different people, Matt," she managed, her voice still unsteady. "I could never love someone who compartmentalizes his personality the way you obviously do. You'd better watch out, though. Keep up the way you're going and you'll end up schizophrenic."

"Stefanie—"

"No! Forget it. Forget everything!" She turned away and stared out the window, suspecting she was being completely unreasonable, but unable to control her emotions. Through fresh tears, she could see Jeffery making his way slowly to the cage.

"I hate that nasty wee man!" she heard herself whisper fiercely. "I hope he does drown out there!"

She stood silently, watching Jeffery inch closer to the trap. He clung firmly to the remote arm as he moved hand over hand along its length. She blinked rapidly. A few more deep breaths and she'd have herself under control.

Then Nessie spotted Jeffery, gracefully arched her delicate neck and rested quietly in the water, watching him approach. Stefanie's tears began to flow once more.

"Weren't you supposed to reload your camera?" Matt asked, his voice strained.

She turned and glared at him for a moment before taking the Pentax from around her neck. She placed it on the console and reached into her bag for a fresh film. She'd shoot a hundred exposures of Jeffery with his trophy. What did it matter now?

She'd take the pictures, but she'd be damned if she'd take any credit for them or take Sound Research's money for this project. Blood money! That's what it would be. She wouldn't touch a cent of it. She'd donate it to the World Wildlife Foundation or some other worthy charity.

She fumbled blindly with the film's box, unable to get the flap unglued.

"Oh, my God!"

Her head snapped up at Matt's horrified whisper. He was staring out the window. Her gaze followed his. She saw nothing unusual. Jeffery had reached the trap, was clinging to the rope netting.

"What's happened? What's wrong?" Her glance flew back to Matt. He was already halfway to the compression chamber.

"Air bubbles! No air bubbles! Something's gone wrong with Osborne's breathing apparatus! I have to take him air. I can buddy-breathe him back in!"

Matt disappeared into the compression chamber, pulling the hatch tightly behind himself.

Stefanie started across after him, then stopped. There was nothing she could do to help. She wasn't a good diver under the best of conditions. If she went out with Matt, she'd only be in the way.

She stared into the water again. Matt was right. The stream of air bubbles from Jeffery's equipment had disappeared. Oh, Lord! What if Jeffery did drown out there? She'd wished that very fate on him only moments ago. What if her wish came true?

She tossed the carton of film onto the console and rushed to the window, pressing her palms and nose against the glass, needing to see every detail she could.

Jeffery was clinging to the net with one hand, facing the *Sea Horse*, making some sort of signal with his free arm. It meant absolutely nothing to her. She stood staring into the cloudy water, feeling completely useless.

As she watched, Jeffery shrugged out of his air tank's harness, pushed himself away from the trap and started swimming in the direction of the sub. His strokes were weak. She knew he couldn't possibly make it to the *Sea Horse* on his own.

Then Matt appeared in view, wearing his dry suit and scuba gear. He clung to the remote arm, moving hand over hand toward the trap, toward Jeffery's struggling form. Matt's motion was slow and deliberate. He pulled himself along the arm, clearly fighting to make forward progress.

But if the currents were working against him, that must mean they were aiding Jeffery. Or did it? Hadn't Mary once mentioned something about the swirling currents in Loch Ness being changing and unpredictable?

Stefanie gazed through the cloudy water at the engineer. He didn't seem to have made much headway, didn't seem any closer to the sub. Damn the water distortion! Damn all that swirling peat. Was Jeffery really still only a few feet away from the trap? He certainly appeared to be.

And his stroke was weaker... practically non-existent. No! That must be her imagination, her fear. But he seemed almost motionless now... suspended in the water.

Matt was drawing closer to him. And then, just as Matt extended an arm toward him, Jeffery faltered visibly. His limbs were no longer moving with any semblance of purpose.

One of his feet pointed down to the bottom of the lake; the other swept gradually forward through the water. Almost imperceptibly Jeffery's body tilted to one side, his face slowly turning away from the sub.

Stefanie watched, horrified, as his arms, like those of a rag doll, floated limply from his body, drifted beyond the reach of Matt's outstretched hand.

Jeffery seemed to be stumbling in slow motion, trying to catch his own arms, moving first in the direction of the *Sea Horse*, then, like a drunk, staggering off to one side. She couldn't tell whether he was still conscious or whether the currents had seized control of his body.

All she was certain of was that Jeffery was gradually moving away from Matt, away from the safety of the sub, into the cold black abyss of Loch Ness.

Matt let go of the manipulator arm and lunged through the water after Jeffery's limp body. He began swimming, kicking furiously, stroking strongly. He seemed to be closing the gap between himself and Jeffery, but with the churning of the water, it was impossible to be sure.

And then Jeffery disappeared into blackness. A moment later Matt duplicated the vanishing act.

Stefanie stared out, no longer able to see either man, not knowing if Jeffery was alive or dead, not knowing if Matt could save him . . . or if Matt could save himself. What if . . . ?

No! She wouldn't even think of that possibility.

She glanced back at the trap, her eyes filling with tears once again. But this time they weren't for Nessie. What if Jeffery drowned? What if Matt drowned? The possibility was too awful, too horrifying to contemplate.

She focused on Nessie, trying to force herself to stop thinking of death. The creature had gone back to examining the sides of her enclosure.

Stefanie looked out into the darkness once more, in the direction the men had disappeared, and she prayed.

TIME WAS STANDING STILL. It had to be, because Matt and Jeffery had been gone forever. They were someplace in the black hole that was Loch Ness. She couldn't see them. Did that mean they couldn't see the *Sea Horse*? That they were lost?

No! She fought to control the panic growing inside her. The light from the sub must reach farther than she could see. Matt would know better than to go so far he lost sight of it. But Jeffery... was Jeffery even alive? And Matt... what if the currents...?

What would she do if he didn't return? She stared blankly at the sub's control panel for a moment, breathing deeply, ordering her mind to continue functioning. She could try to free Nessie. She could try to surface the *Sea Horse*. She could try...but her odds on successfully managing either were probably one in a million.

If she was left alone here, if the men didn't return, she'd die.

It didn't matter. If Matt was dead, nothing else mattered!

That realization stunned her. As angry as she'd been, as cold and unreasonable as Matt had been, she didn't want to live without him. And yet... as long as the specter of Nessie was between them... she knew she could never live with him, either.

But she didn't want him dead! That was the critical factor right now. No matter what, Matthew Garrett couldn't be dead!

Stefanie peered out into the darkness once more, willing the two men to materialize. She'd see them any moment now. Matt would be helping Jeffery along. They'd be sharing Matt's oxygen. They'd both be fine. That was the only possible outcome.

But she knew it wasn't. This was the real world. The cold black depths of Loch Ness . . . a lake Rob had told her never gave up its dead. Things weren't going to turn out well simply because she wanted them to.

She stared through the observation window for another eternity.

And then, at the far side of the trap, she saw a moving shape . . . or a mirage . . . which? She strained her eyes. Nessie swam slowly across the cage, blocking the view. Stefanie silently begged the creature to move.

When she did, Matt was visible.

Stefanie began to sob with relief. Matt was there . . . safe. But he was alone.

Guilt stabbed sharply at her heart—guilt over wishing Jeffery dead, guilt over her relief at seeing Matt alive when clearly Jeffery wasn't. Her sobs became a confusion of sorrow and joy.

She watched Matt's progress. He looked totally spent, as if each step might be the last he could manage. Slowly he made his way along the side of the trap, to the arm, toward the sub, until he finally disappeared from her line of vision.

She raced across to the compression chamber, knowing she shouldn't open the hatch. She heard a scuffling noise in the compartment.

"Matt? Matt, are you all right?"

The door opened and Matt stood before her, dripping water, his tank on his back, his mask pushed up on top of his head.

Still crying, Stefanie threw her arms around him, oblivious to the cold wetness against her body.

He wrapped one arm around her waist, stroking her hair with the other. His wet fingers caught in its tangles. Her clothes were quickly soaking through. It didn't matter. He was safe.

"I couldn't find him, Stefanie." Matt's voice was thick, sounded forced. "He just disappeared from view. I looked. I looked until my air was running low. But I was afraid to go out of sight of the sub's light and I couldn't find him." His words ended in a muffled choke.

Stefanie hugged him even more tightly, pressing her face into the wet hollow of his neck.

"You tried, Matt. You did everything you could. He should never have gone out there alone."

Matt shivered against her, then pulled back a little. "I'd better get out of this suit," he said, his voice unsteady. He turned quickly away and moved to the compression chamber.

Stefanie couldn't see his face, but was certain he was crying. She waited quietly, trying to calm the turbulence of her feelings.

When Matt returned, he was wearing dry clothes once more. Tiny bits of peat clung to his skin here and there.

"I've never dived in water as cold as this lake before," he told her, smiling a smile that didn't come close to making it. "Even with the dry suit, it's a wonder I didn't freeze to death."

He blanched visibly at the word death and wiped his hand quickly across his eyes. "Lord, Stefanie, the brass at Sound Research is going to go berserk. Yesterday they learned one of their vice presidents was selling secrets to the Soviets. And today I have to tell them I let their pride-and-joy sonar engineer drown."

"You didn't *let* him drown, Matt! You did everything you could to save him."

"Did I? I should never have let him go out there by himself in the first place. I knew it was dangerous, but I was so fed up with his antics I was past caring what happened to him.

"All I cared about was having a chance to be alone with you for a few minutes—a chance to straighten things out with you. And I didn't even manage to do that. If I'd been out there with Jeffery instead of in here with you, he'd be alive."

"You weren't his keeper, Matt. He insisted on going out there by himself. He wanted pictures of him and Nessie, not of you and him and Nessie.

"We're quite the pair," she added, swallowing hard, willing herself to retain control. "I'm the one who said I wished he'd drown. How do you think that makes me feel?"

"Wishing doesn't make things happen, Stefanie."

"I know. It's just that . . . as sorry as I am Jeffery's dead . . . I'm so glad you're alive it makes me feel guiltier than I've ever felt before in my life."

"You're *so glad* I'm alive?" Matt smiled a question at her. This time his smile made the grade.

"Tremendously glad."

"Well, that makes me feel a million times better."

Matt drew her to him and hugged her tightly to his body. "I only hope Sound Research is glad I'm alive—that they don't decide to string me up. But I guess our having Nessie will do a little bit to mollify them."

Stefanie felt her body tense. She pulled away, gazed at Matt for a moment, then turned to look out the window. She was incredibly glad he was alive . . . yet there was still that part of him she couldn't accept.

Matt stepped behind her, rested his hands on her shoulders and drew her back against his chest.

She didn't resist. But she felt no comfort from his nearness . . . no sense of warmth at his touch. The fire between them had burned out. She stared blindly out at the trap. And all she felt was a hollowness inside.

CHAPTER FIFTEEN

"STEFANIE," Matt said gently, "I know you're upset about Jeffery. So am I. He may not have been the most likable person in the world, but his dying that way just doesn't seem real . . . or right."

"No." Stefanie shook her head sadly, glad her back was to Matt, glad he couldn't see she was crying. She hated crybabies and she seemed to be bursting into tears every other minute. "No, his dying doesn't seem right at all. And I feel terrible about the awful things I said and felt."

Matt squeezed her shoulders gently. "I know. I also know trapping Nessie and my not wanting to let her go doesn't seem right to you. But I can't explain how I feel about this situation any better than I have, Stefanie. Please try to understand. No matter how much I love you, I can't turn my back on something as incredible as this discovery."

"Matt . . . I do understand. While you were out searching for Jeffery, I thought about what you'd said. Trapping a Nessie and loving me are two entirely different things for you. Just as freeing a Nessie and loving you are two entirely different things for me.

"But understanding something and agreeing with it aren't one and the same. The way you feel about Nessie . . . the way I feel about Nessie . . . are all tangled up in what sort of people we are, in what we're like deep down inside, in what our values are.

"If we're as fundamentally different as we seem to be when it comes to Nessie, that difference would have surfaced eventually, over some other issue. It's just as well we learned about it now. I understand your point of view, Matt, but I still don't agree with you."

"Stefanie—"

"Don't worry!" She stepped forward out of Matt's arms and turned to face him. "I won't try any more emotional ploys to change your mind. But since Nessie's fate is up to you now, just listen to me for one more minute."

"Stefanie—"

"Please, Matt. Give me the satisfaction of knowing I tried to convince you with logic, not simply with what you called 'emotional blackmail.'"

"All right." Matt smiled a weary half smile. "But just logic. I can't stand your tears."

Stefanie nodded, taking a slow, even breath. "Matt . . . how much can you learn from a single animal? For research to have any validity it has to involve thousands of subjects, doesn't it? I'm no scientist, but I can't believe anything conclusive could come from examining one Nessie—at least nothing that's going to benefit mankind. She'd simply be a scientific curiosity, wouldn't she?"

"Not necessarily, Stefanie. She might help us unravel a bit of the mystery of evolution. Even one specimen of a new species could help us do that."

"*Might . . . could*. You're talking about sacrificing her freedom, her life, for a maybe—for a possible clue to something most people don't give a damn about, anyway.

"Look at her, Matt. She's not an abstract *specimen*. She's a living, feeling, thinking animal. What benefit is taking her out of her world going to give humanity? A little amusement? A look at the famous Loch Ness Monster? Matt . . . can you honestly tell me it would be worth destroying her for that?"

"Stefanie, don't you think your question's a little academic? If you and I don't give her to the world, someone else will. It's simply a matter of time. We tracked her. We managed to trap her. If we could do it, others can. At most we'd be putting off the inevitable."

"Matt, what about your silt theory? What if this is the last year the Nessies make it into Loch Ness? Or maybe next year will be the last. If they stop using the passage soon, no one else will have a chance to trap one of them. That's possible, isn't it?"

"It's possible, Stefanie. But it's just as possible their entrance will be passable for centuries yet. We simply don't know."

"But, Matt, it might not be. And people have been searching for a Nessie for a long time without ever capturing one before. It might be years before anyone does again. It might never happen. The Nessies may be gone from the lake before anyone can trap another one."

She stared at Matt, trying to tell if any of what she'd said had impressed him. It was impossible to read his thoughts.

"Matt, I know this is only an animal . . . I know I'm being overly emotional . . . and I can't make you do something you don't want to do. But—"

"Stefanie . . ."

"Matt . . . we can't prevent what happens to Nessie in the future . . . but we can determine what happens to her right now . . . today. We can't control what others do, but we can decide what we do."

Matt shook his head wearily. "I'm sorry Stefanie. But scientifically speaking, your arguments are weak. They just don't hold up. To the scientific world, to my world, Nessie will be an incredible find . . . possibly the most important discovery of its type ever."

"I see," Stefanie managed stiffly. "I see. Well, I guess we live in different worlds, Matt. And we both have to play this the way we feel it should be played. I can't have any part in taking this animal out of her environment . . . won't have any part in recording what happened down here. If there's going to be a definitive picture of the Loch Ness Monster, it isn't going to be mine."

Stefanie took her Pentax from the console, opened its back and removed the film of Nessie exploring the trap. Slowly she pulled the film from its casing, exposing it to the light.

"Those pictures you just destroyed," Matt said quietly, "those shots of Nessie entering the trap, were priceless. They would have made you famous."

"Possibly. But I guess I don't want to be rich and famous. At least, not that badly—not that way. We each have to live in our own world, with our own conscience, don't we?"

Stefanie stared evenly at Matt, knowing she was beaten, yet clinging to a final, vain hope that he'd miraculously change his mind. She willed him to say what she wanted to hear.

Instead he slowly shook his head. "Stefanie . . . I can't. I just can't. I've explained my reasons to you a hundred times. And now there's another one. Nessie was Jeffery's catch, his 'trophy,' as he called her.

"And Jeffery, far more than you or me, was part of Sound Research. Nessie belongs to them. This was their search, their money backing it. And I'm responsible for the results now. I have to turn Nessie over to the company. That's what Jeffery was planning to do. Even if I could set the whole scientific question aside, it wouldn't be ethical to free her now that he's dead."

Stefanie stared at Matt, barely believing what she saw. His face belied his words. Despite all his logical arguments, despite the weakness of her own, despite what he'd been saying two seconds ago, he was considering freeing Nessie. She was reading that in his eyes.

"Ethical?" she asked quietly, praying for the right words. "Matt, Nessie is a living being—a wild creature. She doesn't belong to anyone. Doesn't she deserve more of your ethical consideration than some fat-cat corporation?

"All she'd do for Sound Research would be add to their profits, increase their bottom line. But at what cost? Look at her. Just look at her. Then let her go, Matt! If it's ethics you're concerned about, that's the only ethical thing to do."

Matt stared out the window. Stefanie's gaze followed his. Nessie was clearly oblivious to them, was still prodding at the side of the trap with her nose.

"Let her go, Matt," Stefanie pleaded, knowing she wasn't using any logical argument. It didn't matter. Matt could call this blackmail if he liked, was welcome to call it anything he wanted . . . as long as he listened to her.

The *Sea Horse* was so silent that she could hear her heart beating over the low hum of the engine.

"I imagine," Matt offered finally, his words slow and measured, "if we didn't have a Nessie to turn over to Sound Research, I could trust you to never breathe a word...to anyone...about us having even seen one, let alone having trapped one?"

A rush of exhilaration swept her. *"If we didn't have a Nessie"!*

"Oh, Matt! If we didn't have a Nessie to turn over to Sound Research, you could trust my silence to the ends of the earth!"

Matt smiled a weary half smile. "I imagine I could. But, Stefanie, I meant what I said about none of your arguments holding water. Just because we'd have only one Nessie wouldn't diminish her scientific importance. Perhaps it would even heighten it.

"If we set her free, it would only be because you want that so badly... and I want to do it for you. You haven't convinced the scientist in me, but I guess maybe you've convinced the man in me.

"But it would still be a case of emotional blackmail, Stefanie. Could you live with that?"

"Could *you* live with that, Matt?" she whispered.

"I suspect that would depend on who I was living with."

Stefanie held her breath, afraid that if she spoke, she'd say the wrong thing.

"Well?"

"I'm not certain what you're asking me, Matt."

He reached across the space between them, drew her against his chest and rested his hands on her shoulders. "I'm asking you whether a photographer who spends half her time away on assignment has to be based in Chicago. I'm asking you if New England would be a possibility.''

"It would be a definite possibility, Matt.''

"I don't mean just living in New England, Stefanie. I mean living in New England with me.''

"With you and Buffy.''

"You remembered my dog's name.'' He smiled at her. "You're pretty sharp. I only mentioned it once.''

"Haven't you picked up yet on my being an animal lover?''

Matt laughed quietly. "I was beginning to suspect you were. But you haven't picked up on my last question. Maybe my wording was too subtle. I'm asking you to marry me, Stefanie. What do you say? Is New England with me...and Buffy...a definite possibility?''

"That's not a definite possibility, Matt. That's a definite definitely. I'll marry you and live anywhere on earth with you!''

Matt brushed her forehead with a kiss. "Then I'll make you a deal. Shoot another roll of film of Nessie. After that, we'll release her.''

"Release her...! Marry me!"

Stefanie's heart was soaring. She smiled teasingly at Matt. "Shoot another roll of film, Matt? First you wanted me to promise I'd never breathe a word about Nessie...now you want pictures? Surely you've heard a picture's worth a thousand words. And you want me to shoot an entire film?''

"Oh, we won't let anyone know about these shots for a long, long time. If luck is on the side of the Nessies, you and I will be the only two people in the world who know for certain the creatures exist. "I just thought that sometime in the future it might be nice to have photographs of one to show my grandchildren.''

"Your grandchildren? Matt, I didn't even know you had children!''

"I don't. So I guess we'll have to get started at square one, won't we?'' Matt leered wickedly at her for a moment, then captured her lips in a kiss that sent shock waves rocketing all the way to her toes.

When he finally released her she was breathless.

"Matt . . . before we get started at square one, let's release Nessie. The rate you're going, we're liable to forget all about her.''

"First the pictures.''

"Right.'' Stefanie reached into her gadget bag. "I'll use my Leica this time. I use it in special situations, and I can't imagine any situation being more special than this one.''

Quickly Stefanie shot off the roll of film in her camera, then turned to smile at Matt. "That's it. An entire series of definitive photographs.''

"Too bad they won't see the light of day until we're old and gray.''

"That's all right, Matt. Freeing Nessie is more than worth the price.''

Matt took her by the hand and started over to the navigation console. "Come up here with me. I could use a little help with the controls.''

They reached the front of the *Sea Horse* and Matt placed her hand on the lever that operated the manipulator arm. "Ready?''

Stefanie gazed out at the trap and smiled. Nessie seemed to be gazing back at her. Of course, that was undoubtedly just her imagination, but . . .

"Ready?'' Matt repeated.

"Ready," she whispered.

Matt flicked a small switch, then covered her hand with his own. The warm pressure felt so right it made her smile once more.

His hand guided hers in a slow, almost imperceptible motion. "Watch the locking mechanism."

Stefanie stared out into the murky water. The manipulator arm was grasping the large, circular control on the near end of the trap. She could see its mechanism begin to turn.

Nessie fled to the far end of the cage and hung motionless in the water, her large body almost invisible, her dark shape camouflaged by the blackness surrounding her.

Gradually the mechanism moved upward, until the lock was released.

"Now this way," Matt said quietly, guiding Stefanie's hand gently backward.

Slowly, ever so slowly, the arm pulled the hinged end of the trap open until it stood ajar.

All was still for a moment. Gradually the bait fish began making their escape. Then Nessie swam tentatively forward. Hesitantly she explored the opening. Suddenly, with a rapid, S-shaped switch of her body, she darted out of the cage and vanished into the darkness without a backward glance.

A swirling stream of peat and a tiny trail of bubbles remained. The bubbles dissipated; the veil of peat gradually closed. Except for the giant cage, no clue remained of Nessie's presence. She might easily have been an illusion.

Stefanie swallowed over the lump that had formed in her throat. "She's gone, Matt...she's safe. Thank you." Her words seemed totally inadequate. Matt would never know how happy he'd made her.

"I'll just get rid of that damn trap," he muttered. "No point leaving it standing there. If one of the other teams came down and saw it, they might pick up on Osborne's idea." Matt's voice cracked on his final words.

Stefanie gazed out the window, smiling a little. So much for Matt lacking in the emotions department.

He removed her hand from the lever and maneuvered the arm along the steel beams of the trap. Gradually the cage collapsed in on itself to became a nondescript pile of beams and netting.

"In a few weeks…maybe even a few days," he said, "that'll cover over with peat. It'll just be a mound on the floor of the lake."

He started the engine, then wrapped one arm securely about her waist. "Let's get out of here, Stefanie. On the way back to shore, we'll get our story straight about what happened down here today. We're going to be facing a lot of questions."

ROB MCFARLANE SAT FORWARD on the stuffed chair in Matt's room, listening intently as Matt and Stefanie recounted first the episode with David Finch and the FBI, then the story of their disastrous outing…of Jeffery's drowning.

Mary sat wide-eyed beside Rob, on the chair's arm, clutching his large hand tightly with her own. "I can't believe we missed all that excitement by being away for two days!"

Matt stopped pacing for a moment. "Believe it. Saying we had an action-packed time would be a definite understatement." He looked at Rob. "We certainly owe you an apology. Osborne was so convinced you had some part in the intrigue that he had us all suspicious.''

Stefanie glanced a quick rebuke at Matt.

"Well . . . not all of us . . . but he had me suspicious. I'm sorry about that, Rob."

"It's understandable. No harm done."

"But Jeffery dead," Mary said softly. "That's so difficult to believe."

Rob shook his head slowly. "I certainly can't claim I liked the wee man, but I'd have never wished a kelpie to get him."

"A kelpie?" Stefanie asked.

"A water sprite. Nasty little fellows. They delight in bringing about the drowning of wayfarers."

Mary shot Rob a censorious look. "I don't think you should be joking. None of us were too crazy about Jeffery, but his drowning is nothing to joke about."

"I'm not joking at all, love. Kelpies are every bit as real as the Loch Ness Monster. But you didn't even see a sign of Nessie?" he asked, turning his attention back to Matt.

"No, not a trace."

"Aye. That was to be expected, though. Our beastie's far too clever to be seen unless she wants to be."

"Well, not seeing Nessie was the least of our problems. Nothing went right. As I told you, after Osborne drowned I was so upset I even managed to lose the trap. It's just a good thing the sonar's intact. At least Sound Research still has that. If I'd lost it, they'd have probably put a price on my head."

Mary gazed across the bedroom, her glance flickering curiously from Matt, who was continuing to pace the floor, to Stefanie, who perched nervously on the edge of the bed.

"I still don't understand," she said slowly, "what Jeffery was doing outside the *Sea Horse*."

"I told you," Matt said quickly. "He thought there was something wrong with the trap—insisted on going out. I guess he was right, because when I tried to retrieve it . . . well, I told you how it collapsed . . . sort of disappeared on me."

Mary pursed her lips. "It isn't like you to be so careless, Matt. How could you possibly lose a trap as big as you say that one was?"

"We were awfully upset," Stefanie explained, hoping she sounded more believable than Matt had. "Actually, it was my fault. I was trying to help Matt with the controls and . . . well . . ."

Mary nodded slowly, looking closely at Stefanie's face. "I think I understand."

Stefanie gave her a weak smile and swallowed hard. She suspected Mary indeed understood . . . probably understood far more than they'd like her to.

But Mary could be trusted. Matt was certain of that. They'd even considered telling her the truth, then had decided to make no exceptions to their cover story. The fewer people who knew the truth, the safer the Nessies would be.

"What did the police have to say about the drowning?" Rob asked.

"Surprisingly little," Matt told him. "They didn't question us for nearly as long as I had expected."

"Aye. It's far from the first drowning in the loch. She's a treacherous body of water."

"How was your trip to the Moray Firth?" Stefanie asked, eager to change the subject.

"Uh ... fine." Mary looked suddenly anxious. She gazed down from her perch on the chair's arm at Rob.

He smiled encouragingly at her. She glanced over at Matt. "As I was telling you before we went, some of the research that's going on there is pretty closely related to my thesis topic. Very closely, in fact."

There was a long silence. Stefanie felt like prodding Mary to continue. There had definitely been an unspoken *and* at the end of her statement.

"And?" Matt finally asked.

Mary took a deep breath. Then her words poured out in a torrent. "And, Matt, I was wondering if you thought I could finish up my thesis work in Scotland. I'd still need you to supervise it, of course. I couldn't switch thesis advisers at this stage of the game. But I thought ... if you could see your way clear to keep in touch long distance ... if you think I can manage without being closely supervised ... if Rossmuir would go along with the idea ..."

Matt grinned at her. "If I thought all that was possible, then you could stay in Scotland with Rob ... right?"

Rob laughed loudly. "I told you he wasn't as thick about this sort of thing as you've been making out, Mary."

"'Thick'?" Matt repeated in an indignant voice. "Mary, did you call me 'thick'?"

Mary's face turned crimson. "No! That's Rob's word. I simply said that when it came to romance you ... that you weren't exactly ... that ..." She glanced frantically at Stefanie.

"Stop teasing her, Matt!" Stefanie grinned across at Mary. "Actually, he's improving in the romance department. He's hardly thick at all anymore."

"So this trip to the Moray Firth was all part of a plot to let you stay in Scotland," Matt said sternly, obviously fighting back a smile.

"I must admit the plot was initially mine," Rob interjected. "And that reminds me of something. Even though you know now that I wasn't involved in your espionage caper, I should set your mind at ease over something you were all curious about."

"What's that?" Stefanie asked.

"My visit to the *Sea Horse* the other night—my reason for seeing Ian. The bank I'm with has done much of the financing for the Moray Firth project, so I didn't want to be the one to ask about a place on the research team for Mary. I didn't want anyone to feel obliged to accommodate her. But Ian's brother is involved with the project, so I thought that if he sounded things out, we could get a feel for the situation without anyone's feathers being ruffled."

"And you obviously did," Matt said.

"So, Matt?" Mary pressed. "What do you think? Would you go along with it?"

"Mmm . . . I might."

"And Rossmuir . . . would they?"

"Well, since I'm the department head, I guess I get to be the 'they.' "

"Then what do you think, Matt?"

"I think it's a definite possibility."

"Possibility?" Mary echoed hesitantly.

"Well," Matt amended, grinning over at Stefanie, "why don't we call it a definite definitely."

Mary bounced up off the arm of the chair, rushed over and hugged Matt. "Thanks, Matt! And I really didn't call you 'thick'!"

"Come on," she said, turning back to Rob. "Your mother made me promise to tell her the minute we knew." She grabbed Rob's hand, pulled him from the chair and rushed him to the door, pausing only to shoot Matt and Stefanie a quick grin before leaving.

Matt shoved the door closed, turned the key in the lock and walked over to the bed. He sank down beside Stefanie and wrapped his arm around her shoulder.

"Think Mary bought the story, Stefanie?"

"I don't think she's going to ask any more questions. That's good enough for me."

Matt nodded slowly. "So we've made it past the Inverness police and Mary. Now as long as Sound Research doesn't ask too many questions, we'll be home free. They certainly won't be happy, but I don't imagine there's a whole lot they can do. Aside from never offering either of us another job, of course," he added ruefully.

Stefanie leaned comfortably against his chest. Sitting there beside him felt so right that nothing else could possibly matter.

"Who cares about Sound Research, Matt? I didn't even like their offices. And we don't need them. You still have Rossmuir. And I always manage to turn up assignments."

Matt turned a little and kissed her forehead. "Speaking of your assignments, I was wondering if you'd given any thought to cutting down on them a little. I was serious about those children."

Stefanie laughed. "I haven't had much chance to think about anything. But I could hardly travel all the time and leave you with both Buffy and a horde of children to look after."

She paused, glancing hesitantly at Matt. "I'm sorry you won't get to be a world famous scientist, Matt...at least not because you discovered Nessie."

"Discovered what? I don't recall discovering anything called a 'Nessie.' You must have been dreaming."

"Thanks, Matt. It is all starting to seem like a dream, isn't it? I almost feel I should rush down the hall and develop that film—just to assure myself the creature was real."

"Your film will wait. Let's not do anything to arouse Mary's suspicions further."

Stefanie nodded slowly. "I'll never be able to put into words how much your freeing Nessie meant to me, Matt."

"Well, there are some times when actions speak louder than words, aren't there?" He leaned closer, drawing Stefanie against his body and claiming her lips in a searing kiss. The shock waves not only rocketed all the way to her toes, they reverberated all the way back to her heart.

Harlequin Superromance.

COMING NEXT MONTH

#358 MIDNIGHT BLUE • Nancy Landon
Their families had been feuding for generations. And
things got worse—Caroline McAlester tried to stop
Luke O'Connor from developing his theme park in
their town. Then, with one look into Luke's
midnight-blue eyes, Caroline forgot their feud. One
kiss and Luke remembered he'd loved her forever.

#359 AIRWAVES • Suzannah Davis
Chattanooga deejay Summer Jones was number one
in town—until the station was sold to Ryder
Bowman. He joined Summer in the control booth,
and radio's hottest new duo was born. The public
loved it . . . all but one mysterious fan.

#360 A PRIVATE AFFAIR • Kelly Walsh
Ever since Laurel Davis—personal manager to a
famous actress—had walked into the office of
private investigator Nick Malone, his life had felt like
a particularly confusing adventure film. There was
everything from blackmail to mysterious deaths to a
beautiful, aloof heroine. . . .

#361 PLAYING WITH FIRE • Risa Kirk
Cal Stewart and Mary Nell Barrigan were two
Tacoma-based engineers competing for the same
contract. Each needed desperately to win it.
Determined to remain apart, they refused to see
that by antagonizing each other they were only
tempting fate. . . .

Harlequin Regency Romance™

Romance the way it was *always* meant to be!

The time is 1811, when a Regent Prince rules the empire. The place is London, the glittering capital where rakish dukes and dazzling debutantes scheme and flirt in a dangerously exciting game. Where marriage is the passport to wealth and power, yet every girl hopes secretly for love....

Welcome to Harlequin Regency Romance where reading is an adventure and romance is *not* just a thing of the past! Two delightful books a month, beginning May '89.

Available wherever Harlequin Books are sold.